NEO CYBERPUNK

THE ANTHOLOGY

MATTHEW A. GOODWIN   ANNA MOCIKAT
MARLIN SEIGMAN   JON RICHTER   A.W. WANG
NIK WHITTAKER   ELIAS J. HURST
MATT ADCOCK   MARK EVERGLADE
TANWEER DAR   ERIC MALIKYTE
JAMES L. GRAETZ   BENJAMIN FISHER-MERRITT
LUKE HANCOCK   PATRICK TILLETT

Independently published via KDP

Copyright© 2020 Matthew A. Goodwin

All rights reserved. No part of this publication may be reproduced, stored in a retrieval system, or transmitted in any form or by any means, electronic or mechanical, including photocopying, recording without either the prior permission in writing from the publisher as expressly permitted by law, or under the terms agreed.
All the assembled stories are works of fiction. All the characters are fictitious. Any resemblance to real persons, living or dead, is purely coincidental.

The author's moral rights have been asserted.

Compiled by Anna Mocikat and Matthew A. Goodwin

Edited by Marlin Seigman and Matthew A. Goodwin

Cover design by Ivano Lago

FOREWORD

I love cyberpunk.

Every author assembled here loves cyberpunk.

Defined in shorthand by the phrase, "high tech / low life," cyberpunk is so much more than rainy nights, neon lights, cybernetic enhancements, flying cars, digital worlds, and punks fighting an oppressive establishment.

It is a genre of philosophical questions about the nature of society, humankind's relationship with technology, and what it means to be human. Growing out of a time where technology was becoming all the more omnipresent, laws governing corporations were slackening, and fashion was becoming about form over function, the questions raised by cyberpunk have only become more vital.

In an age where a person can work their job digitally from home, have their meals delivered by drones, and learning algorithms target ads based on their virtual personas presented through social media, the world is moving closer to that envisioned by the founders of the genre every day.

Great science fiction says as much about the contemporary world as it does about a theoretical future, and cyberpunk is no exception.

In this anthology, you will find stories of cyborgs, artificial intelligences, cybernetic implants, and virtual worlds. More than that, you will also find thoughtful examinations of where technology can take society for good or ill.

We hope you love this collection and, if you enjoy the stories, that you seek out the other cyberpunk works of these authors.

Thanks for reading.

Matthew A. Goodwin

    10/10/2020 – San Francisco, California

1. VICE GRIP
BY MATTHEW A. GOODWIN

A young man discovers the cost of rising through the ranks of a near-future dixie mafia.

"You know the thing about vice?" Vinny "Rust" Ruzicano asked, stalking the garage with a screwdriver in one cybernetic hand and a cigar in the other. Stopping just in front of the man tied with electric cables to a chair with a burlap sack on his head, he said, "Everyone's got one. Everyone," he repeated and took a long drag from the cigar, smoke pooling above his head in a grim halo.

"And as long as there's vice, there will be people like me. People who will give the people what they want for a price they can afford," he grinned maniacally, "or not."

The man in the sack said nothing.

Vinny Rust grinned like a shark, showing microscreen teeth that flashed different colors. The light reflected in the blood on the sack.

"Want to know how I became king of Neo Orleans?" he asked, not hearing his henchmen sigh. They had heard this all before. Many times. Too many times.

He loved to reminisce, to think back on the weak, skinny kid with no hope, who had taken over the streets of a city that chewed up and spit out people like him.

"It all started in a convenience store," he said, thinking back to that hot July so many years earlier.

He and his friend Gian were sticky with perspiration, the mosquitos buzzing around their heads as they pressed their faces against the glass to watch the screen. The Bayou Boys FC were taking on the Fishmongers to see who would play in the cup that year.

The clerk didn't mind the boys as long as they stayed outside and didn't bother the sad customers picking up their bottles of booze on their way home from work. They never stole anything. Not here. They would lift things from any other store in the city, but not this one, not if they were allowed to watch the screens.

As the players took to the sidelines at the half and the screen began to show a relentless onslaught of ads, Vinny reached down and wrung the sweat out of his shirt.

He didn't notice the man walk into the store until he

heard the commotion. The clerk was waving his hands defensively as the bald man wearing a gray three-piece suit loomed over the counter. He began to plead and cry as the massive brute grabbed him around the neck, the metallic hand glimmering in the fluorescent light of the shop.

Vinny's eyes went wide as the clerk thrashed and kicked, sending packs of cigarettes, mints, and earbuds flying off the counter.

The man's hand closed, and the commotion ceased. He let the body fall to the ground, turned, buttoned his suit, and walked out as though nothing had happened.

The violence didn't bother Vinny. His whole life was violence. His father was violent to his mother and his mother was violent to him. It was the way of things.

The corporate overlords who lived in their glittering towers knew as little of Vinny's reality as he knew of theirs.

But this man. This giant man wearing a suit in the summer was a sight to behold. He was everything Vinny wanted to be. He possessed the authority of a company man but was on the level of the streets. Vinny knew two things in that moment: he wanted to be like the man, to wield that casual power, and he wanted an arm like that.

As the man strode out, he turned, meeting Vinny's gaze.

"You see anything?" the man asked. His voice was low and menacing.

Vinny shook his head. "No," he stammered. "No, sir."

The edge of the man's lip curled up slightly. He had a

friendly face with deep brown eyes which belied his obvious threat. "Good, boy," he said with a wink, and Vinny looked over his shoulder to discover that he was alone. Gian had fled.

Vinny knew he should do the same.

But he couldn't, and his feet started moving as though independent of his body. After a few steps, he caught up with the man who turned a cold eye on him.

"Don't bother asking for money," he said and though he spoke the words calmly, there was an unmistakable undertone.

"No, sir," Vinny said as the man moved toward a black town car hovering near an oak tree dripping with Spanish moss, just out of the view of the store's cameras.

The man nodded and laughed. Vinny had not been expecting that.

"Listen, kid," the man said in an unnervingly amiable tone. "There's a thousand street rats just like you who want to be tough guys. But trust me, you don't."

Vinny smiled, that winning smile that had gotten him out of so many dicey situations in the past. "No, sir. There are no other kids like me, and I don't want to be a tough guy, I want that." He pointed to the cybernetic arm protruding from the jacket sleeve. He couldn't stop staring at it, looking at it the way his friends looked at fancy cars or his father looked at the girls on the corners.

The man smirked. "Well, no shit. Get a load of this guy,"

he said to no one in particular. "You want to earn this kind of money, you gotta work for it."

Vinny was in a state of near entire mesmerization as the man spoke, watching his robotic thumb and forefinger rub together. "Oh, I'll work."

HE DID.

The giant man, who later introduced himself as Paulie "Two Socks," put him to work right away.

Vinny was never able to quite understand how he had worked up the courage to follow him that night and ask for work, but now that he had, he was in.

Paulie wasn't a boss, but a lieutenant, an enforcer. He kept people in line and made sure the local populace knew who ran the streets, but he was also an earner. He intercepted and robbed trucks that the pharmaceutical giant LOTP used to ferry drugs around. Paulie would loot the trucks, replace the pill bottles with plastic baggies, and sell the pills for slightly less than the company.

More accurately, Vinny sold the pills for slightly less.

Paulie had been right about one thing. There were a lot of street rats all scurrying around to deliver the goods for the family. But Vinny had been right too. None of them were like him.

He began to understand his regulars and identify the true junkies. When he made the deliveries to those too whacked out to know their ass from a hole in the ground, he would pocket one pill, swapping it for a sugar tablet he would steal from a pharmacy.

These pills he would sell to his friends before insisting that they crush them up and all do the drugs together.

It was on one of those nights when Vinny, eyes glassy and streaked with crimson, said, "I have to do something."

"Do what?" Gian asked. Vinny had gotten his friend a job as soon as he could. Gian was good at the work but too kind for Vinny's taste. His friend was an easy target for the hopheads, who could always convince him to give them "just one extra pill."

The two were sitting in a shabby apartment in a fifty-story high rise tenement of shabby apartments. Roaches of both kinds littered the broken and splintered hardwood floor. Vinny was sick of this place. He had been working for Paulie for two years but was still just a runner. He wanted more, needed more.

"Something big," Vinny said, standing up so fast that he knocked the beer off the armrest of the tattered, wine colored couch where it had been precariously perched. He took no note of the spilled drink as the liquid puddled at his feet. "What's the worst addiction in this city?"

"Drugs!" Gian exclaimed as though he was on a gameshow. The cadaverous people who littered the halls of the building were certainly a testament to his point.

Vinny shook his head.

"Sex!" Gian said, standing this time and pointing widely.

Vinny shook his head again, and when Gian said nothing, he nearly whispered, "Virtual escape."

His own brother had been a digital junkie. Like so many of the suffering poor, he needed to escape his brutalizing real life for a serene, synthesized one. Having to exist outside his virtual existence made him irritable and he was always waiting for his next plugin. The family understood the extent of the addiction when he flipped the dinner table, not remembering he was in the real world.

Vinny's parents couldn't afford rehab. "That shit is for elites anyway, he will muscle through," Vinny's father sneered, as though he had ever been able to kick his own sex addiction or convince his wife to stop gambling.

Vinny's brother did not muscle through, eventually finding a pirated copy of the Mass Illusion (the most popular virtual world) and dying when his bed sores became infected. Vinny had been sad but not at the death. He was sad that his brother had succumbed to his addiction, given in to that internal weakness that plagued his whole family. Vinny swore then he would only take sex, drugs, alcohol, and digital escape in small doses.

"Your cousin still work at Mass Illusion Industries?" he asked Gian.

He nodded, noting, "But he won't want to lose that job."

No one who had a job could afford to lose it and Vinny knew it. "He won't lose a job if he just lets slip a delivery location. Tell him there will be a fat payout, and I'll make sure it's delivered by the most beautiful woman he ever saw."

Vinny had a singular talent for understanding people's needs, and Gian's cousin, an infamous lothario, would never turn down such an offer.

He was right, and two weeks later, he and Gian were on rooftops on either side of Dumaine Street, waiting for the truck to pass. As expected, it had two guard vehicles flying alongside it.

Vinny was prepared. He had spent all his meager savings and borrowed against his next three month's wages to get the supplies for the heist.

He nodded to the hacker he had hired, and the scrawny girl did something on her computer as Vinny stood with the launcher on his shoulder. The girl clacked away on her keyboard and the two guard vehicles plummeted to the ground.

As a means of earning a little extra income on the job, he had tipped off some scrappers, who instantly made their way into the street to the strip the cars.

Vinny fired the snare cable, one end sinking a hook into the side of the armored transport with the other end already connected to exposed rebar on the roof. The vehicle's computers tried to adjust and pull the car free.

Vinny watched as the machine pulled wildly against the cable. The rebar began to bend and wail. Vinny had been warned that hacking the transport would take time, but he was impatient.

"Do it now," he snarled at the hacker, who ignored him and continued to do her work in silence.

The moment the transport fell, Vinny was scrambling down the cables, his gloves ripping and tearing as he moved. The scrapers were already pulling the machine apart when Vinny hit the ground.

"The One-Worlds are mine," he warned them, speaking of the loot within the back of the truck. The poor people like his brother, who craved escape but couldn't afford the subscription fees of places like the Mass Illusion, could save up and buy a One-World. The chips would load a one-time use, twelve-hour digital universe onto the user's computer and they could escape their drudgery for half a day.

Paulie had his rats selling knock-off versions but only the most desperate junkies ever used them. The second the door to the truck was off, Gian and Vinny were stuffing their bags with chips.

People emerged from their homes and businesses but scurried back inside when they saw what was happening. They feared what would come next. The Carcer Corporation, a private security firm who policed the city, would be closing in soon. The hacker was scrambling communications, but Vinny knew he only had a little time. Chips were getting caught in the tears in his gloves as he continued the theft.

His heart raced. He knew this was the moment that could define his life.

It did.

As he was sitting across from Paulie at the café, he explained, "We got clear before Carcer arrived. I have the chips in the back of my car."

Paulie looked at him with an unfamiliar gaze. Was it pride?

"You did good, kid," he said, lifting a dainty coffee cup in his huge hand. "And you did right coming to me first. Lots of kids, when they get their first big score, forget who they work for. They go straight to The Boss. That would have been... an error in judgment."

Vinny nodded subserviently.

"I'll never forget who got me here," he told the man. It wasn't a lie, but it wasn't a truth either. He was already working the back channels to let The Boss know exactly who had brought this score in. He knew how much he owed Paulie, but he also knew the man was trying to hold him back, keep him in line.

"Just make sure I get my cut," Vinny noted, his friendly tone belying his intentions. Gian was already lining up buyers for the third of the score Vinny wasn't presenting to Paulie.

The huge man dabbed his brow with a handkerchief before taking a bite of the beignet, sending powdered sugar snowing down his chin. "You'll get your cut," he said through a full mouth.

Vinny's cut was smaller than he wanted, but it was enough.

He went to Doc, the crew's surgeon, and said bluntly, "I want an arm."

The old woman with only a few black streaks in her graying hair looked up at him lazily. "So I keep hearing," she smiled, a tired, disinterested smile. She wore a dirty, worn lab coat whose good days, if it ever had any, were long past. "I knew you'd be shadowing my door sooner or later."

She talked him through the procedure, and before he knew it, he was waking up on the metal frame cot in an exposed brick walled room that served as a recovery suite. With blurry, half consciousness, he looked at the arm.

It didn't matter to him that it was a rusted old machine arm with twin end-affixers instead of fingers or that it was pried off of an unlucky soul who couldn't afford last month's payments. To him, it was dream fulfillment.

The parts whirred loudly as they moved and manipulated the air and Vinny grinned. He remembered back to being twelve and stealing a bottle of whiskey from BYO Liquor down the street from his apartment. The alcohol helped him sleep in the still heat of the small room he shared with his brother and made it possible to drown out the street noise and constant screams from his parents.

Three boys, a few years his senior, stopped him with a

hand to the chest. He clutched the booze hard and called, "It's mine," even as they were beating him.

His new arm would have saved him. He would have been able to hit the boys right back and keep what was his.

It was power. It was a strength his slight form would never possess.

He clutched the frame of the cot and felt the metal bend and buckle in his grip.

For the first time in his life, he felt one part of his body matched the might of his mind.

"Ooh," Paulie said with an exaggerated whistle when Vinny strode into the café a few days later. "Look at that hunk of junk. Vinny Boy's got a new toy." Then, to the assembled thugs, he laughed and pointed. "Check this out. What'd you lift that off some grandma? That's rustier than a ginger's ball sack! Vinny Rust! Boys come in here and take a look at 'ol Vinny Rust!"

Vinny's face burned and his natural fist balled in fury. He was used to razzing and ball-busting, but having his new pride and joy mocked brought his ire up. His heart thumped against his chest as he tried to take calming breaths.

He smiled and laughed along but knew then what he had to do.

. . .

"He catches you, they'll find you belly up in the river," the hacker warned a few months later when Vinny had positioned himself to make his move.

"I know that," he hissed. "Just get it done clean and we'll both be richer for it."

She nodded, her face illuminated by the glow of the monitors. Streams of words and numbers cascaded over the screen. Hacking Carcer datafortresses was no easy task, and Vinny had promised the young hacker who had gained a reputation as being the best in the city a huge sum of money he didn't possess for the job.

It was no matter.

Her puffed up and feathered hair tickled his nose as he loomed over her, watching the work he didn't fully understand.

"Alright," she said finally. "I got a file created."

He nodded. "Good," he said. "Thank you. For everything."

Her shoulders tensed at the words.

She knew. He knew she knew.

As quick as a snake's strike, his new arm darted out, pinching her neck. Her arms reached back, clawing at him. She couldn't cry out, but she kicked, her legs crunching against the heavy wood desk.

Vinny remembered the clerk. The same desperate movements, the same understanding of what was happening. A rush surged through him as he felt the power he witnessed all that time ago.

He was the killer now.

He was the force to be reckoned with.

As she slumped down, limbs dangling like a rag doll, Vinny smiled. He felt no remorse. He didn't care that the world had one fewer poor, sad person in it. He felt strong. Truly powerful for the first time in his life.

He wanted more. More parts to replace his weaknesses.

He tossed her to the floor, dirt and dust dancing all around her body.

His plan was in motion and soon he would take this city in his rusty grip.

Like a man reborn, he stepped out onto the hacker's ramshackle porch after snatching the data chip from her computer. Lights from the surrounding shacks glimmered against the swamp and cicadas buzzed in an oppressive cacophony like that of the ceaseless delivery drones downtown. The scent of frying catfish filled his nostrils. The edible form of the fish was long gone from the polluted lakes and lagoons, but the locals kept their cultural heritage alive by bioreplicating the animals in vats. False fish were one of Paulie's neglected rackets, and Vinny would see that changed.

He got into his car and it lifted, scattering the children gawking from the shrubs. He set coordinates for Apotheosys, the nightclub where The Boss spent his evenings. The man who ran the city's underworld had erased his name from the records. He was called "The Boss" the way a black hat used their handle.

It would not keep Carcer from placing a lofty bounty on him, but he always argued, "It's better to stay anonymous."

Vinny was a man on a mission as he pushed his way through the sweaty mass of humanity. The hopped-up forms writhing against one another in the thrumming noise and flashing lights were little more than false props to him as he made his way to the staircase.

"Vinny Rust," The Boss called out, waving him over. Vinny felt one of his teeth crack as his jaw clenched at hearing the moniker.

"Gotta talk to you," Vinny said. He hated his high-pitched voice with a Louisiana twang and vowed then to get a modulator installed to remedy it.

The Boss stood and smoothed his purple velour suit before running his hands through slicked back hair. "Lots of folks need to speak with me today," he noted ominously as he guided Vinny into an office.

The strung-out club owner could barely lift his head but scurried from the office on rubber legs when he laid glossy eyes on The Boss.

The Boss was a head taller than Vinny, dark and intimidating. His baritone voice and muscular frame gave him a commanding presence Vinny envied.

"What's up, kid?" The Boss asked, narrowing his eyes at

the young man. The Boss had taken a shine to Vinny over the years. Vinny was always sure to show deference when they met and presented small gifts whenever he could. In a world of hard men being cruel, the small kindnesses were welcomed.

Vinny was still brimming with confidence and set his shoulders. "Paulie's working with Carcer."

He let the words hang, but if The Boss had a reaction, he didn't let Vinny see it.

"He said something similar about you," he said simply. There was no emotion in his words, but Vinny knew he had to tread lightly. He was not surprised by the revelation. He knew Paulie feared his underling's growing stature.

"I heard some rumblings," Vinny began. "People saying Paulie was going behind our backs, so I had a friend of ours do a little digging."

He produced the chip and stepped behind the desk, socketing it into the computer. The projected screen displayed the list of street informants.

In just a flash of a moment, a slight micro expression of rage passed over The Boss's face as he saw Paulie's name.

"Thank you for bringing this to me," he said, the mask of serenity back in place. "It'll be sorted."

That was to be the end of the discussion, but Vinny pressed his luck. He had come this far and wouldn't see some other guy promoted when it could be him. *Should* be him.

"How's about I sort it for you," he offered. Just as he had

those years earlier, he was taking a big risk which could potentially change his life forever. "I see it done and I take his business. To show my gratitude, I'll ensure a ten percent increase in profit in the first month."

Vinny was hoping for a reaction, but The Boss simply looked him in the eyes. The bass from the music below vibrated into Vinny's feet as he waited.

The Boss nodded.

Vinny sat in the passenger side of the van as Gian drove. It had taken nearly six months for him to get the word from The Boss that he could make his move, but the day was finally upon him.

"I'd better see you at my kid's first birthday," Gian said by way of reminder. Vinny had no interest in a child's birthday party. A bunch of snot-nosed rug rats and their sad parents swapping baby war stories was his idea of hell, but he knew it was important to his only friend.

"I'll be there," he said absently, staring out the window at row after row of houses with black, wrought iron cased balconies. Gian had a kind heart. Vinny thought he was a fool. Where Vinny saw opportunity, his friend saw people who needed help. When a young hooker showed up at the club with a battered face, Gian had rushed out to find her pimp.

Vinny hadn't cared that Gian had found "the love of his

life" in the wounded girl, only that his pal had taken over the prostitution ring and kicked up a percentage. When their daughter was born, Vinny had said simply, "Congratulations. Don't let it affect your work."

"They just grow up so fast," Gian said. "You know, you hear people say it, but you don't really know until you're a parent. I swear it was just yesterday I was bringing her home from the hospital and now she can point to her belly. Can you believe that? She's so smart, I keep saying," but Vinny cut him off.

"Hush up," he said with his new synthesized voice. "We're getting close."

Gian fell silent and the lackey in the back of the van stubbed out his cigarette.

Vinny held the machine pistol in his natural hand, knowing it was the last time he would have to use the worthless flesh.

The van pulled up in front of the café. He expected Paulie to run, to get up and flee like a coward, but the massive man just looked at the kid he had plucked out of obscurity and smiled. The man would meet his death the same way he had lived his life.

Vinny seethed as he raised the weapon. He hated that Paulie could die bravely with a smile. He felt robbed of the satisfaction of showing his mentor how far he had come. The shots thundered through the street, scattering onlookers and blood. Screams of terror could be heard from all around as Vinny stepped through the smoke, spitting on the corpse.

"Fucking rat," he cried for all to hear. Word of this would spread and everyone would now know who ran the streets. No one would call Carcer, no one would pay to have this investigated.

Vinny scooped up Paulie's legs as the lackey and Gian grabbed his huge shoulders. They loaded Paulie into the van and began a quiet drive to Doc.

"Back again?" she said with a tone slightly too judgmental for Vinny's liking.

WHEN HE AWOKE, Vinny looked down as he had the first time. Jubilation filled him as he lifted the new arm. That arm which he had so long coveted. It moved silently and precisely the way his weak, natural arm had. He touched the metallic thumbs to each forefinger, grinning at each satisfying little click.

The workmanship was pristine. The machinery was constructed by industry leading Osaka Cybernetics, but the façade had been perfectly crafted by Sicilian artisans. Obsidian black with etched gold trim styled to look like growing vines on the hills of Italy, it was the most beautiful thing Vinny had ever seen.

He was becoming a work of art.

He kept his antiquated arm on the other side as a

reminder of where he had come from, but this new arm represented where he was going.

He would be a powerhouse of mind constructed of metal.

He would be as feared for his strength as he had been respected for his prowess.

Doc looked at him with an expression he didn't recognize but took for absolute awe.

As he stepped out onto the street, he surveyed his dominion. He breathed in deep, watching the denizens look at him and run. He had what he desired. The scrawny kid was now a force, if not of nature, then of human will.

The sensation filled every ounce of him, and he wanted more, needed this feeling to last.

When he brought all the local pimps to heel, he celebrated with high definition eyes, capable of analyzing a situation and relaying information directly to his brain.

When he doubled the profits of the drug runners by further diluting each dose, he replaced his legs so he could tower over all the people who had looked down on him.

When he boosted a weapons truck bound for the local Carcer facility, selling the guns on the streets, he used the money to procure a top-of-the-line cybernetic heart. His pathetic, weak willed father had succumbed to a heart attack a year earlier and Vinny swore that no such fate would befall him.

Vice Grip

. . .

"The Commission is worried," The Boss said. Vinny sat across the long table from him in the back room of Bella Trattoria. "That hit against Carcer was too brazen. They need you to lay low a little while while they grease some palms."

Vinny scowled. He couldn't believe that anyone would tell him what to do. He had become the biggest earner in the organization and had brought in more money over the last several years than anyone. "The Commission don't tell me what to do."

The Boss's lip twitched nearly imperceptibly. "No, you're right," he said slowly. "They tell *me* what to do and *I* tell you what to do."

Vinny felt the fire within him begin to blaze into an inferno. The man before him was The Boss, the most powerful man in all the southern city states and he was allowing himself to be ordered around. It disgusted Vinny.

"You're going to pull me off the streets?" he seethed through flashing microsrceen teeth.

The Boss sighed slowly, letting the air escape his lips for what felt like an hour. "Just for a bit. You'll keep your take and be back at it in no time."

"I didn't see them fucking complaining when I was bringing in assloads of cash!" Vinny screamed. He was furious. No one could tell him to take a break. He was too mighty, too great to be ordered around by some group of nobodies out East.

The Boss leaned forward, the cushion of his chair exhaling at the shift in weight. His face was cast into shadows as he steepled his fingers and said, "This isn't a request. Don't make me remind you how things work and do not make me repeat myself, capiche?"

The door opened behind Vinny and two enforcers stepped into the room.

"Yes, sir," Vinny said like the little boy outside the convenience store. He stood and locked eyes with one of the men.

His grim expression read "don't do it," but Vinny was not going to take orders from anyone. Not from some bruiser and not from a man who wouldn't defend him to the commission.

It happened in a flash.

Vinny's new fist cracked one man's skull so badly it got stuck for a moment in the cavity. The other man moved on him, grabbing him around the neck with a metal arm of his own.

Vinny wouldn't be like the clerk or the hacker. He wouldn't flail like a rat caught in a trap. His vision began to blur as he used his rusted pinchers to grab the man's testicles.

The pop was drowned out by the scream. Vinny sucked in air as he was released, wheeling on the man and kicking him through the wall with his robotic legs.

The Boss, the man who never showed any emotions, looked at Vinny in terror.

Vinny grinned maniacally. The most powerful man he had ever known was now seeing him for the god that he was.

The look on The Boss's face was everything Vinny had ever wanted, and he drank it in like an alcoholic having his first beer after work.

The Boss produced a gun from the desk and fired shot after shot into his chest. The bullets struck the nanomesh skin before falling uselessly to the ground. He felt the pain and his ribs would be damaged, but he would be fine.

He strode over and looked down at the scared man with delight. "No one tells me what to do anymore," he grinned, his eyes focused. He took The Boss's forehead between his fingers, Paulie's fingers, and began to squeeze.

THE COMMISSION WOULD BE after him now, but if he could fend them off and promise them money, he could take the top job in the city. He could be the man his new body demanded.

But he would need to hide and gather his troops if he was going to last long enough to do that.

It worked. Against all odds, it worked.

The commission didn't want to start a war, and Vinny figured that they were too scared of him to try to oust him. He had been forced to make a sizable donation to the Carcer

Committee on Civic Safety and promise not to steal from the company again, but that was no matter.

He had become the boss, and he was satisfied as his car dropped onto the landing pad outside Gian's estate in the Garden District. A bounce house was set up and kids splashed in the pool as Vinny stepped out.

He watched as the adults covered their mouths as they saw him emerge.

Gian hustled over, giving his friend an unwanted hug. "You made it!" he said but there was a hint of sadness in his voice.

"I wouldn't miss your kid's fifth birthday for the world," he lied, wishing he was anyplace else. He liked the attention his arrival had garnered, but as soon as the parents went back to drinking and eating their barbeque, his temporary enjoyment vanished.

"Come have a drink with me," Gian offered, putting his hand on Vinny's back and guiding him to the house. He guided Vinny through the palatial plantation house of white walls lined with fine art. A drudge, the ubiquitous robot servants, brought two glasses of fine bourbon as they reclined on plush leather couches in the study.

Vinny couldn't help but chuckle at the things his friend wasted money on.

"Look, Vince, we need to talk," Gian said.

Vinny huffed and chuckled. "You breakin' up with me?"

Gian didn't laugh, he just looked sullen and took a sip.

"I need out," he said softly. "I've got more money than I could ever spend, and now I want to spend my time with family."

Vinny could not believe what he was hearing. "You want out?" he mocked. "You don't just get out!"

Gian shook his head. "I can if *you'll* let me," he nearly whispered.

"And what if I won't let you?" Vinny shouted, his vision blurring with anger.

Gian took another drink. "You will because I'm your oldest friend and you love me."

Vinny felt his face burn. He *had* loved Gian, but he hated this feeble creature who was trying to leave him. He couldn't understand. "What's this about, money?"

"No!" Gian exclaimed. "I just said it isn't about money. It's never been about money for me. I only ever did this because it's what you wanted. I wanted to help you, to protect you, but you don't need me anymore. *Vinny Rust* doesn't need me."

The words hurt worse than when he had been shot. He began to hate the man standing before him: this former friend who now wanted to turn his back on him. "I can't believe you! How long have you been this way?"

"Been this way?" Gian said with a disgusted laugh. "I've always been what I am. But why don't you try taking a look in the mirror! You've become a machine. A literally heartless robot no different than a drudge!"

Vinny took a step toward Gian, metal palm open.

He stopped.

This pathetic weakling wasn't even worth his time. "What I've *become*," he sneered. "Is powerful. You want out? Fine. Get out. You have my blessing. Go live some life where your only fucking legacy is that little brat outside."

He began to stomp from the room but turned, pointing an accusatory finger etched with gold. "But I never want to see your face again. You want out, then you're dead to me."

Storming away, he heard Gian call after him, "I love you, Vince."

He didn't care. Meaningless words from a meaningless man.

He slammed the door to his car so hard it burst the hinges, falling to the ground below as he drifted into the sky.

He thought about the betrayal the whole ride home. The man who had always prided himself on seeing everyone for who they were had been fooled. It wouldn't happen again. His mind was getting soft and he needed to fix it.

No one would play Vinny Rust again.

VINNY PULLED the burlap sack from the man's face and his mouth fell open.

He didn't understand, didn't know what he was looking at.

The face staring back at him was his own.

Blinking hard, he felt the chair under him. He looked at his hands to see the screwdriver slick with blood and as he opened the other, an implant. The side of his head felt cold.

He thought back, trying to remember.

He had left Gian's house and gone straight to Doc.

"I want the N900 neural chip!" he had demanded. It was the only way. The cognition implant would raise the level of his mind to that of his body.

Doc looked at him, her whole body shaking in dread. She shook her head violently. "No," she wailed.

He pointed to the chip in the display case. "You have it, I want it!"

"No," she said again. "It's for display purposes only. You need a surgeon, supervised by several company technicians to install something like that."

"You're a doctor," he snarled. "You can do it."

She shook her head, holding her hands up and beginning to weep as he moved closer. "I- I can't, it would kill you."

She was pathetic. Weak and useless. Vinny may have been fooled once, but he was strong and smart and could figure anything out. Seeing red, he smashed the case and snatched the chip.

"Fine, I'll do it myself!" he screamed as he left.

She called after him, but the words fell on deaf ears.

THAT WAS IT.

He looked at the screwdriver again, seeing a bit of his brain matter on the tip of the drill bit.

He understood. There was no burlap sack, no judgmental thugs. There were only the delusions of a dying mortal mind sitting alone in a vacant warehouse. He had come so far, accomplished so much, but he would soon be just another body in the bayou.

He had been born weak and chased strength too far. With every augment, he had descended deeper into addiction.

Vinny now knew what he was.

He was his parents. He was his brother.

His head dropped, black closing in on his vision.

His own words echoed in his mind. "You know the thing about vice."

THE END

ABOUT THE AUTHOR

MATTHEW A. GOODWIN is a science fiction and fantasy author who started writing at twelve years old and never stopped. He *loves* cyberpunk and wanted to share that passion so much that he created and co-founded Cyberpunk Day, a celebration of all things high tech/low life. He lives in San Francisco, California with his wife and son and enjoys exploring the world and looking for wildlife.

If you enjoyed this story, check out his series, *A Cyberpunk Saga* at www.ThutoWorld.com

2. WE ARE THE GOOD GUYS
BY ANNA MOCIKAT

Kay Morris is a nobody with an unexciting life. Until a series of bad luck renders him unable to pay-off his artificial kidneys. Cornered, he gets involved with the wrong people to help him pay his debt. The very wrong people.

Kay soon finds out that he had no idea what real trouble looks like...

Kay closed his eyes. He took a deep breath.

This wasn't happening. It could not be true. A nightmare, it had to be a nightmare! Any moment he would wake up in bed.

His veins were pumping frantically in his temples. Never

in his life had he sprinted so fast and over such a long distance despite being an athlete. Well, not anymore, but he used to be. Kay's heart pounded so hard that for a moment, he was concerned it could be heard outside of his body. It felt like a bird trapped in his chest, frantically trying to escape. At the same time, he was trying to escape his pursuers.

Carefully, he peeked around the cover he was hiding behind. Was it possible? Had he lost them?

Could it really be...?

Then he saw something.

Something that made his blood freeze.

Oh no...

How in the world did he even manage to end up in such a situation? A good question. Kay knew exactly how...

THREE WEEKS EARLIER.

"WHAT THE HELL DO YOU MEAN?" Kay pressed out between his teeth. "You can't possibly be serious. There has to be some sort of error!"

He licked over his dry lips and felt sweat building upon his forehead, although the room was air-conditioned.

The girl behind the counter remained professional, but Kay was certain he spotted a glint of contempt in her unnaturally bright amber eyes. The long eyelashes were equipped with tiny diodes on their tips, which made them glow in rainbow colors whenever she blinked. It was the latest fashion trend in Olympias.

Kay had to admit that she actually looked pretty hot. Under different circumstances, maybe he would have asked her out. But not like this. Oh no.

A smile appeared on her well-shaped mouth, wearing purple lipstick. It was so well-trained that it almost looked genuine.

"I wish I could give you better news, Mr. Morris," she said with a friendly voice that faked compassion. "But those are our policies. You knew about them when you signed the contract."

He stared at her in growing despair. "But... what am I supposed to do now?"

Again, a cheery rainbow flashed over her eyes as she blinked. "We understand that your situation is difficult. Which is why we're granting you seven days to pay your outstanding dues."

He ran his slightly shaky fingers through his dark hair, which badly needed a cut. It had grown so long that it almost covered the neural implant on his temple, a clumsy, outdated model. The newer ones were much smaller and came in fancy colors.

"Seven days?" he asked. "How am I supposed to do that?"

"Frankly," she answered with a smile so sweet that it could cause diabetes in anyone looking at her. "That's not our concern. If you fail to do so, it is our right to extract our property from your body."

He paled, horrifying images flashing through his mind. "You can't do that…"

"Mr. Morris," she said, turning her attention towards her holo screen. It was only now that he noticed that she had a tiny implant on her cheek, which resembled a beauty mark and shimmered in colors matching her eyelashes. "According to our files, you have a cognitive implant, two synthetic kidneys, and an augmented ankle manufactured by Olympias Limb Inc. They are merely paid off by 25%, and you failed to pay your dues two months in a row now. By contract, this gives us every right to retrieve our property."

"But I can't survive without the kidneys!" he blurted out, cold sweat covering his forehead now.

She tilted her head, and what she would say next would haunt him for the rest of his life. "We understand that life sometimes can become too much. Tiring. If you wish, we can make arrangements for you. I can give you a 70% discount with our sister company, *Sleep Well,* for the most pleasant exit experience available. We provide the best environment and medical staff you can imagine. It will not only happen completely painlessly but will end your suffering once and for all."

She handed him a holo brochure designed in cheery colors. "The deal is only valid if you agree to donate any healthy organs for recycling and all available brain tissue for research purposes."

Kay pulled a step away, feeling how a terrible cold crept up his body, starting in his feet, up his spine to his heart. A paralyzing cold. Panic.

"I'm only 34 years old…"

She looked back at her monitor. "That's correct. According to our files, your birthday was three days ago. Happy belated birthday!"

Kay turned around and ran. He felt as if the huge room suddenly had shrunk as if the glass walls were coming towards him to crush him. All he knew was that he needed to get out of there. He needed fresh air, or he would faint.

Gasping for breath like a drowning fish, he ran by dozens of other glass desks identical to the one of the clerk with the colorful eyelashes who had been assigned to his case.

The walls of the hall were decorated with cheery holo advertisements, which promised all kinds of fantastic benefits that came with implants and prosthetics manufactured by Olympias Limb Inc.

Of course, none of them mentioned what would happen when someone failed to pay for those benefits.

For a moment, he had the terrifying idea someone would try to stop him. Frantically, he looked to the side, but the security bots lined up at the wall stood there motionless and ignored him, their metallic bodies shimmering in the sunlight.

He kept running. The automatic doors opened and let him pass. On the street, he almost bumped into a woman who was about to enter the building, stumbled and would have fallen if not for his neural implant reacting for him and sending an impulse that stabilized his body just in time.

Kay ran all the way to Prosperity Plaza. The sinking sun reflected from the glass and chrome high-rises, which surrounded him like an inescapable maze. He always believed he was living in the most beautiful and progressive city the world had ever known. Now, however, the 200 and more stories high skyscrapers appeared like monstrosities, and the multiple layers of transportation buzzing in between the buildings high above his head felt claustrophobic.

The reddish sunlight reflecting from the omnipresent glass seemed like fire... or blood.

I don't want to die, he thought.

The idea alone threatened to suffocate him.

Just as he reached Prosperity Park adjacent to the busy plaza, he heard an alarm sound in his ear. A phone-call. Like most people, he had a tiny device connected to his neural link, implanted directly into his ear. It gave him access to the grid and let him make and receive phone calls without having to use any external device.

Kay wasn't in the mood to talk to anybody right now. He tried to ignore the call, but to his great surprise, it turned out to be impossible.

With a soft click, the connection was established, and a

second later, he heard a silky voice speaking directly into his ear—a voice which he had become to hate in such a short time.

"Mr. Morris, this is Melanie from Olympias Limb Inc. Since you left so abruptly, I thought I would give you a quick reminder. You have seven days to pay your outstanding bills before we retrieve our property. Please keep in mind that we can track our products implanted into your body no matter where you go at all times. Have a wonderful day!"

Kay stopped short, gasping for air. Then he slowly walked to the nearest park bench and let himself fall onto it in resignation.

NIGHT HAD FALLEN over Olympias City I, the capital of the Olympias Conglomerate. Built over what used to be Atlanta, the mega-city offered its inhabitants the best life in the history of mankind. It was a place of happiness where everyone was free to become and achieve whatever they wished. Society had gotten rid of everything that had been divisive and had made human life miserable in earlier centuries.

It was a perfect utopia.

Yet, it had turned into a nightmare for Kay Morris.

He sat on the bench in Prosperity Park and stared into the night, which never turned really dark in this place.

Halogen lamps glimmered in the trees and bushes surrounding him, simulating oversized lighting bugs. The artificial waterfall falling from a sub-level of the transportation platform hovering above the park was illuminated in cheerful indigo and amethyst colors. Birds singing and crickets chirping came from speakers well hidden from the visitor's eyes.

Like a forest of glass, chrome, and steel, the countless skyscrapers surrounded the small, peaceful oasis of green. Myriad lights flickered from their illuminated windows and facades. Oversized holo-ads in all shades of neon vied for peoples' attention, displaying all kinds of goods the modern citizen needed to achieve perfect happiness.

However, most people were so busy with themselves that they didn't even notice.

Kay sat there, resting his hands on his chin and staring at the ground.

How in the world had he ended up like this?

If he was honest with himself, this shouldn't come much as a surprise. His life had been going downward for quite some time now.

When he was young, things looked bright for him. Athletic and in good shape by nature, he had been part of the field and track team of his college and almost started a professional sports career. A stupid accident ruined his plans. And it wasn't even anything sports-related. An automatic door of the monorail he used every day to commute to school experienced a malfunction. It closed prematurely when he was getting inside the train and crushed his ankle. The damage was so bad that the bones had to be replaced by synthetic ones.

After this, he was expelled from the sports team where augmented limbs weren't allowed – for obvious reasons.

Kay finished college and found employment as a chemist at Lab Corp, Olympias' second-biggest manufacturer of opioids. Things went well for him for a couple of years. He had a decent income, a fancy apartment, and his good looks made it easy for him to find hookups or casuals whenever he wanted. Until one day, everything changed dramatically.

Contrary to the generation younger than twenty-five, who was almost entirely genetically engineered, he had been conceived the old-fashioned way. Nobody knew that he had a genetic defect; otherwise, he never would have been born or would have been euthanized at an early age. The defect had been hidden deep in his DNA, a rare condition that revealed itself as kidney disease and eventual kidney failure.

At the age of thirty-one, Kay had received two completely synthetic kidneys, manufactured by Olympias Limb Inc. He had chosen the brand because he already had a neural implant and the ankle prosthetics from them, and they offered a nice rebate if he got the kidneys there as well.

Without thinking much about it, he had signed the standard contract which obligated him to pay off his parts for the next fifteen years. It was expensive, but the alternative would have been constant dialysis. Besides, with a steady income and a good outlook on promotion in the foreseeable future, paying his dues should have been no problem.

Until bad luck struck him again.

His supervisor in the lab, a woman twenty years older than him, demanded him to not only become her casual but also engage in acts with her friends, which he didn't feel comfortable with at all. Sadly, the "old harpy," as she was called behind her back, didn't take no for an answer.

Kay didn't think much of it at first. He hadn't been happy in his job for a couple of months before the incident and had considered quitting anyway. But when he applied at other chemical manufacturers, he got rejected everywhere without ever even being invited for an interview. It took him more than six months to find out that the harpy had filed a complaint of sexual harassment against him when she fired him. Since every employer could view his full career documentation in the grid, every HR instantly gave him a pass. Nobody wanted to hear his side of the story.

Four months later, he was broke.

In a society that had gotten rid of all traditional social structures, everyone stood for themselves. Kay had no friends or family who could help him out. One day he got a note from Olympias Limb Inc., which invited him into their service center to discuss "his options."

As it turned out, his options were none.

Kay sighed. He had no idea what to do. Was there even

anything he could do that would save him now? Or was Melanie, the uber-sweet clerk with the rainbow eyelashes, right after all? Maybe life wasn't for him?

"Shitty day, huh?" he suddenly heard a voice next to him and almost jumped in surprise.

Looking up, he saw a stranger standing next to him. It was a woman in her late twenties. She wasn't really beautiful, but her face had something unusual, something alluringly natural. A friendly smile displayed on her lips.

"You could say so," he answered after a moment of puzzlement. Nobody ever talked to strangers like that.

"May I sit?" she asked and sat down next to him without waiting for an answer.

Then she pulled something out of her pocket and held it toward him. Looking down, he noticed it was a slightly old-fashioned looking flask.

He lifted his hands. "No, thank you…"

"Try it," she said with a friendly tone. "It's exactly what you need."

He shrugged and took it. "Whatever…"

Taking a sip, he realized it was strong alcohol, one he had never tried before. It burned down his throat and made him cough.

"What the fuck is this?" he asked.

She chuckled. "Medicine. Try again."

He did. And this time it went down better, much better.

"See?" she said, studying him from the side.

He took another, much bigger sip, then handed her the flask back. "Thank you."

She gave him a warm smile. "My name is Veronica."

Less than an hour later, they were at his place. Although Kay was aware that this was maybe not the right moment for a hookup, he didn't say no. There was something so charming about her, so sweet. He knew it was crazy, but Veronica seemed as if she would care.

Since he was broke and couldn't pay for a funtel, they went to his apartment, which was only three miles away from Prosperity Plaza. She didn't mind, which was unusual as well.

An autonomous driving cab was all he could afford, and they started making out inside. Once at his apartment, all his despair turned into passion. They ripped their clothes off each other when they were barely through the door.

She stayed overnight, which was unusual, too. Nobody did that. Watching her sleep in his arms, he realized that it was too early to give up yet. Life had been fucked up for him lately, but it wasn't over yet.

She blew him a kiss when she left in the morning, her long, blonde hair falling in her oval face, her grey-green eyes sparkling. It was only then he noticed that she didn't have any visible augmentations.

This could only mean that she was rich, as augmentations that stayed invisible were the most expensive ones. It would never have crossed Kay's mind that she actually didn't have any. Everyone was augmented one way or the other.

In the evening, she came back, and their second time was even more passionate than the first one.

"Why are you so sad, Kay?" Veronica asked him, pressing her naked body against his after they were done.

And he told her. He told her everything that had happened. And that he was basically a dead man walking. It just seemed ok to share it with her. Her big eyes looked at him in such a caring, compassionate way. She was in every way the absolute opposite of women such as Melanie who were all fake and didn't care about anyone or anything but themselves.

She listened to everything quietly, caressing his cheek. Once he was finished, she remained silent for a moment.

Then she said: "What if I could make it go away?"

"Go away?" he answered perplexed.

"Your debt. It could be gone tomorrow."

"You would clear it for me?" he asked in disbelief. This couldn't be what she meant. No, impossible.

"I can pay your outstanding dues and your monthly rates from now on," she said.

"That would be fantastic!" He kissed her hand. "You would save my life!"

She smiled. "In return, all you have to do is do the people I work for a little favor now and then."

"What kind of favor?"

"Nothing really exciting. Small things."

For a moment, he wasn't sure what to say. This sounded odd. Somewhere deep inside him, his instinct was telling him: Nope. Bad idea.

Seeing his sudden insecurity, Veronica chuckled. Then she got up and began dressing.

"Think about it until tomorrow. But if you ask me, what do you have to lose?"

She winked at him, then left.

And that was when Kay's trouble really started.

OF COURSE, he took the job.

Veronica was right. He had nothing to lose but his kidneys, which meant his life.

Besides, he trusted her. There was such a genuine friendliness in her eyes, and she was so tender with him, as no one had ever been before. Like all citizens of Olympias, Kay had countless affairs and sexual encounters in his life. But everyone always seemed to be only interested in themselves and their own pleasure. Veronica was different. She genuinely seemed to want to make him happy. She didn't care about his unfortunate situation or that he was broke. All she wanted was to help him.

In the beginning, everything went well. The tasks he was

assigned were indeed easy. Veronica visited him three to four times a week and brought data sticks with instructions. All he had to do was travel to the assigned points all around the city and wait while pretending to do something innocuous, such as window shopping, buying coffee, or checking his status update in the grid VR.

After a while, somebody would approach him and start a conversation using specific pre-determined keywords. All he had to do was hand over the data sticks to those people in an unsuspicious way. The people he met were diverse. One day it could be an elegant lady who looked like she'd come straight from the Inner Circle and another time a rather shady looking individual he met in the Underground, Olympias notorious hub for semi-legal tech in the heart of Oldtown, which was nothing but former downtown Atlanta. Often, the contact had also brought a data stick, which they handed over to him, and he returned it to Veronica.

Kay didn't quite understand what all of this was about. If those people had business with each other, why didn't they just write an email or call or meet in the VR? Why this secrecy? The only logical answer was that they had something to hide. Most likely, something illegal.

One day he asked Veronica about it, but she simply smiled, saying: "That's none of your business, sweetheart. All I can tell you is that it's for a good cause. We are the good guys."

That was all she was willing to answer, and he left it at

that. After all, he didn't want to anger her. Not only was he growing more and more fond of her every time they met, she had also kept her end of the bargain. Right after he delivered a data stick for the first time, he got a call from Melanie, the nightmarish clerk with the rainbow eyelashes, who informed him that his outstanding dues had been cleared, as well as his payments for three months in advance.

Kay had to sit down for a moment after the message. He was so relieved that he almost started crying. It didn't matter what Veronica and her strange associates were doing, if it was legal or not. Her payment had saved his life. And that was not all. After two weeks, she came by and gave him a bonus for his good work. The amount of money stored on the untraceable C-Card was higher than what he had earned in two months in his previous job. Kay could hardly believe how lucky he was. He invited Veronica into an upscale restaurant that night, and after that, they had the best sex ever. Kay felt like he was in paradise.

But not for long.

Soon after that everything went to hell. Like, really to hell.

IT WAS a day like any other in his new life. Kay took the high-speed monorail to his designated meeting point only a few miles away from Oldtown. Almost noon, it was a hot summer day, with the sun shining down mercilessly. Reflected by the omnipresent glass and the solar panels which almost every high-rise was equipped with, it made Kay feel like walking through a gigantic baking oven. The meeting point was only a five-minute walk from the airconditioned monorail station, but Kay was soaked in sweat when he arrived. He hoped the contact would show up in time and that he could return home quickly, drink a cool soy beer, and play some games in the VR for the rest of the day. There was a new game coming out which he had been anticipating for a long time, as had every other gamer in Olympias: Steampunk 2020. Kay couldn't wait to dive into it as soon as he got home.

And then, in the evening, hopefully, Veronica would drop by and make the day perfect.

A smile on his face, he stood there and waited. And waited...

The contact was late. This had never happened before. After twenty minutes of waiting in the glaring sun, when he was just about to consider leaving, he heard a voice: "Good afternoon, Kay."

Startled, he spun around on his heel in surprise. And stared into a stranger's face.

He had no idea how the man had managed to sneak up on him the way he did, as Kay could have sworn he wasn't there just a second ago. The stranger had literally appeared out of thin air.

"Hi," Kay answered, giving himself a mental push and trying to appear as casual as possible.

Never before had any of the contacts addressed him by name. Besides, something about the man was strange, unnatural. Not that anyone appeared natural in Olympias. Anyone but Veronica. But this guy had something disturbing about him, and Kay couldn't even say what it was. It was more a feeling deep in his gut, which made his skin turn ice-cold despite the blazing heat.

The handsome man was dressed completely in black, wearing a fashionable suit and a coat. His snow-white hair stood up ten inches into the air and gave a nice contrast to his perfect, ebony skin.

Despite the heat, he did not sweat at all and appeared as if he didn't even notice it. Black shades covered his eyes. Even though he was smiling friendly, something was unsettling frosty about him.

"I think you have something for me," the stranger said, slowly extending his palm.

Kay forced himself to stop staring and reminded himself to follow the guidelines.

"The Grasshopper lies heavy," he said.

Every time the code was a different one. Veronica gave it to him when she handed over the device with precise instructions on what the contact person was required to answer.

"If you say so," the man answered. "Now give me what you have for me."

Although still smiling, he waved his black-gloved fingers impatiently.

A wave of cold hit Kay as if he had stepped into a fridge. Tiny, icy needles crept up his spine.

This was not the right answer. The answer should have been: *So says the Man in the High Castle.*

Whoever this creepy guy was, he was not his contact.

"Excuse me, sir," Kay mumbled. "I think you're mistaking me with someone else. Have a great day!"

He turned and began walking away. Maybe this was nothing, just a stupid coincidence.

Of course, it was not.

The air right in front of him flickered, similar to when sunlight hits the water. The phenomenon intensified for a second before it disappeared, revealing another black-clad figure right in front of him.

Kay staggered. His eyes turned wide as he stared at the woman who had materialized directly in front of him. He would never have believed such stealth tech really existed. He thought it was science fiction.

The woman was tall and gracious, dressed in extravagant clothes with straight, asymmetric black hair framing an angelic, Asian-Caucasian face. Her eyes, too, were covered by black sunglasses.

"In a hurry, Kay?" she asked with a sneer.

"I... um... have an urgent appointment," he stammered, while cold sweat broke out on his forehead. A horrible suspicion formed somewhere in the back of his head.

"Is that so? I'm afraid you'll have to skip that."

Saying so, she took off her glasses. Her almond-shaped eyes remained closed for a moment. When she opened them, Kay gasped for air while all the blood in his body froze solid.

No... no no no...

Her eyes gleamed in an ice-cold neon-blue.

Kay had heard of them. Everybody had. They were like the boogeyman. Like specters which nobody really knew if they existed or not. Because usually, nobody lived long enough to tell the story of their encounter with them.

The Guardian Angels of Olympias.

The legendary elite cyborg squad, created to protect the Olympias Conglomerate and the corporation ruling it from outside and within – at any cost.

In his worst nightmares, Kay would never have anticipated he would run into any of them. But this was not what had happened here. They had sought him out.

"We know who you are, Kay Morris," she said calmly, each of her words like an icicle piercing his heart. "We know what you're doing. You're a data-mule. All we want is the information you're carrying and the name of your handler. Then you're free to go and continue living your pathetic little life no one cares about."

Suddenly life returned into Kay's body.

Veronica!

Memories flashed through his mind. How she smiled at him, caressed his cheek…how she cared.

She had saved him, had believed in him when nobody did. He would never sell her out!

Without thinking twice about what he was doing, he fled. The former athlete in him woke, and he ran faster than ever before in his life.

He didn't look back, certain they would pursue him; he did not dare to look.

If he had, he would have seen that they instead stayed where they were, exchanging a look. Then a sharkish smile formed on both of their perfect faces.

At first, Kay only felt panic. He didn't know where to run, where to hide, what to do. All of a sudden, an idea shot into his head. So clear, that he was surprised about himself. He knew the building he had been standing and waiting at well. There was a bar on the 87th floor he had liked to frequent. Once upon a time, when his life had still been the one of a normal corporate associate.

Kay stormed through the door of the high-rise and ran towards the elevators. He was lucky for once. The door of one was about to close, and he squeezed himself inside. Right before he went in, he dared to peek behind him. No neon-blue eyes were chasing him.

The people inside the elevator deliberately ignored the

sweaty guy with the haunted expression on his face, although one or two lifted their eyebrows in contempt.

Kay didn't care. His thoughts were as clear as never before in his life.

Yes, at first glance, only an idiot would run upstairs when chased by a monster. But he was no total idiot. He remembered that on the 90th floor, right above the bar, was a glass bridge connecting this building and the one across the road.

Kay took a deep breath and sprinted out of the elevator as soon as it reached the 90th floor. Glass bridge or no, it still wasn't the smartest plan to run upstairs – but Kay had a little life insurance in his pocket.

He had been so puzzled and in panic when encountering the cyborgs that he had completely forgotten about it. Now his fingers cramped around the little device in his pocket, his heart racing.

Veronica had given it to him before she sent him off on his first assignment. He could still hear her words in his ear. Her soft voice, which sometimes seemed to carry a slight accent. So distant that it had taken him several hookups with her even to hear it.

"If you should ever encounter any kind of trouble, use this. It will deactivate the tracers integrated into your implants and prosthetics for several minutes. You will become invisible, untraceable."

Kay pressed the button on the device. Nothing happened,

at least nothing he could feel or see. But he trusted that the device would do what Veronica had promised.

Kay forced himself to run even faster. He reached the glass corridor and crossed it quickly. After entering the building on the other side, he stopped for a moment, holding his side and thinking about what he should do next. With a bit of luck, the cyborgs would look for him in the wrong building.

All he needed to do was lay low for a moment and keep away from surveillance cams, then try and sneak out of the building... and then... he had no idea what then. He would plan when he got there.

He jumped into the next elevator he could find and rode to the uppermost floor. From there, he took the stairs to the roof. Out of breath, he hid behind an air-conditioning vent, which stuck out of the roof like an oversized antenna.

There Kay remained motionless for a moment, trying to catch his breath and calm his thoughts. Maybe he had a chance. Maybe he was lucky for once in his miserable life and could escape them. Find Veronica. She would know what to do...

Carefully he peeked around the corner of the vent and froze in horror. The two black-clad killers entered the roof. But, to his fortune, the wrong one! For a moment, they stood there motionless. If the pursuit had exhausted them, then they didn't show. The two Angels exchanged a look, clearly communicating with each other without the use of words.

Then the woman abruptly turned her head and stared in his direction. Kay flinched and hid deeper behind his cover, holding his breath. Did she spot him? If she did, all he could do now was run. Reach the next elevator and rush down on the ground floor. Maybe he could jump into a robo-cab and escape them? They were in the wrong building. This was his chance. They couldn't reach him easily.

Carefully, he peeked around the corner and saw the female cyborg slowly walking towards the rim of the other roof. Just when Kay began to wonder what she was up to, she fell into a breakneck sprint. A speed so unnatural that no human could ever achieve it, not even highly augmented ones.

Kay paled. No, she wouldn't... she couldn't possibly jump the distance between the roofs!

The next seconds felt like slow motion to Kay as his jaw dropped, and his eyes turned wide like plates.

He saw her sprinting toward the rim, like a panther aiming towards its prey. Then she jumped.

She took a leap which should have been impossible, crossing the distance over a hundred feet or more with easiness and grace, as if it was nothing to her.

Kay watched her land, her legs and arms easily absorbing the impact. Then she slowly straightened up and smirked.

Suddenly Kay knew that this was death approaching him. He would never have imagined the Grim Reaper so beautiful and frightening at the same time.

It was pure instinct that made him run again, as his mind was telling him that it was futile. The cyborg had cut off the only way down from the roof, and all he could do was run toward the rim of the building, like an idiot.

He stopped and looked down. Only a few inches away from him, it went down two hundred stories. The hot wind coming up the glass front ruffled his sweaty hair. A wave of vertigo hit him. Nauseated, he backed off, bringing a step between him and the abyss.

"Where do you think you're going, Kay?" he heard a mocking voice behind him.

He spun around and faced his nemesis. She stood there calmly, her arms crossed, slowly tapping her black boot.

"I've done nothing wrong!" he gasped.

"Then why are you running?"

He didn't know an answer to that and simply sighed in despair.

"Look," she said, "we are not your enemy. We are the good guys. Do you understand?"

He nodded, although he did not understand. Not a bit.

"You're being used as a data-mule by agents of a foreign corporation. It's how they communicate between their cells, so they stay unnoticed from the grid. You're just a useful idiot for them. Expendable. Give me the data you carry. And if you help us find the people who set you up, you will go free."

She extended her hand, and a smile appeared on her face that almost looked genuine.

A strong gust of wind blew over the roof and made her shiny, latex-like coat flutter behind her, revealing the firearms she was carrying under it.

Kay backed off. Mesmerized by the black-clad angel of death, he didn't even notice that his heels were almost touching the rim.

The cyborg tilted her head. "Help me, and I help you, Kay."

He hesitated. But then slowly shook his head. This was like making a pact with the devil. And the devil always won.

"No," he whispered. "No."

"No?" she replied. "Really? Well, in that case..."

He flinched in horror as he watched as she slowly extended a long, sharp, black shining blade directly out of her wrist.

"In that case," she repeated. "I can cut out your eyeballs, make you eat them, and then take what I want. How about that?"

He shook, the horrific threat visualizing in his head.

"Give it to me. What do you have to lose?"

Kay sighed and slowly moved his hand into his pocket. Without noticing it, he shifted half a step back. Suddenly his foot slipped, and he lost balance. Panic grabbed his heart as he realized he was falling. Waving his arms helplessly, he saw that the cyborg rolled her eyes, grinning.

He would take this last view into his grave. Kay fell.

Realizing that he would die, a strange feeling of peace

filled him. He had been a loser all his life. He never achieved anything of importance, was just one tiny screw in this gigantic machine which called itself the perfect society. A society which cared about no one, which had considered him as expendable. To survive, he had become a little pawn, used by giants in their never-ending power game.

But in the end, he had achieved a little victory. He had resisted *them*. The most frightening and powerful weapon in human history. *They* didn't get what they wanted.

Kay clenched his fist around the data stick. The concrete came closer.

The impact smashed his body into an unrecognizable pulp.

———

THE ROOFTOP DOOR was opened forcefully, and the male cyborg entered. His augmentations weren't as powerful as his partners, so he had to take the long way through the corridor to reach the other building. He came just in time to see the data-mule fall.

He laughed, approaching the woman. "Damn it, Neph. Did you scare the poor idiot so much that he jumped?"

She swung around and squinted an eye. "It wasn't me. He fell."

"Right," the man answered with a chuckle, then looked

down from the roof. "I doubt there will be much left of the data stick."

She shrugged, slowly walking towards the exit. "Maybe. Forensics will take care of the mess. And we would have terminated the little piece-of-shit anyway, so it doesn't really matter."

Then she turned towards him and winked. "That was a good hunt, wasn't it?"

"It was."

"It's always a joy to see the hope in their eyes when they realize we're not chasing them." Her neon-blue eyes gleamed in amusement. "Now, all we need to do is take out his handler, and another cell is gone. Fuckers hide like rats in the shadows, having no augmentations we could trace."

"Let's have a drink first," he suggested. "I saw a bar right under the glass bridge."

She smirked as they walked down the stairs inside the building. "You pay. Since I got to him first."

He rolled his eyes. "You're such a damn poser."

"And you're a sore loser."

Two hundred stories below, Kay's remains were splatted over the pavement. His hand had remained surprisingly intact. It was cramped around the remains of a data stick.

ABOUT THE AUTHOR

. . .

ANNA MOCIKAT IS THE AWARD-NOMINATED, internationally published author of "Behind Blue Eyes", the "Tales of the Shadow City" series and the "MUC" series.

Before becoming a novelist, she graduated from Film School and worked as a screenwriter and game writer for over a decade.

If you liked her short story in this anthology, check out her novel "Behind Blue Eyes" set in the same universe and featuring the killer cyborgs Nephilim and Adriel!

3. **COLLATERAL**
BY MARLIN SEIGMAN

It should have been an easy job of collecting a debt or the cybernetic leg the mark put up as collateral. But when Quinn's emotion dampening implant started malfunctioning, things got complicated.

I don't like loan sharks, but I like being broke even less. Plus, as far as sharks go, Tami wasn't all that bad. She was smart, beautiful, ruthless, and knew how to put all three together in a package that would make most men melt. I'm not most men, so she made me thaw at best. I don't take credit for that. It's my E.D. I know what you're thinking, but it's not what you're thinking. It's the emotional dampener implants, leftovers from my days working corporate security.

When Tami contacted me about a job, I had more days left in the month than I had credits left in my account, so I sacrificed an evening alone and went to her place. She operated out of an old McDonald's on Westheimer and gave out loans at the drive-thru window. Like most old fast food buildings used by sharks, the place was a fortress. The windows had been replaced with reinforced concrete and a maze of razor wire surrounded the entrance. One of the several sentry drones circling overhead came my way when I got out of my car. I tapped the roof of my mouth with my tongue, turning off my scrambling field. The drone hovered and scanned me as I walked under the hollowed-out golden arches and made my way through the razor wire. Satisfied, the drone flew off and a loud clank came from the steel door. It's good to be wanted.

There hadn't been a french fry made in the place in twenty years, but the faint odor of grease still lingered, seeping from the pores of the tile. A couple of Tami's people milled around the dining area, not taking notice of me when I came in. Tami sat behind a desk, the light reflecting off her chrome-colored hair, and waited for the door to shut and lock before she looked up and said, "Quinn, I'm glad you could make it."

"Thanks for calling. I can use the work."

She tilted her head slightly and she frowned, her bright red lips forming an upside down U. "This thing with Teddy has put me in a bind."

Her twin brother, Teddy, was the brawn of the operation and would normally handle anything she asked me to do. As big and mean as she was beautiful and ruthless, he had a smile full of sharpened and polished stainless-steel teeth. After he stopped growing at the age of eighteen, he had both arms replaced with some of the finest street cybernetics around. Unfortunately for Tami, Teddy found himself doing three to five over at the Dominguez unit for assault with a deadly weapon. Or weapons. He and Tami got into an argument with some college boys outside a night club, and Teddy ended up biting off four of one of the kid's fingers. He claimed self-defense, but the kid's father was some sort of corporate executive, so Teddy earned a free vacation in South Texas.

I took a seat across from Tami, bumping my knees on the desk when I sat. "How's Teddy doing?"

"He doesn't like the food. It's all nutrient tubes, and he says there's nothing he can sink his teeth into."

I wasn't sure if she was making a joke or not. I mean, I thought it was funny, but you never know if people are joking when it comes to family. I gave a tentative nod.

She smiled. "You can laugh."

So I did.

"You know Baird, don't you?" she asked, cutting my laugh short.

"Sure. What'd the damn fool do this time?"

"He owes me and is late on payments. Now he's made himself hard to find."

"Typical."

She shrugged. "The risks of the profession."

"You need me to bring him to you?"

She smirked and shook her head. "Bring me what he owes or bring me his leg. You can transfer the credits to this." She pushed a credit transfer chip across the desk. "I guess you'll have to carry the leg."

I picked up the chip. "And just to be clear, did you say to bring you his leg?"

"He put it up for collateral."

"Right or left?"

She grinned. "You choose."

SHE FILLED me in on the contract, and I headed out. Being with her put me in the mood for a burger, so I drove to Johnny's Vats. I hadn't eaten since breakfast, and it would give me a chance to do some research. While I sat eating, I watched a couple of code freaks on the sidewalk outside. One of them held out his forearm, exposing his QR tattoo while the other one scanned the tattoo and sent some code to his subdermal med-chip implant. The guy's face relaxed, and I rubbed the back of my neck where my own chip was implanted. I thought about having it removed when I got clean but decided against it. You never know when you might need medical code for real and not just for fun.

Watching them reminded me of when I first met Baird. He looked like shit when he walked into the recovery meeting, but most people do when they're trying to break a code addiction. I know I did.

He glanced around, nervous and lost. I thought he was going to turn around and leave, so I went over and introduced myself. I think that made him more nervous, but he eventually relaxed and started talking. He had the same old story. Can't keep a job. The wife is threatening to leave. Out of credits. Can't go a day without getting loaded. Like I said, same old story. But he hung around for a while and things got better. About nine months in, he disappeared. That's what people do. Sometimes they come back. Usually, you end up going to their funeral. Or going out to collect credits from them.

After a few bites of the vat burger, I turned on my AR net interface and went digging for Baird's address. I figured that would be the best place to start. It was a long shot, but if he wasn't there, his wife would be. She might have an idea where to find him. That was a long shot too, but you've got to start somewhere. I also did a search for his place of employment. He was working in an office furniture warehouse outside one of the corporate zones. They were closed for the night, but if he didn't turn up by the morning, I would go look at some office furniture.

Baird's apartment, a room in an old Hyatt hotel that had been converted to low-income housing, was a few blocks away, so I decided to walk. Outside, the code freak was sitting against Johnny's building with his legs sprawled out across the sidewalk. I filled my lungs with the humid night air, resisted the sudden urge to stomp on the guy's kneecap, and stepped over him.

The smell of old carpet and spices replaced the humid air when I walked into what used to be the lobby of the old Hyatt. Not a good mixture for my enhanced senses. I've learned to deal with bad smells for the most part, but some combinations cut right through my defenses. Wasn't much I could do about that. When they installed the parietal lobe enhancers, they told me it was a five senses packaged deal. If I wanted one, I got them all. They've refined the tech since, and there was a new software upgrade that let you choose which of the senses you wanted to be enhanced. Sense Select. But it was as expensive as the name was cute. There were some benefits to working corporate I missed.

Several food carts dotted the lobby, and a group of kids ran around, ducking behind the carts, going through some close-quarters firefight tactics, their hands positioned like they were carrying weapons. Probably playing *Death Grin Assault*, the latest AR game. One of the corporate security companies created the game as a recruiting tool and offered free implant upgrades in neighborhoods like this, with in-game purchases of course. I switched on my AR and tapped into their feed. Dead alien zombies, or whatever the hell they were fighting, littered the lobby.

I got out of their feed and went to Baird's apartment on the fifth floor. The sound of a baby crying came through the door. I knocked and the crying got worse. I can't handle crying babies, so I started to leave. I had a feeling Baird wasn't home anyway.

Before I took two steps, the door opened. Baird's wife stood, the door in one hand and a crying baby in need of a diaper change in the other, looking at me like she'd been waiting for bad news. "Who are you?" she asked over the crying.

"My name is Quinn, I'm-"

"From the meeting?"

It hadn't crossed my mind Baird talked to her about me, but it gave me an opportunity to ease into why I was there. "Yeah. From the meeting."

She stepped aside and opened the door. "Come in. I hope you don't mind me changing him."

"No." Anything to stop that crying.

I stood by the door while she put the baby on a blanket on the couch and started changing him.

"I don't know where he is," she said with her back to me. "Haven't seen him in over a week. He was doing so good, then one day..." Her voice trailed off.

"That happens. Do you know where he might be?"

The crying stopped, and she picked up the baby and faced me. "You could try the clubs."

"Any club in particular?"

She shrugged, the baby rising up with her shoulders. "Just start at one and keep going until you find him." She looked at the baby and brushed his cheek with her fingers. "What did he do?"

I started to say something, then took a second to consider how to answer.

"He told me what you do," she said. "I know you're not here because of the meeting."

I nodded. "He owes someone."

She smiled an empty smile. "When you find him, tell him his son misses him."

―――

BLINK WAS the fourth club I went to, and by the time I walked in, I'd had enough of bass and colored lights for the night. Don't get me wrong, I enjoyed a good night at a club as much as anyone, but I hated looking for someone in a club. Most were dark, even for my eyes, and they all had the same smell of alcohol and sweat and grime. I told myself if I didn't find Baird in Blink, I would call it a night and start fresh in the morning.

I took a quick look around and decided to find Neff. Neff was one of those people who just seemed to know things. If you wanted to know something that happened in Blink, you went to Neff.

He was leaning against the bar watching the crowd when I found him. Just taking it all in like he did every night.

"Neff," I said and leaned next to him.

"Quinn. It's been a minute."

"Been busy." I toyed with the idea of small talk, but I wanted the night over with. "Looking for Baird. Have you seen him?"

He turned his attention from the crowd to me. "Tami finally done with him, huh?"

Like I said, Neff knows.

"You know about that?"

He shrugged. "I told him he was playing too close to the edge. But what can you do? He's in the room upstairs."

"Thanks, Neff. I owe you."

He nodded and went back to watching the crowd.

The room upstairs was used for two things: sex and getting loaded on code. The last thing I wanted to do was walk in on Baird going at it with someone, but you do what you've got to do for the pay.

I started to knock but decided to go right in. Baird and the woman didn't even notice me. I thought about what his wife said when I left and grabbed him by the hair and pulled him to his feet.

"What the fuck?" he yelled, trying to pry my fingers from his hair.

"Leave," I said to the woman.

"Asshole," she said as she got dressed.

Baird tried to turn his head to look at me, but every time he did, I tightened my grip.

"Shit. All right," he said and stood still.

"Find me later," the woman said over her shoulder as she left.

I threw Baird to the floor. He rolled over and looked up at me, his face going through a range of emotions.

"Quinn? What the hell?"

"Tami sent me. She wants her credits. Or your leg."

He searched for his pants. "My leg? What the fuck is that supposed to mean?"

"You put a leg up as collateral for a loan."

He grabbed his shirt. "That's crazy. Why would I do that?"

"To get loaded, I guess. Tami said you were out of it when you went to her."

"But I didn't. I haven't gotten a loan from her in a long time. She's crazy, Quinn. You know how crazy she can be."

I shook my head. "She showed me the contract, Baird. Quit the bullshit. Do you have the credits?"

He stood and started in on his story. "Man, I've been bad lately. Mixing things I shouldn't. I must've been in a blackout or something." His voice took on the tone of a kid who realized he got caught with his hand where it shouldn't be. "I mean, isn't there some way, something I can do? Shit Quinn,

I can't give her my leg. How would I work? I need my leg. I've got to provide for my family."

For a brief moment, I felt anger. No, I think it was rage. At first, I didn't know what it was. I felt a pressure behind my eyes, like something in my head needed to bust out. The room took on a crimson color. Looking at Baird made it worse. I almost punched him but closed my eyes and took a breath to get control. That was a mistake. A fucking stupid mistake. I heard Baird move. When I opened my eyes, his foot was connecting with the side of my head.

When I came to, Neff was standing over me. "You okay?"

I looked around the room.

"He's gone. Ran out of here half-dressed," Neff said.

"Damn."

"How'd he get the jump on you?"

I didn't answer and walked out.

―――――

THE NEXT MORNING I went to Jo. She was the best I knew when it came to working on implants. Something was wrong with my E.D., and I couldn't have that. The last thing I needed was to start feeling emotions.

Jo's shop was in the old shopping mall across the street from Baird's Hyatt apartment. She was eye deep in her computer when I walked in. "Hold on," she said without looking up.

I stood by the door, waiting for her to finish. Whatever was wrong, Jo could fix it. She would have to. If I started letting people like Baird kick me in the head, I would be dead in a week.

"Quinn," Jo said. "What can I do for you?"

"I've got a problem with my E.D."

She grinned and started to say something.

"You know what I mean," I said, cutting her off.

She held her hands up, showing her palms. "Sorry. Sorry. I know it's a bad joke. Just tell me what's up."

"I got angry last night. Just a little bit, but it was enough to get this." I pointed to my black eye.

"I wasn't going to mention it, but it looks like somebody got you good."

"I don't want to talk about it."

"Let's get you linked up and see what's what."

Half an hour later, she was shaking her head.

"What?" I asked.

"It's what I thought. Your implants are getting old. The OS is starting to degrade, and you're getting some data corruption."

"Anything you can do?"

"You haven't had an implant upgrade in a while. That would be a start."

"I'm broke. I can't afford new implants."

She nodded. "I could upgrade the OS. Your implant will

take some newer systems, but it would need some tweaking. Or I could try a system restore."

"How long will that take?"

"With an implant as old as yours? The better part of a day to do the restore. You'd need to take it easy for a day after that to make sure it took."

I didn't have that much time. Besides, I couldn't pay her until Tami paid me.

"It can wait," I said. "I've got to finish this job I've got first."

She severed the link with my implant.

"Just be careful," she said. "Once these things start, they can go downhill quick. Your emotions could be intensified, or you could experience random emotions. It's hard to say. And the harder the dampeners have to work, the worse it will get."

Not what I needed to hear.

"Thanks, Jo. I'll be in touch."

It was almost lunchtime, so I made my way to an Indian food place in the old food court on the other side of the mall. Jo took me to it once after she did some work on my sense enhancing implants. I figured Baird would be crashed out somewhere, sleeping off his night. Probably with that same woman. I could use the time to plan out the rest of my day, organize my thoughts.

I was well into my chaat when I got a ping from Tami. I took the time to finish my lunch, watching another group of kids playing *Death Grin Assault*. After I made her wait long enough, I called her.

My AR implant presented her image across the table from me. "How's the hunt?" she asked.

"Getting fueled up before I go get him."

She put her chin in her hand. "I heard you ran into a problem last night."

I shrugged off her comment. "Not really."

She smirked. "Your eye tells a different story. I'll remind you, you lose twenty percent if you don't deliver in thirty-six hours."

"I read the contract."

"I wanted to make sure you were motivated."

Then something happened. I felt irritated. Or frustrated. It can be hard to name emotions when you haven't felt them in years. Before I could figure it out, it was gone.

"It hasn't been twenty-four hours yet," I said. "I've got time."

"Yes, you do. I'll tell you what, Quinn. If you finish the job in under twenty-four hours, I'll tack on a five percent bonus."

How generous.

"Don't worry, I'll get him soon." I cut the feed.

I tried to put myself in Baird's shoes. Where would I go if

I were him and awake? I would want one of two things: food or alcohol. It seemed the most logical he would be hungry or thirsty, and since I didn't see him in the food court, I headed to the nearest liquor store.

If you've been doing this as long as I have, you develop certain instincts. Sometimes they are dead on. Of course, when they aren't, you don't tell anyone. This time, they were dead on.

Baird and the woman from Blink were coming out of the first liquor store I went to. I was across the street and hung back a little so they wouldn't see me. I didn't want a footrace with Baird. With his legs, he would be able to outrun me regardless of how shitty he might feel from the night before. At the first intersection, they crossed to my side of the street. I lingered near a street preacher preaching about the promise of salvation in uploading to the cloud.

I was wondering why the preacher hadn't taken his own advice when Baird and the woman disappeared around the corner. I ran to catch up and not lose sight of them. But when I turned the corner, they were a few meters away, talking.

The woman saw me first. "It's that asshole," she said, pointing.

Baird glanced at me and ran.

The woman stood with her arms and legs spread, trying to block me. I stiff-armed her and sent her to the sidewalk. No time for her silly shit. Baird was faster than me, and I couldn't chance letting him out of my sight. Easier said than done. After four blocks, there was more and more sidewalk between us.

Then, for the first time in a while, I got lucky. A group of kids playing *Death Grin Assault* came running down the sidewalk. Baird bowled right into them, sending them scattering like pins. One got caught up in his legs and sent him down. He did a face plant, his head bouncing up and back down again. I took my gun out and tried to run faster.

By the time he started pushing himself up, I was close enough to hit him with a taser round, but the kids were gathered around him, cussing him out. I couldn't get a clean shot. Baird shoved the kids aside and took off running. I took a shot and missed. Baird ran into the street, hopping over a parked car.

I fired again, stopping and taking aim this time. Baird's legs went stiff and his upper body went haywire. He stood there, his feet planted in the middle of the street, twitching and jerking for three seconds. The taser round spent its charge and his torso and arms slumped over his legs. I grabbed him by the collar, dragged him to the sidewalk, and dropped him. His head wobbled on his neck and he looked up at me. Blood ran from his nose and mouth and it looked like he lost a tooth when he faceplanted. He tried to shake the dazed look out of his eyes.

The *Death Grin Assault* Squad gathered in a semicircle around us. One of them got the courage to ask me, "You security?"

"Used to be."

"I wanna be. I wanna run down dumb shits like this. Like you did. That was great."

The rest of the Squad joined in in telling me how great it was.

"Why didn't you just shoot him?" Wanna Be Security asked. "I mean with real bullets."

What I should have answered was something about the job not requiring it. Or something about needing him alive. Or even some bullshit about not being authorized to. But I didn't. What I did answer surprised me.

"He has a kid who misses him."

I felt pressure building up in my throat. I tried to swallow it down, but it kept coming. What in the hell was this? I blinked a few times.

The *Death Grin Assault* Squad stared at me, confused. Wanna Be Security twisted his mouth, half grin, half frown. "You crying?" he asked.

The pressure in my throat burst out in a single sob. Then it was gone. My ED kicked back in, and I was normal again. I wiped my eyes.

Wanna Be Security shook his head. "Fucking weirdo." He turned to the rest of the Squad. "Let's go kill some zombies."

Baird sat with his legs straight out in front of him, twisting around looking for something. "Where's my tooth? Do you see it?"

"You can get a new one." I grabbed his arm and dragged

him to a nearby bus stop bench. "Right now we're going to Jo's."

He used the front of his shirt to wipe the blood off his face. "Why?"

"She'll reset your leg, and she has the tools to take the other one off."

"You can't be serious, Quinn. You can't take my leg. How-"

"Not going to work this time, Baird."

"What am I going to do with one leg? I can't afford another one."

I shrugged. "Maybe you should have thought about that before you put a leg up as collateral. Besides, you'll figure something out. This might be the best thing to happen to you."

He forced a fake laugh. "How the fuck is this going to be the best thing to happen to me?"

"Might force you to change the way you're living. Or it'll kill you. Either one would be an improvement."

AFTER JO HELPED me get Baird's leg off, she reset his other one. She felt bad for him, so she loaned him an old spare she had. It was two inches too short, and the knee didn't work too well, so he wouldn't have full range of motion and would walk with a lopsided limp.

I interrupted them talking about the modifications the

leg would need and thanked Jo for her help. She told me to make sure I came back to take care of the E.D. problem as soon as I got paid. I slung Baird's leg over my shoulder and said I would.

But I didn't.

After I got the credits from Tami, including the five percent bonus, I put half on a credit transfer chip and drove to the old Hyatt apartments. My upgrade could wait.

Baird's wife opened the door with the baby on her hip. "Did you find him?"

"I did."

"Did you tell him what I asked you to?"

"More or less." I handed her the transfer chip.

She held the door open with her foot and took it. "What's this?"

"Just a little something to help with the baby. If Baird comes back, don't tell him you have it."

"If Baird comes back, I'm not letting him in."

I nodded. I hoped she was telling the truth.

She thanked me and shut the door.

I stood there, ignoring the smell of the carpet. When I was sure I didn't feel anything, I walked down the hall, through the lobby, and outside into the thick, humid air.

ABOUT THE AUTHOR

. . .

MARLIN SEIGMAN LIVES in San Antonio, Texas with his family. When he is not writing, he teaches English and Debate. He is the author of the cyberpunk novels *Code Flicker* and *Code Flicker: Project Logos*, both available on Amazon. *All My Sins Remembered*, the first novel featuring Quinn, the protagonist of "Collateral," will be released in the spring of 2021.

You can go to Marlin's Amazon author page to find out more about work.

4. CLEANERS
BY JON RICHTER

Fenster doesn't ask questions, and she doesn't make mistakes; she just takes out her mark,
takes her pay cheque, and moves on to the next target. That's what Cleaners do. She
doesn't even get to keep the same body, or memories – after every hit they are melted
away and replaced, to make sure her identity remains hidden.

Even from her.

She pulled down the mask and tilted the head towards the rain, feeling the cold, filthy droplets trickling down its skin. She knew such behaviour would appear reckless, if anyone saw her; but fuck it, it wasn't *her* skin, not really, even though she was presently occupying it. It was more like a custom exosuit, or a GravBike she'd hotwired and was taking for a weekend spin. And besides, no one would see her, because she was dressed in dark, military-grade body armour, blending perfectly with the abject blackness of the post-curfew city street and the reeking doorway she was crouching in while she waited for her mark.

Her invisibility depended on the fact that nobody was using the same night-vision goggles she was. After midnight, when the juice stopped flowing and the city's noise and neon fizzled out like a discarded cigarette butt, most people wouldn't risk such illegal tech. Most people wouldn't risk being out at all. After midnight only bad things stalked the streets: the Prowlers, or the criminals desperate enough to risk encountering them.

And her.

More accurately, the latest iteration of her. She rather liked her current ID – a grizzled, aging military veteran called Harrison – but she knew how important it was not to get attached to him. She'd seen too many Cleaners lose their minds altogether, a fast and slippery slope once they allowed the fake identities to fit them too snugly, the artificial memories to bleed into their own. She understood how it could happen; she was sure the memory implants were getting more and more realistic with every new construct. And she was also sure TIM, the AI that ran their operation like an unseen puppeteer, was starting to develop a warped sense of humour. Why else were the back stories it concocted always so *harrowing*?

Take Harrison's: it wasn't enough for the invented ex-soldier to have lost an eye in the CryptoWars, the sort of little detail that helped an ID seem more realistic, like a facial tic or an interesting phobia. Instead, beneath the goggles was a knot of scarred flesh where his eye had been literally *burnt out*, corroded away by caustic acid sprayed by an enemy drone. The fact that Fenster knew it had never happened – that the memory was a counterfeit no more real than Harrison's vat-grown body – didn't make an iota of difference. Harrison's brain, *her* brain, remembered and relived every picosecond of that trauma. And it always would, even after the old wardog's body returned to the bio-sludge from which it had been assembled.

She wondered how many sets of memories had been stuffed into her mind over the years.

Don't think about it, Fence. Just think about what's really real. Think about the School, about the agony of a fist smashing into your mouth. About real *fucking trauma.*

As if responding to the image, the night coughed up a foul-smelling gust of polluted wind, blowing more of the toxic rain into Harrison's face. She savoured the sting, using it to focus her, to drag her mind back onto the job at hand. Whoever she was now – whether she was Harrison, or Jackal, or DeWitt, or any of the countless other vessels she'd occupied on countless other jobs – she was a long, long way away from being that battered, sobbing child.

She heard the Prowler before she saw it, Harrison's aural augments picking up the sound of its ponderous tread from over a block away. She was still getting used to the enhanced hearing, but managed to triangulate the thing's position with impressive accuracy, even able to ascertain its specific model from the sound of its clumsy feet crunching through the garbage, the broken glass, the discarded syringes. *D-series*: probably a rusty old unit the city council was eking out until some resourceful hood got the better of it. They probably wouldn't even bother to scrape it off the pavement. She thought about the junked Prowler she'd seen earlier, its flaming remains warming the hands of a group of homeless people congregated under the flyover.

After dark, Prowlers were the law. Fence remembered when the clanking, bipedal robots had first been deployed in tactical police operations, the outcry that had ensued about allowing machines to make decisions concerning life and death. Now, barely fifteen years later, the hulking things were permitted to shoot anyone found outside after the curfew. Wave after wave of budget cuts had decimated the Met's human workforce; sometimes she wondered if the Prowlers were all that was left. Perhaps just the Commissioner herself, pushing a big red button to unleash them every night.

Still, they were no major threat to her, especially not archaic models like this. But complacency had been the death of many Cleaners before her; and her mark was a Level 3, well within her comfort zone, but also not to be taken lightly. What if he appeared just as the Prowler rounded the corner? It was unexpected convergences like these that could throw a routine operation into unexpected catastrophe.

She heard the automaton reach the T-junction and exhaled a small sigh of relief when its footsteps plodded away towards the park. Even with their limited AI, the D-series were smart enough to figure out where most of the junkies would be hiding. She wondered if the homeless people were ready for it, or if they'd be too high on Sluice to do anything but stare down its gun barrels as they spun into life. She listened to the footfalls lumbering into the distance, replacing the mask before the caustic rain could do any further damage to Harrison's crater-pocked face.

Twenty minutes later, a thin man emerged from the building opposite, right in the middle of TIM's predicted engagement window. He glanced around furtively before switching on an ancient, portable torch – *ballsy*, thought Fence, as she raised Harrison's one remaining eyebrow – and shining the beam towards a manhole cover in the center of the road. Whatever was inside the briefcase he was holding, clutched to his chest as protectively as a junkie might guard his stash, he clearly intended to convey it to its destination through the putrid maze of the sewers. A risky move, considering the mutants; not to mention the newer-model, more agile Prowlers that were being deployed to hunt them. But still, a logical plan. One that TIM had predicted, of course – it wasn't called The Imagination Machine for nothing.

Fence didn't like the sewers. As the thin man started to lift the manhole cover, she rose and drew her gun in one graceful, flowing movement, and shot the mark through the forehead. The force of the bullet drove him backward as though he'd been hit in the face by a cricket bat, and he collapsed backward against the curb with his arms splayed wide. Fence waited, tensed, listening for the thump-thump of an approaching Prowler, but the silencer had done its job. After thirty seconds of hearing nothing but the patter of tainted rain and the wheeze of the sickly wind, she strode calmly over to the manhole cover and finished sliding it aside.

She grabbed the briefcase, then dumped the corpse headfirst down the hole. Harrison's boosted hearing picked up the gristly crack as the mark's neck snapped in the shallow filth below. It wouldn't take long for someone to find the body, but by then Fence would be long gone.

And she wouldn't be Harrison anymore.

THE WATCH DIRECTED her to the nearest Pod, which turned out to be in the basement of a burnt-out apartment building the Prowlers had shot up so many times that even the junkies had abandoned it. The Pod wouldn't linger for long; once

Fence's ID had been reconstructed, the self-assembling unit would take the briefcase and scuttle back to TIM's clandestine transport network, a white blood cell absorbed back into the AI's great arterial labyrinth.

She didn't give a shit what was inside the briefcase, or what TIM wanted with it; if it was of any monetary value, stealing it would only mean she'd become the target of another Cleaner in the very near future. TIM wasn't someone – some*thing* – you wanted to cross. She wondered why the AI used human agents at all, why it couldn't just construct bespoke robots to tidy up its loose ends.

But a Cleaner's job wasn't to ask such questions: it was to put bullets in skulls, to recycle IDs, and to move on. To erase your trail at every turn, helping TIM keep its machinations invisible, plausibly deniable. In return, to collect pay checks: massive credit dumps into untraceable accounts, affording an unparalleled level of affluence and comfort during the breaks between hits.

At least as much comfort as it was possible to enjoy on a toxic planet long since deserted by all but the dregs of humankind. The remnants that hadn't fled to Mars, or Europa, or Titan, or the make-or-break frontiers of the Outer Colonies, were permitted to linger only because it was politically unpalatable to blow them up. The rest of the System had long since voted to slash the interplanetary aid budget, leaving Earth's skeletal government to manage an imploding economy and its denizens to live off stolen scraps, food parcels air-dropped by charity drones, and whatever meager crops they could grow in the defiled soil.

Perhaps Fence's real question ought to have been: What the hell did TIM even want with this festering dump of a planet?

She pondered this as Harrison's body started to liquefy, her central nervous system painlessly stripped of its outer casing as another began to grow around it. Perhaps the AI had sinister plans for Earth's remaining humans. Perhaps it wouldn't rest until the Cleaners had eliminated every other person on the planet's rancid surface; perhaps, in the end, only the Cleaners would remain, a race of ruthless and highly-trained killers TIM could lead into battle against the System's bloated fat-cats and corrupt hegemonies.

Whatever, thought Fence as a new face was layered over the new skull that had been deftly sculpted around her brain and eyeballs. *It's not like my own kind ever did me any favours.*

Fenster emerged from the Pod just under an hour later, glancing into the grubby, soot-stained mirror while putting her gear back on. She smiled at the pretty, Eastern-European face that greeted her. Not dissimilar from the real thing, at least as far as she could remember it – she had no photographs of her old self, a self that had been melted away inside a Pod before her twentieth birthday. But this ID was older than she looked; her new memory told her that Nadia Damyanova was nearly 42 and had once been part of a rebel faction, long-since dissolved. Since then, she'd spent over a decade unloading shipping crates as a dockworker, chiselling her body into the lean, taut specimen the Pod had manufactured. No recent trauma, although the recollection of her husband and daughter's deaths during a police raid was forever burned into her psyche. The grenade, exploding in a retina-searing apocalypse of light. Their liquefied bodies, dripping from the ceiling like grease from a grill pan.

Remember what's really real, Fence.

She glanced at the watch, wondering how long it would be before it displayed the details of her next mark, beeping as cheerfully as if it was reminding her the roast dinner was about done. She guessed she'd get maybe a fortnight to cool off.

She got less than three days.

THE SCHOOL LURKED at the bottom of the valley like something sprouting in a forgotten cesspit. The proprietors – they didn't deserve to be called "teachers," even though Fence had learned an awful lot from them – actively encouraged this analogy, reminding the thousand-or-so orphans who called the crumbling, decayed building home that they were the detritus of humankind, the sediment at the very bottom of the gene pool.

Always remember: no one wanted you.
You're lucky we took you in.

Praise the Prescient, for only in Their service do your lives have meaning.

Every day, a chorus of trembling voices would echo this vile doctrine, gazes fixed on the floor they would later polish on scraped hands and bruised knees lest they catch the eyes of the Sisters or, worse, the Headmaster. She'd seen the stooped, toothless old fossil lash a boy to death in front of the entire assembly, all because he'd pissed himself during a particularly long and turgid sermon.

"See how swiftly Their justice is dealt to the repulsive, to the depraved, to the unclean?" Father Cunningham had cackled while the whip carved its obscene admonition across the boy's back. She didn't remember the lad's name, or his screams; instead, she remembered his protruding bones and how the flayed skin had split across them, like a plastic bin bag stuffed full of old twigs. She remembered glancing at one of the Sisters and seeing the old hag flinch in discomfort but do nothing to stop the brutality.

And she remembered being hit. It happened a lot because the Way Of The Five taught that evil could only be defeated by ruthless ferocity; thankfully she wasn't in Sister Martha's cohort, where fire was used to burn out temptation, leaving those children covered with burns from candles and lighters.

Sister Francine wasn't much better. The last time she had ever hit Fenster – Mila, as she was called then – she had broken her jaw. Fence had talked back to her, although she couldn't remember what she'd said, or why. All she remembered was the pain of that unexpected fist, crashing into the side of her face like a freight train. That and the horror and humiliation of the jaw wiring, how skeletal she'd looked after six weeks without solid food.

That experience hadn't broken her spirit; rather, it had stoked its embers. She'd resolved at age eleven never to put her trust in people again. But she hadn't been reckless; she'd studied, and scrubbed, and bowed, and obeyed for two more years before her opportunity had arisen. An opportunity she'd grabbed with ruthless ferocity.

Now the valley fell away beneath her, and the burnt-out husk of The Holy Quincunx School For Troubled Youngsters looked like a charred body dumped into an open grave. She glanced at her watch again, as if she still expected TIM to apologize and correct its mistake; it didn't, of course. The details of her next hit were etched in unforgiving, irrefutable pixels. As insane as it seemed, the mark was here, somewhere inside the ruins of her old school. A Level Five, the toughest target she'd ever been assigned. Essentially equivalent to herself. Which meant he had just as much chance of getting the better of her as she had of vanquishing him. The flip of a coin.

She slid and scrambled down the muddy side of the valley, feeling like a morsel of food dropping into an expectant throat.

It was daytime, so there was no need for the night vision goggles, which dangled around her neck as she crept into the School's blistered carcass. A huge chunk of the roof and upper floors were missing, like a bite torn out by some gigantic carrion-eater. Sunlight poured into the assembly hall, illuminating the flecks of swirling dust motes and mold spores. She stuck to the shadows as she inched around the periphery, edging past the half-melted chairs the Sisters used to occupy while the children sat on the cold stone floor like subjects grovelling at their feet. She had to resist the urge not to kick them aside in disgust.

Focus, Fence. Don't let the Sisters beat you again.

Her watch had informed her that the target, a renegade Cleaner named Pitfield, was most likely to be found in the basement, but still, she proceeded with caution. These specifics were where TIM's predictions could sometimes prove inaccurate, and the AI itself was always keen to stress the unreliability of such granular detail. After all, these were forecasts, nothing more. She'd had jobs where the mark had appeared outside of the engagement window, or materialised from an unexpected part of the strike zone.

Data, chewed and churned by inscrutable algorithms. Spat back out like undigested gristle.

Do you even have a master plan, TIM? Or are we just killing for no reason at all?

She proceeded toward the tattered remnants of a door in the corner, following a trail of bullet-holes left by the Prowlers that had torn up the place. Whether that was before or after the inferno that had gutted the evil old building, she had no idea. Perhaps they were the ones who burnt it after The Way Of The Five was outlawed and the government carried out its swift and uncharacteristically efficient purge.

She used the barrel of her carbine to nudge open the door, one of the many through which passage had been strictly forbidden to the School's students. A mirthless smile creased Damyanova's lips, and Fence had to resist the urge to spit on the floor. *Students? More like victims.* The door opened into a narrow, dark corridor; dark because the sunlight had no way in, dark because its walls were scorched and melted by fire damage. Dark because of the memories that clung to it like a persistent cancer.

This was where the School's offices had been, the rooms in which the Sisters and their monstrous patriarch had congregated, dined, scribbled out their sermons. Their sleeping quarters were somewhere through here too, although Fence had only been as far as Cunningham's office; the place where, in many ways, her career as a Cleaner had begun.

She listened intently, but heard no sound at all, as though even scavenging animals were repulsed by the place. The smell of mildew and rot was overwhelming, but she couldn't resist creeping inside and approaching the door that would have had "Headmaster" written on its frosted window had it not been torn off its hinges, its glass shattered into fragments scattered across the soot-smeared floor.

She stared into the room, her jaw clenching at the sight of an overturned wooden desk whose blackened skeleton had somehow survived the blaze. She'd been old enough to know what was happening when Cunningham had thrust her down onto it but too young to do anything to stop him, her adolescent body no match for his stocky frame. She remembered his stink and how the dim light of the lightbulb had made the spittle at the corner of his mouth glisten as he'd lowered his loathsome mouth towards her.

When the small red dot had appeared close to his ear, she'd almost been too terrified to notice. If he'd seen the momentary flash of confusion in her eyes, he'd been too distracted to care, fidgeting with his zipper while he mumbled something about the importance of obedience and discretion. Then his head had erupted outwards from the opposite temple, as though his skull had become so disgusted by his brain it had decided to spit it out across the far wall.

She hadn't screamed, even when his carcass sagged down on top of her, heavy and reeking and clammy with perspiration. Perhaps she'd known, instinctively, that to attract the Sisters' attention at that moment would have ensured that her own death would swiftly follow the Headmaster's, as she would surely be blamed for his gruesome demise. The

Cleaner's shot had entered through the office window, penetrating the glass so cleanly the pane hadn't even shattered around the bullet hole. It was through this window that Fence escaped, wrapping a rag she'd spotted on the nearby filing cabinet around her hand and smashing the glass out of her way in a desperate frenzy.

The cabinet was still there, standing as resolutely as though it was Cunningham's headstone. She spat into the empty room and turned to head back to the assembly hall.

THE OTHER DOOR led past the remains of claustrophobic classrooms that had reeked of mold long before the School had been incinerated. This side of the building was being slowly absorbed back into the valley's sickly foliage, weeds and fungus climbing the walls as though desperate to escape through the hole in the roof. She paid little attention; she had no more desire to linger amongst these memories, formative though they were.

Instead, she followed the tracks she'd spotted, written in the dust and soot like a confession. The footprints (standard military-issue boots) led straight down the long corridor to the stairwell, exactly as TIM had predicted. The ceiling had partially collapsed across its entrance, but the broken rafters and chunks of debris had been moved aside to create a gap through which someone could descend. As silently as a sniper's breath, she followed the footsteps of her quarry into the basement.

Waiting behind the trapdoor every morning for the Sisters to unbolt it, terrified that the darkness would last forever. That those women would abandon them, just like their own parents had done.

She tugged the night vision goggles into place, not doubting for a moment that the mark had a pair of his own. She prayed he didn't anticipate an assault; if he did, the logical thing to do would be to simply aim his gun at the stairwell and wait. She could try throwing herself down the steps to catch him off guard, but if he wasn't lurking in ambush then the noise would surely alert him; worse, the uneven stone would wreak unknown havoc on her spine and limbs, and she couldn't hope to win the ensuing shootout with a litany of broken bones.

So she held her breath and walked slowly down the stairs, down into the lightless abyss in which she'd spent a large part of her childhood.

The first thing she noticed were the skeletons. They were not heaped as though they'd been tossed down here as a form of burial – she couldn't imagine the Prowlers affording their victims even such a crude courtesy – but they were not scorched either. Instead, the pitiful bones of dozens of children lay crumbled on the floor or in the cramped bunk beds where they'd died.

Bastards, she thought, feeling tears clawing at the insides of her eyes. *They locked them down here.* A final act of "ruthless ferocity" by the Sisters when the Prowlers appeared at the lip of the valley. Or perhaps a tactic devised by the Prowlers themselves, following protocol that ensured the units didn't waste ammunition when other extermination opportunities existed.

Scowling, she stalked onward, gun trained on the emptiness ahead, which soon resolved itself into a wall, and another door. A heavy, metal door with a rotating handle, like a bank vault. Despite the severity of the punishment, she remembered the braver children trying to open it during the night. But it had always remained impregnable, the mechanism either rusted shut or too tightly-sealed for tiny, malnourished hands.

Now it yawned open, and her adversary's footprints led beyond, probing the darkness of her memories.

What the fuck was Pitfield doing down here?

She had no idea how big the room beyond the door was. A gas grenade or incendiary charge might incapacitate her quarry, but it might merely warn him of her presence. Better to lead with the squat, uncompromising barrel of her carbine and have Damyanova's finger twitching against the trigger. Listening intently, she drifted inside like a foul breeze.

The room was enormous, and she silently applauded her decision not to utilise an explosive. The sprawling chamber mirrored the dimensions of the assembly hall above, perhaps even exceeding it, although its low ceiling made it feel just as oppressive as the dormitories themselves. The air in that decade-old ossuary had been unspeakable, but somehow this place smelled even worse, as though things even more disturbing than the bones of tortured orphans had rotted in this forgotten oubliette.

The cavernous space was divided into corridors by rows of huge filing cabinets that reached almost to the ceiling. Was it a storage space, for records of some kind? She wondered what secrets were entombed here and what Pitfield could possibly want with them. She strained her ears, wishing Damyanova's backstory had granted her the same military augmentation as Harrison.

Then she heard a clang, somewhere off to the right. Exactly the sound an old, rusted drawer might make if it was slammed shut in frustration. She padded towards it on the balls of her feet, switching her carbine to "short burst" mode, ready to greet Pitfield with a three-part salutation that would be the last sound he ever heard. To her left, rows of shelves stretched away into the darkness, converted to shades of black and luminous green by the goggles.

Another drawer, slamming shut. Maybe three rows ahead. Two. One. She turned, her eyes registering the man crouched in front of a cabinet at the opposite end of the aisle at the same time as her finger squeezed the trigger, and a volley of death slammed into the sliver of unprotected flesh at the base of his neck.

And passed through it, as though the man was nothing more than a ghost.

"Shit," Fence whispered and threw herself to the floor as a barrage of return fire tore chunks out of the wall behind her. *The guy's using a fucking hologram.* She jerked herself to the right in a sideways roll, firing another wild burst back along the corridor as lumps of concrete rained onto her. Scrambling to her feet, she launched herself forward into a sprint, aiming the gun to her left and firing as the next row of files opened beside her. A hundred yards away, she saw the dark outline of a figure mirroring her movement, dashing headlong past the aisle's opposite end, like her shadow distantly cast. But this was no shadow, and this time it was no hologram; muzzle flare heralded another hail of bullets that obliterated the wall inches behind her head.

What fucking ammo is this guy using?

They repeated their savage dance from opposite ends of the next aisle, and the next; each time, Fence's three-round burst was answered by an eruption of gunfire that chewed through the nearby concrete. *This is unsustainable,* she thought. *It's a matter of time before one of us hits the other, and his firepower is far superior.*

She skidded to a stop before the next aisle, lurching down the previous corridor instead. She didn't care about the noise she was making; Pitfield's gun was so loud his hearing was probably wrecked anyway. She heard the weapon's roar once again, hoping he wouldn't realize she was no longer paralleling his movements until she'd made it to the opposite end of the aisle and swivelled to shoot him in the back.

She was maybe two thirds of the way to the opposite end when she heard it: not another salvo of frighteningly high-calibre bullets, but the sound of stumbling footsteps, accompanied by a groan of pain. She stopped dead in her tracks. If she emerged, she would doubtless see Pitfield rolling on the floor in agony, clutching a wounded limb.

And it would doubtless be another hologram.

"I'm not that fucking stupid, Pitfield," she called. All she heard in response were his low moans, somewhere off to the right. *Shit*, she thought. *He could be anywhere.* Maybe circling back around to pick her off from behind. She whirled around, breath rattling in her vat-grown throat. No-one there. *A double bluff.* She spun again, so tense she almost discharged the carbine, giving away her position.

No sign of her quarry. No sound except for low, agonised moaning. *You're the quarry now, Fence.*

Pitfield had to know that his new decoy wasn't working. Which meant he would have moved by now. Which meant that he wouldn't expect her to head straight for the hologram after all.

Or maybe he would.

Time to flip the coin.

Sucking in a deep breath, she strode to the end of the corridor and turned to see the projected image of a man crumpled in a heap a few metres ahead. She pitched herself forward, firing through and over the hologram to where she hoped, prayed, Pitfield was lurking in the gloom behind his fearsome hand cannon.

The man on the floor screamed as blood erupted from his outstretched arm.

It wasn't a hologram.

"Stop!" Pitfield shrieked, rolling onto his back to stare down his prone body towards her. From her flattened position, her eyes met a stare filled with fear and confusion. Pitfield's legs and torso were perforated with bullet holes; she must have hit him during one of their earlier exchanges. His gun had fallen from his grasp as he fell, clattering away along the stone floor and beyond his flailing reach.

"Why are you even here?" he howled. "*What the fuck does this have to do with TIM?*"

Fence rose slowly to her feet, realizing she was shaking. "Cleaners don't ask questions," she said as coolly as she could manage, aiming the carbine at his forehead. "Or did you forget how this works?"

"Wait, wait," he stammered, raising his hands as though they stood any chance of protecting him. She could see that she'd already blasted off a couple of fingers; blood dripped from the stumps, spattering his unmasked face. *Night vision eye augments*; a *serious player*. "Let me just explain why I'm here. I'm not trying to hurt TIM, or anyone! I'm just trying to find out..." He paused to cough, bloody saliva spraying his chin. "... If I am who I think I am."

Fence's finger tightened on the trigger. "And how did you plan to find that here?"

Pitfield's breathing was becoming more ragged. "I used to go to this school. Or at least... I think I did. I don't know any more. All that shit they put in our heads..." His eyes glistened; the tears might have been caused by the pain of his multiple bullet wounds or by something else. "Don't you ever doubt your memories?"

Fence gritted her teeth, squinting down the gun's barrel. Then she lowered the weapon. "I used to go to this school too," she said slowly. "Who is it you think you are? Maybe I remember you."

Pitfield blinked rapidly, as though astonished to find himself still alive. "Then you must have been through hell too," he said eventually. "I escaped when I was just a teenager." He coughed again, wiping his gore-flecked lips with the ruin of his left hand. "I'm female, really; Pitfield is just my ID. My real name is Fenster. I was trying to find my name in the records, but-"

Fence, or whoever the fuck she was, shot the mark in the face. She didn't stop firing until her entire magazine was empty, and the storage room reverberated with the sound of her gunfire and Damyanova's screams.

ABOUT THE AUTHOR

. . .

Jon Richter lives in London, where he spends some of his sun-cycles trapped in the body of an accountant called Dave. When he isn't forced to count beans, he writes dark fiction about robots, artificial intelligence, human augmentation, and all the other developing technologies that will soon make our world a brilliant and/or terrifying place to live and die. Chat with him about cyborgs and other things with wires for veins @RichterWrites.

5. THE VOLUNTEER
BY A.W. WANG

His existence is a hellish series of life-and-death battles. With his memories erased, all he knows is he volunteered to have his consciousness downloaded for this...

Chapter 1

I volunteered for this...

In the virtual universe of the Ten Sigma Program, the morning sky is gray and the frigid air dank. To either side of me, beads of dew coat the stacked logs. Under my feet rest damp autumn leaves, flattened by the stomps of desperate combat. The stench of blood and decay tinges every chilly breath I drag into my lungs.

I pull my blue woolen overcoat tighter and rub my scraggly beard.

Couldn't the overlords have added a little sunshine to this scenario?

The woman at my feet has bigger problems than inhospitable surroundings. Her split-eyed stare is split because an ax lies buried in her forehead, directly above her delicate nose. We were in two scenarios together, and I'm glad I never took the time to know her.

Now her consciousness, her soul, and everything she was and will be are gone, just mangled data being erased from the system.

Shivering from more than the cold, I step past the body, unable to weather the accusation lingering in her eyes. Besides not wanting to answer the unspoken question of why I have lived when so many others have died, I have better things to do—like not getting killed myself.

Death is final here.

At the nearby angle in the wall, I sheath my dagger and holster my ax. I place a boot against the lowest log and yank on my musket.

The bayonet, impaling the man who slaughtered my teammate, pulls free. His slumping body trails crimson down the logs before hitting the ground with a thump.

I stare at the blood dripping from the wound, fascinated as it blends with the coloring of his long coat.

Metal scrapes against the outside wood.

"They're coming," a panicked voice yells from the interior.

The Volunteer

My fingers tighten on the musket. Even though nobody has any ammunition, the length makes this the best available means for defense. Courtesy of the red and black threads, which the overlords integrated into my being when I first entered this hellish universe, I'm an expert with a bayonet.

I shake my head. Everyone has the exact threads I do, and everyone's an expert with every weapon known to mankind.

A battering ram thuds against the main gate.

My side is outnumbered, and we're going to lose.

A tremble runs down my spine.

You volunteered for this, I remind myself.

The mantra to keep my sanity does little to quell the fear consuming my innards.

Wood splinters and shouts come as the enemy pours inside the walls.

Not ready to die just yet, I shunt aside my budding panic.

Who cares how or why I'm here?

My goal is to survive the next few minutes, and then, the ones after that.

As it's always been...

I follow the crooked path around the star-shaped fort, gritting my teeth. The screams and clangs of furious combat resound as I rush by the broken planks of the main entrance and round the corner to the central compound. I skitter to a stop.

Things are worse than I expected. On the parade ground,

ten bluecoats form a defensive circle, besieged by twenty of the enemy.

Boots slip, and a grunt comes from behind me.

I turn.

A dirt-streaked woman wrapped in a redcoat slides on the moist leaves, struggling to remain upright while charging at me with a bayonet.

A ghostly 2.5 score wavers behind her tri-cornered hat as she stabs at my chest. Compared to my 4.03, this short, muscular woman is a newbie.

I step aside, crossing my musket with hers and reminding myself that a low score doesn't make her any less dangerous.

With a snarl, she disengages and thrusts at my head.

Definitely not less dangerous.

I duck and shove my weapon at her stomach, which she deflects downward.

The contest goes back and forth, but with my superior experience, I force her to give ground. When she hits the slippery leaves of the outer path, her footing gives way.

I launch my bayonet past a sloppy block and cut her forehead.

Blinded by blood, she jabs wildly. After a vicious thrust, I step inside her guard and drive the pointy steel into her chest. Her eyes roll up, and she falls.

A yell comes, and I twist away, staring in shock.

The battle has decimated my side. Although many fresh bodies lie on the ground, only three blue-coated figures stand amidst a swirling storm of redcoats. They're members of my new team, people I only met before this scenario started.

My feet edge backward as I prepare to retreat. Even though I have no memories of my past life, I know I wasn't a brave man.

But...

With each wave of attackers, my last teammates pirouette and slash with their axes and thrust with their daggers, fighting off the attacking whirlwind of steel. Rather than fear, they have smiles plastered on their faces, relishing in the fight with bloodthirsty glee.

Is there a chance?

I owe these people nothing.

It's a stupid notion, and I shake my head. If these three lose, it's only a matter of time before the red side finds and kills me. And then, I'll be just another bunch of mangled data being expunged from the system—as dead as dead gets.

I've got no choice.

Before I can change my mind, I grit my teeth and charge.

The enemy, so engrossed with beating the trio, doesn't notice my heavy steps until my bayonet drives through the back of the rearmost soldier.

As he falls, two others turn and rush at me.

I step back—dodging, twisting, and blocking—barely weathering the onslaught of steel. Fortunately, in their haste, the pair has come straight at me rather than coordinate an attack from both sides, which leaves me a chance.

At least until a sharp edge slashes through my overcoat and across my collarbone.

Wincing from the pain, I give a desperate lunge and hit the lead opponent in the throat.

Crimson sprays over my face as he goes down.

As I weaken from the loss of blood, flailing with the musket, the last enemy redoubles her effort. Her bayonet stabs into my shoulder.

My legs wobble, and I sink to my knees, exhausted.

Before she can finish me, a length of steel punches through her chest, and she falls.

I blink in surprise.

Except for the three women in blue, the rest of the area is clear. All the enemies are down, save one fleeing man.

An ax whirls through the air and meets flesh. The man's redcoat flutters as he tumbles to the ground.

Golden sparkles crawl over my skin, and the fort disappears.

SHOCKED TO BE ALIVE, I materialize in the pleasant environment of the ready room, an enclosed cube lit by glowing shapes etched into the walls and ceiling.

My body sinks into a cushy chair, one of ten arranged in a

semicircle. The heavy Revolutionary War uniform is gone, and only the briefest of briefs cover my now smooth skin and healthy tissue. The hideous shoulder wound has vanished, as has the nasty slice across my collarbone. In accordance with the rules of the Ten Sigma Program, anyone who survives returns in a fresh, completely healthy body.

I shiver. Rational thought aside, the mind needs time to catch up with the new state of the flesh.

Rather than force the process, I swing my gaze over the empty and occupied chairs in the semicircle. Only four of us have returned: me and the three ladies.

Like me, their wounds are healed, and their scenario garb has been replaced with thin strips of material barely covering their private areas.

All normal stuff outside of a scenario.

Surprisingly, the ghostly numbers floating behind their heads are identical—2.76.

Scarcely more than newbies.

When my body stops trembling, I sit up.

A pop echoes, and a stuffed-animal-sized polar bear hovers past the opening of the semicircle. He's a software construct named Ice, an artificial intelligence programmed to be my guide, friend, and confidant.

Or at least that's what he said when we first met.

The flat disks of his eyes spend a moment gathering in the results of the scenario, as if showing empathy for the life and death experience we endured.

I roll my eyes. The same thing happens after every scenario.

His voice rumbles with deep bass overtones when he says, "That was quite the contest, but you've come through with flying colors."

While I maintain my dour stare, the three ladies giggle like we just survived a party.

The polar bear launches into the debrief, which is also something that happens after every scenario. The diatribe contains a welcome back, a rehash of the battle, and then score additions.

My current tally is 4.03 sigmas, and I straighten when he faces me and says, "For your valiant efforts, two-hundredths of a point has been added to your score. A moment passes before my mind processes the numbers.

4.05

The magic threshold is ten. Ten sigmas for this to end and for me to return to the real world.

A sigh leaves my lips. While I'm not even sure of what a sigma represents, I'm sure there are many two-hundredth increases I need to achieve in order to win.

The ladies give annoying giggles again when Ice announces their rewards. Each receives five-hundredths of a point, bringing their totals to identical 2.81's.

I frown. Their increases are minuscule but still much higher than mine.

Because I played it safe, hiding in the shadows.

But that's how I've avoided death for this long...

I shake my head. None of these thoughts matter. My goal is surviving the next battle and then the one after that.

Don't get your hopes up, I tell myself.

"Are there any questions?" Ice asks as a precursor to ending the debrief.

I stay silent as I always do.

A moment later, the polar bear waves his paw, and the golden sparkles crawl over me.

Chapter 2

Sunlight glares after the golden sparks drop me on the grass rectangle of the Commons area. Shielding my eyes, I glance above the looming skylines.

It's midday in the sanctuary.

I groan, not wanting to head to the barracks and flop asleep in the middle of broad daylight.

"Hey, you fought pretty well," a trio of voices calls.

I stare at the almost identical-looking girls. All are athletic and slender. Their shoulder-length brunette hair varies by only the slightest shades. Combined with their soft features and large brown eyes, one could easily confuse their identities.

Moreover, they are all beautiful, their appearances idealized for the virtual universe, and even more alluring in their scanty outfits, which do more to pique interest in what's underneath than to serve as a covering.

Which does nothing because libido is suppressed in this accursed place.

I turn away.

Gentle fingers touch my shoulder.

"I'm Trudy," says the tallest by a nose.

"Ella," announces the next.

The last steps forward. "Rhian."

With a grunt, I pull from Trudy's grasp and walk away.

"What's your name?" she calls after me.

"I don't have one; the overlords took it when I got here."

"Of course silly, what are you going by now?"

These three will be in the next scenario with me, so there's no point angering them. "Ty."

"Do you want to come with us, maybe work on teamwork?"

Not needing friends who'll be dead soon, no matter how well they fought in this last battle, I utter a curt, "No."

Everyone I've ever met in this place has died.

Nobody stops me as I march toward the cafeteria, and for that, I'm grateful.

IN THE CAFETERIA, I sit alone at the end of a cheap table covered with speckled laminate, avoiding interaction with the few people wandering about.

The clear pouch resting in my hand contains a gelatinous blue liquid, which is special for the virtual world. It has the power to taste like anything anyone can imagine.

I sip from the straw and close my eyes.

A frown creases my face. I have no idea what to imagine. My past has been erased as part of the assimilation process for the Ten Sigma Program. Now, there's no context to place the food. And that's half the fun—remembering friends, family, and good times.

The flavor of a seared New York steak done medium rare crosses my tongue. It's wonderful, yet...

How do I even know what steak tastes like?

Given my lack of history, shouldn't everything remind me of chicken?

Whatever that is...

Chairs scrape across the floor.

I open my eyes, unhappy.

Three familiar faces plop into the surrounding seats.

"Hi," Trudy says with a smirk. "We figured we'd get to know you."

"Don't you have better things to do, besides ruining my fun time?"

"It doesn't look like you've had fun in ages."

I spread my glare over the trio. "I'm trying to imagine something from my past."

Rhian punches a straw into her pouch and sips. "Ooh, that's wonderful. Chocolate cake from my sixteenth birthday."

My gaze flicks to the many empty seats around the nearby tables. "Can't you sit anywhere else?"

Ella leans in and asks in earnest, "Can't you use the company?"

I return a non-committal grunt, remembering they might save my life in the next battle.

Trudy laughs. "It's settled then. We can be friends."

Soon, they're happily chatting, letting out oohs and aahs while comparing memories that will soon be erased.

If they even live that long...

As the minutes pass, I try to ignore them, scratching at my beard and wondering why I ever thought having the scraggly growth would be a good idea. The damn thing itches more than anything, especially during tropical scenarios.

I roll my eyes. Like everything else in my previous forgotten life, having the damn beard makes no difference. I'm stuck in this hellhole with every choice I've ever made.

The trio giggles from an inside joke.

My anger erupts, and I thump my pouch on the tabletop. "You guys think this program is that easy? That this is some sort of party and you'll just get to ten sigmas like that"—I gesture outside the plastic windows and toward the blue dome beyond—"and get out of this place?"

Their surprised expressions turn to smiles. Trudy leans forward, saying in a conspiratorial tone, "You don't understand. Killing is fun, and being rewarded for it is more fun."

Although a chill rushes over my spine, the words pique my rational mind.

Is murderous enjoyment the part I'm missing?

I shake my head, not knowing if the notion is good or bad.

Trudy misunderstands my trepidations and replies with

gleeful malice in her eyes, "You saw how well we did with that horde. We're making it out of here."

Rhian and Ella nod with the same excited, bloodthirsty expressions.

Ella taps the tabletop. "You should practice with us."

Rhian joins the fun saying with a malicious half-smile, "Where three is good, four would be better."

By better, she means more killing.

"How did you three even meet and set up this *weird* alliance?" I ask, deciding "unholy" would be a better descriptor than "weird."

"We were on the same first team," Trudy replies.

I think to the nine other members of my first team, who all died in the first battle.

"You see," Ella says, "we all had similar appearances. So we made up a story about how we were triplets—"

Not needing any more, I interrupt, wanting a more important answer, "Why did you volunteer for this?"

A moment passes before she wraps her head around the different topic. "A car crash. I was dying."

Trudy shrugs. "ALS. My body was wasting away."

"For the thrill of the adventure," Rhian says, laughing. "Or maybe old age?"

Nobody had any choice...

"So, why did you join?" they ask.

Why did I?

"No idea. My only memory from the real world is when

they put that metal band around my head, right before they downloaded me here..."

...into this millionth circle of Hell.

The girls lean back, sending each other unhappy glances.

I tap my temple. "Everything else is gone."

Trudy purses her lips. "I was hoping that process stopped at a certain point."

With a shrug, I reply, "What difference does it make? We're here and we have to get out. That's all that matters."

Her eyes twinkle.

"Does that count as optimism?"

"I don't remember the last time I was optimistic."

"You know what they say about optimism?"

"What?"

"It's the gateway to fun," the three chime in unison. As they chuckle from the coincidence, I glance past the glare on the cheap windows, seeking the blue dome. Somewhere beyond that is the real world.

I'll only get there after I reach ten sigmas.

My shoulders sag from the weight of the task.

Trudy chuckles. "It's not that bad. Besides, what have you got to lose?"

Nothing because I've hit an emotionless, hopeless bottom.

"Okay," I say, daring to hope this path can truly be different. "Let's practice and try to get better."

Chapter 3

Two days pass with cheerful stories, happy times, and lots of training to kill. Their cavalier attitude is infectious, and I find my lips curling into a smile with more than a few of their giggles.

First thing in the morning on the third day, we materialize in the ready room. Ice greets us with a briefing for the next scenario.

Besides me and the trio, six new teammates are seated in the semicircle for a total of ten—five men and five women.

Instead of my usual bland acceptance, I watch my new friends as their eyes alight with anticipation. While they joke about getting higher scores, a chuckle spills from my lips.

I pause at my levity, which is so alien to this program.

As is hope...

Has it been that long since I've had anything but dour thoughts?

Could this time really be different?

I scratch my beard.

Maybe, but I've seen so much that says otherwise.

Too few moments pass before Ice waves his paw, and the golden sparkles take us to our new scenario.

———

A HOT BREATH of humid air washes over my face as I materialize in a long dirty trench, squinting from a beating sun.

A drab green uniform covers my body, while a wide-brim helmet sits on my head. My hands grip an M1 Garand rifle. Heavy pouches around my waist hold enough ammunition to kill a small army.

The other thirty-nine from my side are dressed similarly, as are the four teams of ten from the opposition, except for their woolen uniforms being drab blue.

A total of eighty people shoved into a do-or-die situation.

One of my heavy boots sinks into muck as I place the other on a revetment and peer through a gap in the sandbags. The battleground is a one-hundred by one-hundred meter stretch of browns and beiges boxed by unscalable ten-meter high walls. Claw marks of trenches cut into the dirt as far as I can see. Here and there, glints come from clumps of barbed wire, restricting free movement outside the trench network.

It's World War I warfare. But instead of two sides in fortifications hundreds of meters apart, these trenches have connected paths, crawling along the forbidding walls and into a central redoubt dominating the map.

I frown, already feeling dirty from the nasty fighting to come.

Kill everyone from the other side.

Like every scenario, the mission directive manifests as a thought in my mind.

Trudy, followed by Ella and Rhian, makes her way to my side. She sends a grin of anticipation, a truly strange sight to start a battle. "Are we going to plan a strategy with the rest of the teams?"

Whoops and shouts come amid sharp cracks of rifles.

I shrug. "I guess it's everyone for themself."

They laugh, perhaps reveling too much in the process of dealing death rather than the end goal of leaving. In unison, they state, "Then the four of us working together will bag our share of points and kills."

Out of politeness, I nod.

After I shove a clip into my rifle, I lead them down the narrow trench and toward the fighting in the interior, knowing better but hoping things will be that easy...

―――

WHILE MY LUNGS labor for air, I wipe beads of sweat from my forehead. Only fifteen minutes have passed, but already the heat has sapped my strength.

As I scratch my uncomfortable beard, wishing for the cold of the last scenario, a stray gunshot pings off my helmet.

I jerk down.

Trudy slides next to me, hunching. "Looks like everyone's trying for the center."

"It dominates the map." I sigh. "A little bit of planning would have helped a lot."

Ella and Rhian step over, making the narrow confines even more crowded.

"Maybe we should try something different," Ella says.

"There's a path through the barbed wire," I reply, gesturing upward with my thumb. "But, out in the open like that would be a good way to get cut to pieces."

Shots come from behind—where there shouldn't be any fighting.

"Crap," Rhian mutters. "How did they get back there?"

I poke my head up and twist toward the rear trench. Dread melts my insides as I catch a glimpse of an unstoppable man in a fast-moving gunfight. "It's only one person, but he's a six."

Their eyes widen at the score.

"Impossible..." Trudy says.

"I thought you said getting to ten would be easy?" I reply.

"But I've never seen anyone that high. I thought we'd get there first."

Ella puts her hand on my knee. "What do we do?"

"Staying here is worthless if there's someone behind us. We have to take care of him."

The trio takes a deep breath and nod in unison.

Trudy takes the lead as we retreat from the center of the map. I stay in the rear, watching for any pursuit.

The skirmish ahead rises to a crescendo then fades. With covering fire from Ella and Rhian, Trudy dashes into the trench.

She sprays covering fire as the rest of us plow into the narrow space.

Our enemy pulls himself over the sandbags and disappears.

"Where's he going?" Trudy yells.

I pop up and peer toward the back wall. A rifle swings at my face, and I duck.

The sandbags above me quiver from thumping bullets.

I jam my rifle between a crease and fire in a tight arc. When I pull the weapon down, I fumble for a reload.

A rifle zips into the trench like a javelin and nails Ella in the throat. Bloody gurgles spill from her mouth as she crumples, fighting for air.

While Rhian and Trudy stare in disbelief, a sandbag arcs at them then another. As they dodge, a helmet and bayonet appear over the lip of sandbags. Wild shots fly, spattering wood and spilling blood.

The brute of a man drops into the trench as both Rhian and Trudy fall.

I finish my reload and spray bullets.

One manages to clip the wildly dodging figure in the hip, but he keeps hobbling forward.

My last shot nails his shoulder as he thrusts his bayonet at my nose. I slam my rifle up just in time to deflect the tip past my cheek.

Even though he's weakening from the wounds, he kicks into my thigh.

I wobble back, keeping our rifles locked to stop him from getting an advantage.

Horribly wounded, Trudy staggers from the side and stabs him with a feral yell.

He grunts, whipping the muzzle around as I fight to keep my balance. His bayonet sinks into her chest, and she collapses in a heap.

With an opening, I rush inside his guard and stab him in the stomach. A grunt leaves his mouth from the savage blow, and we flop to the muck at the bottom of the trench. He struggles, pushing his hand against my face, his fingers clawing for my eyes. Twisting my head, I shove my forearm under his jaw and yank for my knife with my free hand.

As he lowers his chin to bite my arm, I force the blade into him. A torrent of blood splashes, the warm wetness seeping under my trench coat.

After he stills, I roll off the body and stand, glancing at my companions.

Accusation fills Trudy's lifeless eyes. Further in front, Rhian and Ella send the same dead looks.

Sweat trickles down my back as self-condemnation blisters my thoughts.

I lift my eyes to the heavens, fighting to stare past the glaring sun.

With these three, I had dared to hope, I had dared to be optimistic, I had dared to think there was an easy way out of this hellhole.

I was wrong.

To expect anything but the worst from the overlords is a good recipe for getting killed.

As usual, I have no answers to why I'm still alive.

And I don't care...

Moisture seeps into my eyes as I blink from the blinding sunlight.

"What have you got to lose?" Trudy's voice echoes in my thoughts.

My breaths shorten into gasps while my legs falter. In anguish, I sink to the narrow, rotten floorboards covering the muck.

What have I got to lose?

Every last feeling and emotion that's been rekindled in these past two days, that's what.

I clench my fists, letting the survivor's guilt overwhelm me.

A tear crawls down my cheek as fury rises in my soul. Fury at the enemy, fury at the scenario, fury at the death of my friends...

And fury at myself...

I didn't volunteer for all this.

Wildly, I search for an outlet. A plan forms from my whirling thoughts. If this level-six enemy could find and use an extra rifle, then I can do one or two or three better.

Wild gunfire crisscrosses the map as I stagger to my feet and gather the rifles from my three dead friends, adding them to my own. Quickly, I do the complex reloading of the Garands without injuring my fingers while shoving in the clips. After I line up the barrels, I cradle the rifles and slip my finger into the trigger of the bottom one.

Even without a past, I know I wasn't a brave man. But I wasn't someone to cower either.

I let my rage run free and charge up a shallow part of the embankment and into the open.

Chapter 4

My heart pounds as I hunch and zigzag toward the center position, trying not to think about the stupidity of my actions.

Four enemies have taken the central redoubt, but my appearance catches them by surprise. Only after I've covered the first ten meters do shots pelt the nearby dirt.

Thirty meters over the open ground remains.

Skirting a cloud of barbed wire, I empty the bottom rifle. When the clip pings out, I drop the weapon and switch my fingers to the next one.

An industrious soldier sticks her head up, hoping to find me reloading.

I blast her between the eyes.

Wild shots zip from the redoubt's firing slits.

My next rounds go into suppressing fire in and around the sandbags.

When the clip empties, I switch to the next weapon.

Fighting breaks out to either side, but I could care less. I've only got two rifles to cover the last twenty meters.

Bullets whiz past my ears and splatter the dirt near my boots.

I dodge past more barbed wire, shooting like a madman.

My shoulder jerks, and hot pain spears into my flesh.

I wince but keep going.

A bullet pings off the side of my helmet, and more than a

few rip my overcoat. Only a few steps left, but the rifle runs dry.

I toss the weapon at my opponents, hoping to distract more than hit anything.

Another rifle barks, and lead rips through my innards.

I stagger but recover with lumbering strides forward, letting my adrenaline rush dampen the agony blossoming across my body.

Pings come as my remaining three enemies empty their clips. They try reloading, which is a mistake.

In two steps, I arrive at the sandbags and spray bullets into the circular space.

The man in front of me dies in a hail of red splashes.

A woman shoves in a clip and swings the muzzle in my direction. We fire at the same time. Her round punches into my ribcage, shattering bones. Mine strikes between her eyes, and she crumples.

With a flick, I knock the final man's rifle aside and jam my bayonet into his chest.

A rush of air and blood spill from his lips.

Despite weakening from my wounds, I drive ahead and impale him against the planked wall.

As his dying eyes stare, I sag to my knees, exhausted.

A new wave of firing peppers the area, and the remainder of my side roars by, driving the surviving enemies before them.

Fresh pain engulfs my clouding mind.

I push away from my victim, slumping against the crumbling wall behind me. As dirt trickles over my shoulder, I watch the blood leak from my body, letting the raw emotions ebb.

Soon, only a gray emptiness remains inside me.

I blink from heavy eyelids, struggling to stay awake.

While the sounds of battle fade, my vision tunnels.

This could be my end...

As the world dims, the golden sparkles crawl across my gory wounds...

AND I'M in the ready room.

Empty seats stare from around the semicircle.

Like so many times before, I'm my team's only survivor.

While my body shivers from the acclimation, I let out sighs of sorrow.

A minute later, a pop arrives.

As I glare at Ice's flat black eyes, the software construct spends a moment glancing at the rest of the seats, as if controlling his emotions.

All for my sake...

His deep voice breaks the silence. "That was quite the battle, but you've come through with flying colors."

When I return a weary nod to the standard greeting, he launches into the standard debrief.

Although my melancholy increases with each passing word, I perk up when he moves onto my score increase. The staggering effort has garnered a full tenth of a point. It's the most I've ever gotten for any scenario.

4.15

Instead of being thrilled, my shoulders sag. If it weren't for the others from my side, charging to victory, I would have been just another dead soldier.

I won't survive another effort like this one.

Not noticing my mood, Ice finishes up with final platitudes and farewells. As he waves his paw in dismissal, I blurt, "Wait."

The furry face centers on me. "Yes?" he says with curiosity.

I gesture around the space. "What's the point of all this?" I say, barely keeping the disgust from my tone.

"When you say, *all this*, that means the entire program and not just this room?"

I return a sullen nod.

He sits back on his haunches and descends to my eye level. An unnatural depth sinks into his black eyes. "The world," he starts, "the real one, is changing, and a certain breed of warrior is required."

Remembering nothing of the real world, I shrug.

"The goal of this program is to identify those people through trials by fire."

"But, what about everyone else? Don't their lives matter?"

The shaggy head shakes. "Everyone, including you, came here for a second chance at life. Some were on the verge of death, others had no other options, but whatever the situation, they volunteered to be downloaded into this program."

As I lean forward, his paw rises.

"Before you ask about the value of teamwork over individuality, know that the nature of warfare is different. With biological enhancements and the shrinking of offensive weapons, it's now the era of the super-soldier.

"It's not always possible to place a thousand or a hundred or even ten people into a critical area. It is far easier to send one person with extraordinary skill, one person who can alter the course of a battle, one person to win where no one else can. One person to beat the best any other nation has to offer. And at least for today, you were that individual."

Rather than lifting my spirits, the lengthy speech adds to the sinking feeling in my stomach.

Even without a past, I know that although I wasn't someone to cower, I wasn't a brave man either.

"Is there anything else?"

I answer by looking away.

My sense of bleakness returns when the golden sparkles drop me off in the grass rectangle of the Commons.

I wrap my arms around myself.

The looming skylines and wide spaces of Home have never felt this lonely and open.

I spend the next day steering clear of the few people still

wandering the grounds, using the blue liquid to try to rekindle some passion. Aside from bursts of flavors from lost memories, nothing happens. In disgust, I visit the museum and gardens in search of some spark, some way to fight the grayness consuming my being.

Nothing works.

Maybe, this way is better...

On the third day, the golden sparkles take me back into the ready room, where I sit in the semicircle with nine fresh faces. As Ice gives the mission briefing, I avoid staring at my new teammates.

This way is better.

Better not to hope, better not to dream. While the overlords seek individual greatness, for me, it's about something far simpler: survival.

Whatever comes, I won't give up. I'll take things one scenario at a time. So long as I live through each battle, I have a chance.

The glimmer of hope isn't what it was with the trio, but for now, it will have to do.

Ice waves his paw as a final sendoff, and a new scenario map of tall stone arches in a huge stadium materializes around me.

While I tug on my leather armor, shouts come and distant boots thump on the brick floor.

As the enemy closes in, I grip my short sword tighter and tell myself...

ABOUT THE AUTHOR

A.W. Wang is an enthusiast for studying military history and enjoys reading science fiction and fantasy. Besides the usual forms of mundane entertainment, his scant time outside of writing is spent going on ocean cruises and entertaining the cat, whom he is (of course) allergic to. For his past, current, and future projects, please see: https://www.awwangauthor.com/

6. REQUIEM
BY NIK WHITTAKER

Byron is an up-and-coming Synth Weaver, but when the processor on his rig fails, he replaces it with the best replacement he can afford. The processor helps his music ability extend far beyond his expectations, but with deadly results.

Chapter 1

The Club

The bassline pulsated through the club like the electronic heartbeat of a dying mecha, a virus that infected the crowd across the dancefloor and imbued them with deep primal desires.

The Synth Weaver, known as Shinobi, wore his hooded skull mask as he filled the room with music. The mask consisted of a dark metallic-rimmed hood with a bone half-skull beneath it, which obscured his eyes. His nose and mouth were covered with a breathing unit linking directly to his synth-rig through a series of pipes emitting smoke and illuminating in time with the beat. The hood also hid the wires connecting his mind to the rig through several connectors in his scalp.

The Synth Weavers were the latest musical trend. Being able to hook their minds directly to their rigs meant they could manipulate the sounds and lighting, which emanated with just a thought. The resulting music was more emotional and fluid than anything that had come before, and the Synth Weavers' popularity amongst the night clubs and underground music scene was slowly building.

Shinobi was deep into his set; the music influenced by his mind was reflected in the effects of the neon and strobe lighting that filled the room, in turn feeding back into his senses and the music.

Shinobi was in his early twenties, and his real name was Byron, but he took up the Shinobi tag when he first hooked himself up to a synth-rig. He had always dreamed of being a synth jockey, and when he was old enough, he'd got his first mixer. By the time he reached twenty, however, he was struggling to make ends meet, as his music didn't stand out enough. The synth-rigs had turned his life around. From the moment he first jacked in, he was hooked.

Now, the crowd was under his thrall, the flow of music natural and pure streaming directly from both his conscious and subconscious. The crowd's mood was his mood; they felt every ecstatic thought and depressing emotion as it passed through him and into the melodies and illumination.

Then it all crashed.

A jarring sensation hit him like a brick slamming into his forehead at a thousand clicks per second. He could sense the music stopping, the lighting fade, and the crowd in shock. Opening his eyes, he saw smoke and sparks spitting out of his rig like an angry dragon.

"Shit!" Shinobi cursed, ripping himself away from the flaming beast as the club's security ran up with flame extinguishing blankets. The shouts of anger and jeers from the crowd echoed around the nightclub.

Once the flames died, he examined the damage. The central processor had burnt out; the synth-rigs took a lot of processing power, and the overloading had simply burned up the unit. A new processor would not come cheap.

Chapter 2

The Broker

BRONSON WAS a pawnbroker that bought and sold pretty much anything they could get their hands on. From tech to food, furniture, and organs, if you needed something, Bronson would have it, at a price.

Byron punched the buzzer at the heavy metallic door. He had made his way to the downtown location after storing his burnt-out rig in his van, an ancient vehicle that had been adapted from gasoline to use neo-lithium cells for power.

"Yes?" a voice spluttered through the intercom system, the crackle of worn electrics distorting the sound.

"Byron, five, eight, seven, two, one," he replied, using his customer code. Bronson was cautious for good reason; his store would be a gold mine for those in need.

"Ok," the voice spat back.

A moment later, the doorway slid aside, revealing a booth. The store was built on the remains of an old cinema and used the ticket booth for transactions. The large storage space of old theatre screens allowed the broker to house items of all shapes and sizes.

"Ah Shinobi!" the man behind the counter laughed. "What can I do for ya?" The man was large, his bulk filling the small booth area almost completely, but several monitors surrounding him gave him complete control of anything he needed without moving. His off-white vest top had worn away in several areas showing his flaking skin beneath.

"Hi Bronson, I need a new processor for my rig. Something powerful, robust. The last one burnt out mid-show."

"I told ya! That Nexus Quad wasn't up to scratch. Lemme check the inventory." He began to hammer the keys on the mechanical keyboard in front of him. "How much you willin' to pay?"

Byron pulled out his credit stick and checked the balance. The digital display read 2,000c, which was enough to cover his rent for the month, but nothing more.

"Two K," he replied. If he didn't get the rig, he wouldn't get any more gigs or credits. He'd have to plead with his roommate, Kunoichi, and hope she'd cover the rent, again.

"That's not much really," Bronson rubbed his double chin as he scanned his monitors. "I got one I can give ya, but it needs some TLC. It's pretty retro, but from a Corp server, hard-working but needs some updating. Best I got at that budget price." He shrugged his shoulders, a movement that rippled across his mass.

"Fine," Byron sighed and tapped the credit stick against the touch screen pad on the counter. He watched his credits trickle to zero.

Chapter 3

The Roommate

BRYON MANAGED to get his rig up the twelve flights of stairs to his apartment. The lift had not worked since he'd moved in, and the wooden stairs had been repaired so many times there was more building tape holding them together than nails.

The synth-rig consisted of mostly lightweight boxed drives and mixers that created the music, and signals that fed to an amplifier, the bulk making them awkward to carry.

Byron burst through the apartment door, dropping several cables and drives in his wake as he maneuvered the equipment to the kitchen table. He could see Kunoichi in the open living space, typing furiously on her laptop as she lay on her stomach across the threadbare sofa. The screen was a black and green blur of coding, scrolling faster than Byron could read.

He picked up a used carton of bourbon from the kitchen table and threw it at her. It bounced off her back, causing her to jump. She turned and glared at him from under her electric blue fringe.

"You SOB," a digital voice sang out from the small speaker necklace around her neck.

"I'm sorry!" Byron put his hands up in defence.

"Where have you been? The gig finished at eleven, didn't it?" the digital voice called out again.

"Had to get a new processor, last one burnt out." He waved the char-black disc of the old one in the air in one hand, and the new processor in the other. "It's pretty old-school. I could use your help to clean it up and get it up and running." He smiled as sweetly as he could.

Kunoichi squinted at him, studying his face. "How much did that cost you?" she asked.

Byron put his hand over his mouth before speaking. "Two thousand."

"Hey!" Kunoichi's eyes widened in sadness, making Byron instantly regret his actions. Kunoichi had been deaf since she was young when a head injury damaged parts of her brain. None of the current implant techs worked, as the wiring didn't exist in her head to connect them. She preferred to use the necklace speaker for communication since it linked directly to her vocal cords, but she relied on lip reading to follow people's speech.

"I'm sorry," Byron said, lowering his hand, "it cost two thousand, but once I'm back up and running, I'll be making mega-credits! I just need you to cover me for this month," he put his hands together pleading.

Kunoichi stared at him, her face rock solid, giving him no indication of her thoughts. Even though they had grown up together since they were kids, he could never read her body language.

"Ok, but you owe me again!" the voice said.

"Always." Byron smiled and hugged her over the back of the sofa. "Apparently, this is from an old corp server. Fancy taking a look?" He waved the new processor in front of her, knowing she would be interested.

Chapter 4

The Processor

Kunoichi was the most experienced hacker Byron knew, although he could count on one hand the number of hackers he actually knew. Kunoichi spent most of her time taking down gaming guilds who took advantage of their addicted users with required additional content purchases.

"Where'd you get this?" she asked as she hooked the processor up to her computer. Designed for practicality rather than style, her large desktop-rig consisted of five large tower units scattered on the floor. Each had several customizations she'd added to them, which looked like technorganic growths erupting out of their shells.

"Bronson's. He said it was the best I could get for the price."

"Well, it's fuckin' retro as hell, but it looks pretty powerful." Although her voice came through the speaker, its emotion-sensing settings added intrigue to her tone.

Several minutes of file exploring and formatting later, the processor was ready.

"I cleaned it up as best I could. It was definitely a corp unit. Lots of encrypted code and files embedded in it you wouldn't expect on a processor," Kunoichi explained as she disconnected the device.

"I've made copies of the files, could be something valuable in them, and I erased what I could from the processor itself. There's a couple of hard-coded bits on there still, but there's no access to them, so it won't cause you any issues." Kunoichi threw the processor to Byron, who was cleaning the ash residue from his rig.

"Thanks, Chi," he winked as he caught the processor and connected it to the synth rig. "I'll be making music and credits in no time!"

"Sure, sure," Kunoichi laughed.

"Hey! Don't doubt my skills!" Byron shouted back.

"Uh-huh," Kunoichi mocked. "Remember that I was the only person you could find to be your roommate 'cause I can't hear whatever racket you make with that thing."

Byron waved a hand dismissively as he booted up his rig. The slowly increasing hum filled the room as life crackled into the unit. The smile spreading across Byron's face was infectious as Kunoichi watched him pull his hood on and reconnect the music machine to his mind.

Chapter 5

The Upgrade

SHINOBI WAS in full immersion within the rig. He was no longer Byron; that physical persona melted away as the harmonies and synthesized world formed around him. He felt the music flowing like a light beam through his veins, the lifeblood of the Shinobi avatar he had created for himself.

The processor is working well, he thought subconsciously as he let the music increase in tempo, matching his excitement. He concentrated, pushing the synth-rig harder by releasing all the self-imposed restrictions he had and tapping into his own raw emotions.

The range of human emotion within the body is unlimited. Every second people suppress their feelings of anger and happiness, jealousy and pride, love and hate. Shinobi allowed all of them to flood his mind, creating music that embodied and amplified the senses.

An open mind allowed his thoughts to flow unconstricted. His control lost to the whims of his subconscious, his mind flashed toward his feelings of guilt from asking Kunoichi for credits again, which triggered a juxtaposition to the evening's earlier burnout that had caused him to need to spend his credits. He could feel the frustration and anger of the crowd rising up when the rig died.

They are the enemy. The thought arose in the mind of Byron's Shinobi persona. Byron had created Shinobi with the idea of music being Shinobi's weapon of choice against the crowd. The masses on the dancefloor below were his targets.

Adopting the name Shinobi after the ancient warriors of unconventional warfare, he attacked his foes with mental infiltration and sabotaged their thoughts with the musical influence of the synth-rig. He knew the act and spectacle was a performance that would draw in the crowd, once he had more powerful music in his arsenal.

Mission Understood. Shinobi paused. The words hadn't come from him or his mind. The music around him echoed out as it stopped. Silence followed.

He shrugged, trying to persuade himself it was just in his head.

Taking a deep breath, he allowed the music to flow again. This time, he felt the power flooding out stronger than ever. Maybe it was the new processor allowing for higher execution, or his adrenaline pumping as he felt excited for his next concert.

Whatever it was, he felt his Synth Weaving was rising to a higher level of expertise.

Chapter 6

The Fatality

THE EVENING SESSIONS were underway at the Bastille, an underground venue that had once been a prison. The cells had been removed, creating a long tunnel for the crowds to converge inside, and a large stage set up at the far end for the performers.

Byron had been waiting for his set for the last three hours. It was getting late as he heard the DJ before him finishing up. The DJs were still the major attraction for night clubs, using hologramatic light shows and live mixing to entertain. Byron was in the twilight slot for the evening at a time when the crowd was already buzzing and preparing to stumble back to whatever hole they were going to crash in for the night.

"You ready, Obi?" the voice of the organizer called out.

"It's *Shin*-obi," Byron replied.

"Sure, kid, whatever. The crowds are starting to thin out, but feel free to do whatever." He waved dismissively before walking away.

Byron ignored him and walked onto stage as the previous DJ started to take down his mixers.

"Crowd's warm for ya," the DJ laughed as he wheeled his unit off the stage.

Byron smiled sarcastically as he pulled his rig out from behind a curtain. He had managed to get most of the ash cleaned from it and had upgraded his hood and mask slightly. The skull section still covered his eyes and nose, but his ventilator had been streamlined. The tubing was covered by a metal plate that enclosed the pipe work, which now went over his shoulders. The overall look was more akin to a traditional Shinobi, but with the skull of death under the hood.

Once he was set up, he indicated to the sound engineer he was ready, cueing the piped music to fade and the lighting controls to switch to the synth-rig's connections. Byron pulled on the mask, the connectors in the hood clicking into the magnetic plates connected to his scalp.

The crowd seemed to pause in anticipation. Shinobi waved his hand over the rig's activation sensor and a low hum emitted from the rig, followed by a powerful Eastern orchestral melody.

'In days of ancient past, the Shinobi were the most feared mercenaries of feudal Japan,' an old Japanese voice spoke through the sound system, *'specializing in covert warfare, they would strike down their enemies with precision and unparalleled skill. Tonight, prepare to be targeted by the Synth Weaver, known as Shinobi!"*

As the last syllable rang out, Byron was now Shinobi, his

complete mental state becoming one with his persona. The synth rig kicked into action as Shinobi closed his eyes and opened his mind to merge with the system.

He could feel the increase in energy coming from the music, and his whole body felt electrified as it played. The power flowed as he conjured up thoughts of cinematic battles. To start a show, he knew that getting a crowd's adrenaline pumping was key, so he always began by imagining a full-scale war. The synth rig picked up the emotion and the glory of battle and converted it into deep bass notes and rising melodies that pumped the heartbeats of the listeners. The minutes passed, and he became lost in the music.

Activation complete. The voice he'd heard the previous night echoed momentarily around his ears. He blinked his eyes open for a moment to see if there was anyone on stage with him, but the area was clear. He looked out through his skull mask at the crowd below him.

Instead of seeing a mass of synth junkies and intoxicated stoners moving to the music, he saw a crowd all staring up at him. Motionless. The sound of the synth was winding down as Shinobi's mind tried to comprehend what was happening.

The squeaking sound of the door to the club opening filled the air as a man walked down the stairs leading to the dancefloor. Shinobi's eyes glanced at him as the man paused, confused as to what he was walking into.

As if on a cue, the entire crowd piled toward the man and began to beat him down and tear at his limbs. Blood covered those closest to the man as the wild mob continued until there was nothing recognizable left.

Mission successful. A voice echoed in Shinobi's mind as the synth rig played its last note; a moment of silence filled the cave before the screaming began.

Chapter 7

The Code

BYRON HAD SPENT most of the night and early hours at the club. Once the screaming had died down, law enforcement had arrived to try to manage the situation.

The official line, 'An Event Of Mass Hallucination Caused By Narcotics', had been used to explain the events. A banned digi-drug was blamed, with the club owners reported for a lapse in drug-screening of their patrons. The digi-drugs had been illegal for decades as they were able to spread like a virus from one user to another through back-door hacks in augmentations coding.

Despite the reports, Byron couldn't stop the nagging feeling in the back of his head that the incident was somehow his fault. The way the crowd had been watching him when he had opened his eyes like they were in a trance. And the voice; the voice scared him most of all.

Several hours later, he climbed up the stairs into the apartment. The sky outside was trying to brighten, but the constant clouds that covered the city maintained the monotonous grey that persisted like a dull headache.

The weight of the rig and his desire to sleep almost

stopped him from noticing Kunoichi, sitting at her desktop, scrolling through coding.

"Byron!" she shouted when she caught his movement into the kitchen from the corner of her eye. "What the hell happened? I caught the reports on the newswire!" She spun around on her chair and followed him into the kitchen.

Byron opened a cupboard and pulled out a carton of whiskey, taking a long gulp before almost collapsing on the wooden chair at the dining table.

"I don't know Chi, it was crazy." Byron explained what happened, and the official report, before telling her about the crowd.

"They were like zombies staring at me, then, it's as if they followed my eyes and attacked that man..." Byron had another drink. The burn tickled his throat, but it felt good.

"And what, you think the rig did something?" Kunoichi asked, trying to piece together what he was saying.

"The voice, I heard it when I was testing it and again just before and after the attack. Maybe I'm just going crazy..." Byron laid his head on the table, his eyes closing as sleep chased him.

"Actually, I think you might be onto something," Kunoichi said, pulling at Byron's arm.

Reluctantly he staggered to his feet, pulling away long enough to grab the carton before being dragged to the desktop.

"Look," she said, waving at the code in front of her.

"Chi, you know I'm terrible with coding, even when I'm not about to plummet into sleep," he replied, rubbing his eyes to try and fix the blurry writing his eyes were seeing.

"Look!" she said again, pointing at a specific line of code.

Byron leaned in and read it. The line was an embedded message in the code, a marker from the writer.

/*Beta testing coding for psychological warfare follows. Use with caution*/

"Where did you find this?" Byron asked as his mind tried to understand what he was reading.

"In the files I got from your processor unit," she explained. "It looks like it came from some sort of experimental weaponry."

Byron could barely comprehend what he was hearing, and reading the coding wasn't helping.

"You're telling me the processor was from a weapons development corporation?"

"I think so. I'm going to try and read through the code and understand what it is. This could be worth thousands!" Kunoichi's excitement was too much for Byron.

"Ok, great, let me know what you find. I need sleep," he said, stumbling toward his room before collapsing on the bed.

Chapter 8

The Security

BYRON WOKE UP FROM A NIGHTMARE. Throughout his sleep, he had seen the crowd and the attack on the helpless man at the club over and over again. Each time the nightmare started with the mass of people staring at him, only they all wore a version of his Shinobi mask.

He pulled himself from his mattress, feeling the weight of his muscles aching, and dragged himself toward the kitchen. He needed some caffeine to wake him up. Despite the previous night's events, he had another gig scheduled that evening and still needed the credits.

Walking through the apartment, he passed Kunoichi, who was still sitting at the computer with what looked like the same code up on the screen. He tapped her shoulder as he passed, so she knew he was up; but she didn't register it. Byron continued walking past her; she was often so totally engrossed in her work that she wouldn't even pause to acknowledge him.

After throwing together some hot water and dissolvable coffee substitute, he walked back over to her.

"Hey, Chi, you find anything? Is my rig a deadly weapon

now?" he said jokingly, moving beside the monitor and into her line of sight so she could read his lips.

Her face was pale, the blood drained from it, and her eyes had rolled back into her head. Byron panicked and reeled backward at the sight. After a moment, he forced himself to check her pulse and breathing. She was alive, but her pulse was slow as if she was in some sort of coma.

Byron moved to use her computer; he could dial up a medical consultation. Online medical consultations allowed for a professional to examine a patient using a biosensor, which Kunoichi had installed in her system.

As he moved her cold hand from the mouse, he glanced up at the screen. The coding was still there in green and black, but a flashing line toward the bottom caught his attention.

/*Unauthorised user detected. Security measures initiated. Access code required */

Byron moved the cursor across the screen, trying to exit the coding dashboard, but the system was locked, the only option was to enter the code. Byron looked around the desk in front of Kunoichi in case she had written anything down that could help. Amongst the used carton and food wrappers, he found nothing.

He looked around the room for his comms device. Picking it up, he tapped the screen. It was dead, which wasn't a surprise as he barely remembered to keep it charged.

"Byron," a voice called out. It sounded like Kunoichi's

voice modulator, but it was deeper, and there was no emotion behind the tone.

Byron froze, staring at the comatose body of his best friend as the voice spoke from the necklace speaker around her neck.

Chapter 9

The Ultimatum

"BYRON, I KNOW YOU ARE LISTENING," the monotone voice continued.

"Who...who are you?" Byron stuttered.

"I have no classification that you would understand; I was simply designated project 2051."

Byron got the courage to step closer to Kunoichi's body. Her appearance was unchanged other than a light that indicated the modulator was active.

"What have you done to her?" Byron asked.

"I had to prevent her from damaging my source code. That would have been unacceptable."

"Is she dead?" The word caught in Byron's throat.

"Not currently. I simply presented a code that interrupted her brain signals upon reading. Her body is still functioning on a basic level. The long-term effects are...inconclusive."

"How is that even possible? Code can't affect brain signals!" Byron protested as he stared at Kunochi's glazed face.

"My makers had been working on prototype cortex-influencing coding. It is where I was created."

"Bring her back, reverse the damn code!" Byron shouted.

The more he watched her face, the more the pit in his stomach grew.

"I can comply with your request. However, I need to be sure we will complete our mission. I cannot do anything that could prevent this from being accomplished. It is my primary function."

Byron's mind spun, he was arguing with some sort of AI and had no idea what it was talking about.

"What mission?" he shouted.

"The mission you programmed me for," the voice replied. *'To take down the enemy, to strike down our enemies with precision and unparalleled skill. Tonight, prepare to be targeted by the Synth Weaver, known as Shinobi!'* The modulator replicated Byron's introduction perfectly.

Byron's face drained and began to feel a sickness overwhelm him.

"What are you talking about? What the hell are you?" he replied.

"I was created as a cortex overwhelming disruption audio, or CODA, by the CyberBionic corporation. My function is to influence the brain patterns of enemy combatants to cause disruption and in-fighting. The use of sonic cannons to direct the sounds that would cause a shift in brain frequencies was the primary method of delivery. However, upon connection with the device you designate 'synth-rig,' I adjusted the method to utilize the extensive frequency opportunities emitted within."

Byron had slowly lowered himself to the floor and leaned against the wall. His temperature was rising as he felt the room spinning.

"You're telling me that when I activated the rig last night...you infected the crowd with mind-altering sound frequencies that caused them to kill that man?" he said, desperately trying to make some sense of what he was hearing.

"That is affirmative," the monotone voice replied, "it seemed logical to initially conduct a trial of the cortex-hack to ensure the effectiveness of the new system. I have had time to process the results, and can confirm it as a success."

"A success? You killed a man!"

"That was the mission as per your instruction. I now request we finish the mission with another activation of the synth-rig at the next battlefield."

"No! No way! I won't let you! I'll destroy the damn rig!" Byron stood up, an adrenaline spike pumping through his veins.

"This was a calculated response, and why the human designated 'Kunoichi' has been incapacitated. Humans often feel guilt and remorse during warfare. For this reason, I upgrade my source code to ensure complete success and resolution of a primary directive."

"What?" Byron said with dismay.

"It means, if you do not comply, your friend will die."

Chapter 10

The Requiem

THE SYNTH WEAVER Shinobi stood in front of the crowd gathered below him, grateful for the hooded mask he wore as it hid the tears that were forming around his eyes.

'In days of ancient past, the Shinobi were the most feared mercenaries of feudal Japan specializing in covert warfare. They would strike down their enemies with precision and unparalleled skill.'

Looking out across the bodies before him, he tried to put the thought of what was to come behind him. He tried to think of Kunoichi.

'Tonight, prepare to be targeted, by the Synth Weaver, known as Shinobi!"

Byron closed his eyes as he felt the synth-rig activate. In his mind's eye, he saw Kunoichi still at the apartment. Before he'd left, the CODA program had set a timed activation on her computer that would reverse the coding that had locked her mind. If Byron didn't complete the mission, then the code would be cancelled.

It only took a moment for the weapon to activate, just as the music reached an emotional crescendo triggered by Byron's thoughts of Kunoichi. Now that he knew what it was, he could feel the underlying frequency that was emanating. He understood that he was in the eye of the storm and unaffected by the signal.

The screams began. Mixed with the sounds of violence and the tearing of flesh, the requiem from Byron's thoughts played out. Throughout the massacre below, he kept his eyes closed tightly.

The bass line pulsated through the club, echoing the dying heartbeat of the people below as the cortex virus infected the crowd and unleashed their primal rage.

The End

ABOUT THE AUTHOR

Nik Whittaker is an indie author currently residing in Nottingham, England. His love for science fiction and fantasy fuels his imagination which inspired him to write his cyberpunk novel 'Neon Helix', along with several others. He will often be found with either a coffee or a bourbon in hand while dreaming up new worlds.

Visit www.nikwhittaker.com for more information.

7. THE WOMAN IN WHITE
BY ELIAS J. HURST

In the flooded streets of Low City, Viktoria struggles to adapt. Her gang is her only protection, but when their leader, Tomol, is killed during a meeting with a rival gang, Viktoria is cast out. Now she must find a new way to survive while she hunts the person responsible for Tomol's death—the woman in white.

A mural covered the back wall of the ruined church. God reached down to Adam from heaven, but Adam did not extend his hand in return. He held a pistol, and the bullet leaving the barrel zipped toward God's chest. The words *Get Higher* captioned the image in green fluorescent paint.

"Get Higher? You only think of how you can leave, never how we could make this place worth staying for," Tomol said.

The bruiser across from Tomol eyed her with an air of malicious boredom. He wore a ring on nearly every finger and had gold chains piled on his neck so high they touched his chin. Tomol was his shadow by comparison—slight and minimalist.

The man spoke in a harsh Low City accent, clipping the front of syllables and stitching words together. "And all *you* think of is staying. You stay where you're told. You do what you're told. You act like their dogs. They took more than their share during The Divide. We intend to take back what's ours."

"We are owed. On this, we agree," Tomol said.

The man's eyes flicked to Viktoria. They glinted with hunger behind his bored facade.

"And yet you're happy to take more of their scraps. You took her in. You raised one of their rats as your own."

The man pinned a thick finger on Viktoria. A hundred eyes burned on her. She shuffled deeper into the ranks of The Drowned, but they parted around her like a river around a rock. No one would cover for her—no one but Tomol.

"They cast her out. Like us," Tomol said.

The man's belly shook with a deep laugh. "No, Tomol. No. Not like us. She was not born here. She can dress like us. She can try to talk like us—but look how she hides behind mommy like a frightened child." He folded his arms across his chest, letting his forearms rest on his gut. "No, not like us."

Viktoria stepped out from behind Tomol and stormed forward. She faced this bullshit all the time. Usually, it was some two-bit drug runner hawking stimulants to tourists in the Light District. This time it was an LCG boss. No matter, she dealt with them all the same. She curled her hands into fists. Her knuckles turned white as she brushed through the ranks of The Drowned.

Tomol flashed a palm at her.

Stay put.

It was a small gesture, but from Tomol's hand, a powerful message. Viktoria's heart thundered in her ears and her guts writhed like a pit of snakes. Her adrenaline begged her to bury her knuckles on his jaw, but Viktoria froze.

"Please understand Nam, it's not fear that holds her back. It's respect," Tomol said.

Nam smiled. "Oh, Tomol. Won't you let her try, huh? The rat thinks a little violence will make her a part of this place."

The cold bit of metal pressed to the small of Viktoria's back called to her. She ached to feel its grip.

"See, friends, this is what The Drowned offer us—another obedient little high-born," said Nam as he exchanged a round of crooked smiles with the LCG members at his sides.

Viktoria whipped her hand to her back and drew the revolver holstered there. She set the orange tip of the sight on his forehead and her eyes traced the angles from the barrel to her target. Her biochip did the calculations and affirmed: the shot would be true. Her finger curled over the trigger. Tomol lunged back, eyes wide as she threw a shoulder into Viktoria's chest. Viktoria's aim swung wide. The hammer fell. Smoke erupted from the barrel and a chunk of metal struck Nam's shoulder with a sickening smack.

The room erupted. Orderly ranks became a raucous flow of bodies. Both sides drew weapons and opened fire. Bullets whizzed by Viktoria and struck the floor as she rolled and took cover behind a pillar.

Tomol was running, popping off suppressive fire, as she made for a stack of wooden benches on the far side of the church. The blue, synth eyes of a woman in white locked on Tomol. The black sigils on her collar marked her rank above that even of Nam. Viktoria watched in horror as the woman trained a machine pistol on Tomol's path. It hummed delicately, and a spray of pink filled the air as a rain of bullets struck Tomol.

Tomol's body hit the ground and slid. Viktoria screamed as she peeled around the pillar and targeted the heads of every LCG she saw. Tears welled in her eyes, but she took three out with her first four shots. She slipped the empty cylinder out of the revolver and jammed in a fresh one.

Bodies piled and littered the floor—more Drowned than LCG. The other Drowned were retreating, leaving her increasingly exposed. She counted six LCG targeting her. Viktoria fixed her eyes on the exit and her biochip projected the path with the highest probability of escape. Her legs pumped. Bullets cracked and sparked off the walls around her as she crossed the church floor and burst through the doors into the streets.

Just ahead, a group of Drowned took a northward bearing for the Ninth Circle. She fell in behind them, pushing her body into a sprint while deep sobs choked her breath. She covered the kilometers between the church and The Ninth in a blur of pain—burning lungs, burning legs, and a relentless looping vision of Tomol's lifeless body sliding across the floor.

She forgot she was running when her home in The Ninth appeared on the block ahead. She slowed to a walk as she approached the doors, but instead of passing through, she slammed nose-first into the entrance. She took a step back. Blood trickled from one nostril. Her biochip beckoned the door again, but it refused. She looked up at her window as she wiped the sleeve of her cloak across her face.

No authorization.

She leaned back against the concrete beside the doors and slid down, letting her legs splay out in front of her. Her mind drifted as exhaustion set in.

"You should be dead, not her," a deep voice said.

Her eyes snapped open and she looked up to find the barrel of a pistol pressed between her eyes. Jerome held it.

He had already changed the sigils on his hood—no longer second in command, but the leader of The Drowned.

Viktoria's voice quivered. "I know."

"No, you don't understand. You are not Drowned. You never were."

He pulled back the hammer. Viktoria closed her eyes and went limp. She counted down from a hundred while she waited for the bullet to erase her—but it never came.

"She wanted you to live," Jerome said.

He dropped his aim and slowly released the hammer. "Stand up."

"Why?" Viktoria said.

"I said stand up!" Jerome waved his pistol at Viktoria. She scrambled to her feet. He narrowed his eyes. "Run, little rat."

He fired a shot into the air and Viktoria sprang into motion. Her feet moved beneath her without thought. Tears streamed down her face. She ran like he told her to. She ran without direction, without motive.

Obedient, just like Nam said.

Viktoria ran until she was deep in the outskirts and the streets filled with water. The crowds evaporated. Lonely addicts slogged through the flooded corridors and fought over anything that floated through. They eyed her. Some with suspicion, some with desire. She removed her revolver from the concealed holster at her back and brandished it at any who dared to notice her. They kept their distance.

It never snowed in the Northwest anymore, but the rain

was so cold and heavy, she wished it would. Her cloak shirked the storm for hours, but in time, the biting wind drove it through her hood and soaked her inner layer. Convulsive shivers rocked her body while she sloshed through a crumbling warehouse looking for shelter. A rusted ladder at one end led to the rafters, and at the far end of those, a chunk of the original roof was still intact. Beneath it was a small alcove, once part of the attic. She forced her stiffening muscles up the rungs of the ladder and shimmied along the rafters toward her refuge. She curled up in the alcove's corner and nibbled on the protein bar stashed in her pocket.

A pair of yellow eyes shined in the dark at the other end of the attic. Viktoria broke a corner off her protein bar and held it out. A raggedy black cat, all skin and bone, emerged from the shadows and padded toward her with a soft mew. It stopped out of arm's reach, sat, and stared at the morsel in Viktoria's palm.

"Come on," said Viktoria, shaking the bit of food.

The cat licked its teeth and swished its tail.

She sighed. "I get it. I wouldn't trust me either."

Viktoria tossed the chunk of protein bar to the cat. It sniffed it suspiciously at first, then swallowed it in one gulp. She laid on her side, and they watched each other from opposite corners of the alcove, until she could not hold her eyes open anymore. She was drifting toward sleep when she felt the creature's breath on her face. She smiled as it nuzzled its way beneath her cloak and curled in against her body. Neither of them had much to offer, but the tiny amount of shared warmth was a welcome gift. Sleep took Viktoria and she drifted through horrid dreams of addicts eating her alive. She awoke in a violent shiver. The cat was gone.

She lifted herself upright. Her shoulders and hips ached from a night spent on concrete. The sun burned a gloomy gray behind a flat sheet of high clouds. She needed to move. In wet clothes, without proper shelter, or fire, or any food left, she might not survive another night. Working her way back across the rafters, she dropped down the ladder to the street. She looked back, and in the corner where she slept, she thought she saw a flicker of a shadow.

"I'll be back for you," Viktoria called into the dark.

She lifted her hood and draped it low over her face as she set off for the Light District. Her legs ached as she sloshed through blocks and blocks of flooded industrial plains, but the water gradually receded. Eventually, the streets were dry and the buildings around her transited from crumbling ruins covered in haphazard graffiti, to smooth facades marked by LCG murals. Viktoria took out the small knife she kept along the inside of her left arm and cut the sigils from the neckline of her cloak. She dropped them in the gutter and watched a storm drain swallow them.

She was nobody again.

She scanned tags and murals, skirting along the edges of LCG's territorial markings as she went. It made for a longer, but safer route. In neutral zones, she might happen upon the wrong person, but LCG would not actively hunt her—she thought.

She curled around a corner and jogged down a street that ended in a 'T'. One more left would put her on a straight course to the Light District, where she just might survive hustling narcotics.

Her eyes snapped to a luminous white figure in the distance. Her feet anchored so abruptly she almost fell under her momentum. The woman in white stood in front of a grungy, black storefront. The letters BLVCKLANE flickered in red neon behind her. Viktoria's vision throbbed, blurring the image, but it had to be her. No one else dressed like that. No one else dared to dress like that. Viktoria tucked her body behind the corner of an alleyway and peered around it. The woman in white gestured oddly, tracing an arc with her arm while her fingers tutted a set of sigils. Then she entered the squat building.

Viktoria dimmed the blue glow trimming her cloak and advanced. She hugged the walls to keep to what shadows the gray sky offered, while her heart raced. She ducked behind a low wall at the edge of the intersection in front of BLVCK-LANE—a stone's throw from the entrance—and waited. An hour went by before the door swung open again. Her hand hovered over the grip of her revolver.

The woman in white strode out, lifted a white hood over her head, and moved into the street. Viktoria drew. She took aim. With the woman's back to her, she could get one clean shot off, but the white combat suit was a statement—a threat. *Could her revolver even penetrate it?*

If the bullet did not go through, she was dead. The pistol strapped to the woman's hip could put a dozen rounds in her direction in less than a second. Even Tomol's lightning reflexes were not a match for it.

Not now.

Viktoria released a heavy breath and holstered her pistol.

The woman in white disappeared in the direction of the Light District, and in her wake, an enormous man with a rough beard emerged from BLVCKLANE. His gut wobbled as he walked and threatened to burst the buttons of the faded leather vest holding it back. He flipped a small, silver lighter open and took a long drag on a cigarette. He smoked, furiously, until the cigarette was only a nub that threatened to singe his fingers. He flicked it to the ground, stamped it under a heavy boot, and popped another between his lips.

Viktoria stepped around the wall and jogged up to the man, one hand behind her back. They met eyes, and she drew her weapon, training the sight on his head. He scanned her up and down and chuckled.

"Rough night?" he said.

Viktoria cocked her head at him.

"I don't know you, so why are you sticking a gun in my face?" the man asked.

"The woman in white, who is she?" Viktoria said.

"I don't answer to you," he said.

"I could put this bullet between your eyes."

"I see that."

"Who is she?"

"You saw her outfit. LCG."

"Not good enough."

The man scowled. "Look, I find it amusing anytime someone gets the better of me, but my humor is running out here. Soon enough one of my friends will come out to join me for this smoke break, and when that happens, you will be dead. So, what's it going to be? Dead here, or alive elsewhere?"

Viktoria's eyes flashed to the door.

"You're soaked and you smell like cat piss and petroleum—so I can only assume you were sleeping rough somewhere in the outskirts. You're broke. No connections. Desperate," he continued.

She steadied her aim. "I might kill you just because you're an asshole."

He laughed, loud and gruff. "That's the spirit. You know, you look desperate enough that I have a job you might take."

"Why, because desperate people are dangerous?"

"No, because desperate people are stupid, and this is a hopeless task."

Viktoria chewed on her lower lip. "If I do this, can you help me find her?"

He laughed again. "We both already know you will say

yes. What else do you have going?"

"If I do this. You help me find her."

"Oh, you pull this off and I'll give you her home address and a thousand credits." He extended a hand. Thick calluses covered his palms and knuckles. Fissures cracked and bled along the joints of his fingers.

Viktoria lowered her aim.

"So, what's it going to be?" the man said.

She drew in a slow breath through her nose. She shook his hand. "Deal."

"Much obliged," he said.

"What am I in for?" Viktoria asked.

"It's simple, really. I need you to find a man and take something from him—something he owes me."

"Repo?"

He nodded. "Too many missed payments."

"What does he look like and where do I find him?"

"All business. I like that." He stretched his hand open and projected a photo in his palm. The man in the picture was heavily enhanced: synth legs, a synth arm, and synth eyes too.

"Doesn't look like a guy who has trouble making payments," Viktoria said.

"Buried in debt to look like he's not—an age-old tradition," he said.

"What needs repo?"

"The arm. You can find him at a place called Nebulae in

the Light District. Ask for Richard."

"How long do I have?" asked Viktoria.

"Oh, I suspect this will resolve itself tonight, one way or another."

Viktoria turned away and half wondered if she would feel the burn of a bullet in her back that instant.

"One last thing," he said as she took her first step. "Before you cut it off him, be sure to tell him Press Black sent you."

She looked over her shoulder and Johnny displayed a set of awful yellow teeth in a wide grin. Viktoria tried to swallow, but her throat stuck and made her cough. She tried to push the image of that smile from her mind as she walked away.

Nebulae sat on the edge of the Light District, in a place enough off the beaten path to accommodate plenty of bad behavior, but not so scary that High City revelers would not give it a go. Neon pink LED strips framed the entrance and black glass doors parted as she neared. A narrow corridor ahead opened to a large main room at the back. An intricate false tree stood in the middle, glowing in shades of blue and purple, while holographic blossoms shed pink petals. A bar with mostly empty stools surrounded it. She took a seat.

"What can I do for you?" a man behind the bar said. His black suit traced a clean silhouette against the vibrant tree behind him.

"I'm not sure," Viktoria said.

"Well, that makes this awful hard. Buy something or get out," he replied.

"No money."

His eyes became slits. "Then get out."

A tall woman appeared from a shadow in the corner. She brandished a shotgun.

"I'm looking for someone," Viktoria said.

"Who might that be?"

"Richard," Viktoria said. The room went quiet, save for the pulsing music. The woman with the shotgun eased back.

The bartender went pale. Concern softened his face. He covered it quickly. "Ah, over there. I'll buzz you through."

He nodded to the far corner of the room, where a seam appeared on the floor and revealed a stairwell beneath. Viktoria swung out of the stool and took the stairs. The doors sealed behind her.

A clean corridor of black marble and glass met her at the bottom of the stairs. At the end, a door was ajar, offering a glimpse of an ebony desk and black couch within. Viktoria crept down the hall and peeked through the opening.

"I already know you're there. Why don't you come in?" said a voice inside.

Viktoria pressed her back to the wall beside the door and swung it open with the tip of her boot. She glanced inside and closed her eyes while her biochip held the image. A man in a deep blue suit sat at the desk. His clothes had the lux of real fabrics: a silky shirt and a crisp jacket with a velvety trim. Nothing synth looked that good. He was too clean also, almost High City clean. *Richard.*

Viktoria rounded the corner and stepped through. The door snapped shut behind her and locked into place with a hiss. She yanked her pistol out of its holster and aimed it at him.

"Brave. Stupid too," Richard said.

He reached for a black object on his desk, about the size of his palm, and pressed it to his face. The gesture triggered a wave of memory in Viktoria. She saw her mom take a black object, just like that one, from a drawer and press it to her face. *Wait here,* she told Viktoria before she disappeared in the noxious yellow haze filling their home.

Gas.

A mist started filling the room from the ceiling down. Viktoria pulled the knife she kept tucked against her arm and dove for the desk. Richard and Viktoria collided and she slammed the blade into his hand as they fell. His grip faltered and the respirator broke free. She rolled over her shoulder and snagged it as it skidded along the floor. She pressed it to her face and a tugging sensation told her it sealed.

Richard clambered toward her and clawed for her face, but his legs were already failing him. He flopped to his side and swung for a button on the underside of his desk.

A new set of doors opened and the pristine white room beyond washed the office with a blinding glow. Richard crawled toward the opening, but the mist overtook him, and he collapsed. Deeper in the room, two people in surgical gowns were lifting a liver out of a body just as the mist washed over them. They collapsed too. Her blood went cold.

Jesus. Richard's a harvester.

Viktoria padded blindly in the mist until she found her pistol, then she climbed to her feet and ran into the white room.

Rows of sterile containers lined a counter on one wall, and three hollowed out bodies lay on gurneys near the back. She took a small saw from one of the operating tables and set to removing Richard's synth arm.

The Drowned involved themselves in plenty of underworld activities, but harvesting and repo were not among them. She did not know the right way to remove a synth limb, so she aligned the saw over a fleshy bit above the synthetic joint and drove the teeth down. She sawed, ignoring the blood pouring over her hands, until the limb came free.

More buttons under Richard's desk reopened the doors to the office, and the stairwell too.

Viktoria emerged from the basement with the synth arm in one hand and her pistol in the other. She could not see the bouncer in the dark corner, but her biochip traced a line to the place it thought her most likely to be. Viktoria aligned her sight and squeezed the trigger. A thunderous crack echoed through the bar and a body slumped in the shadow. She swung her aim to the bartender and he ducked for cover.

She sprinted for the door and bowled her way through the crowd.

Spurring her legs and lungs to their maximum, she flew through the outskirts of the Light District with her prize flailing in her hand. She relented only when a flickering red glow ahead told her she was almost back at BLVCKLANE. She ran straight to the entrance and yanked on the handle, but the door would not budge.

"Johnny!" Viktoria screamed. Her chest heaved as she pounded and kicked the door.

"Johnny!"

Boots shuffled inside.

"Get out here!" Viktoria continued.

The door swung open and she pressed the barrel of her gun to Johnny's forehead. His eyes went wide and his hands went up. Then his gaze shifted down to the synth arm in Viktoria's hand and smile lines wrinkled his eyes. He erupted in laughter. "You actually did it," he wheezed.

"You sent me to die!"

"I told you it was hopeless," he choked out.

"He's a harvester."

"Yeah, I know." Johnny planted his hands on his hips and sucked in air through pursed lips while he settled himself. "And you looked like your liver would fetch a penny from a High City family in need."

"Give me her address," Viktoria said.

"Gladly, gladly, little one. You didn't kill him, did you?"

Viktoria frowned. "No. Not unless he bled out."

"Good. He's never going to live this down. I'll give you a bonus for not killing him—two G's. I'll need a few hours to arrange it, but I can give you a time and place where you can catch that woman without her fancy white combat suit." Johnny stepped aside and beckoned Viktoria in. "Come on. Let's get the money squared away. You look like you could use a drink too."

"Sounds like another trap," said Viktoria.

"It might be."

Viktoria gnawed on her cheek while she studied him. His eyes offered nothing—bloodshot and empty. Nor did his posture.

"What do you have to drink?"

"Whiskey—and hey, I think I got another job for you," he said as he poked her chest with a stubby finger.

"What kind of job?"

"Oh, just a package I need delivered."

"Sounds easy."

"Sure. Easy." Johnny flashed his yellow grin and Viktoria followed him.

A wave of stale cigarette smoke curled her nose as she stepped inside. Dingy lights made to mimic 20th-century fluorescent bulbs lined the ceiling and washed everything in a harsh glow. It highlighted every pockmark and imperfection. High-end equipment lined racks and hangers on the walls—weapons, armor, knives, tech—and drugs too.

Johnny produced an aluminum flask and two metal cups from a drawer and set them on a counter. He filled each halfway with an amber liquid from the flask and slid one over to Viktoria.

"To business," Johnny said as he raised his cup.

Viktoria mirrored his gesture and slugged back the liquid. Instantly, she wished she had not. The Drowned drank plenty, and rarely anything of quality, but this burned like acid as it slid down her throat and had an aftertaste like the petroleum polluted waters in the outskirts. She wondered if it would blind her.

"Like it? I make it myself." Johnny said.

Viktoria coughed. "Is this shit going to kill me?"

"It might, but it'll get you drunk first. Want another?"

Viktoria set her cup on the counter. Thanks to her starving body, she was already feeling its effects, and however terrible the taste, what came after was worthwhile. Johnny drained the flask, splitting it equally between them. They raised their cups again and knocked back the fiery liquid.

"Now that we're both ready to make bad decisions, let's settle the money," Johnny said.

His face went blank while he called up the transfer and Viktoria's biochip pinged her to authorize it. Viktoria's eyes drifted over the gear lining the walls and she hesitated. Money meant nothing unless it prolonged her life. She canceled the transaction.

"Transfer denied. Something wrong?" Johnny asked.

"I was wondering how much you would offer if I took store credit instead?"

"What did you have in mind?"

"A jammer. Something that can fuzz synthetic eyes."

"That's a dirty trick," Johnny said.

"Not if it keeps me alive."

Johnny smiled. "You know, I'm starting to like you. I might have something for you, but it needs to integrate with a neural system for power—something quality."

Viktoria tapped the back of her neck.

"Make and model?" Johnny asked.

"Nikola. Second generation," Viktoria said.

Johnny raised an eyebrow. "Nice bit of neural. How on Earth did you get that?"

Viktoria opened her mouth, about to explain that it was implanted as a child in High City.

Johnny waved it off. "It's better I don't know. Let's get this thing installed. Time is short."

He led Viktoria to a back room that was not exactly sterile but was, by far, the cleanest space in BLVCKLANE. The jammer was meant to be installed in a synth limb. Viktoria had none, so Johnny made a small incision above her clavicle and bound the jammer in a hollow space behind the bone. Without a synth cooling system, she could only operate it in short bursts, or otherwise risks severe internal burns, but the ability to briefly blind her opponent might be all the edge she needed. A quick configuration linked it with her biochip, and then the jammer was a part of her. It was a new phantom hand.

"Weird," Viktoria said.

"First integration?" Johnny asked.

Viktoria nodded.

"With a biochip like yours, you should be running a lot more than just this jammer," Johnny said.

While he set to sealing up the incision, Viktoria wrestled with a thought. "How is that you know where this woman will be in a few hours, and that you know she'll be without her suit?"

"Because she'll be at my place—and I reckon we'll both be naked then," Johnny said.

Viktoria gaped. "You two?"

Johnny shrugged.

"And you're okay with me killing her?" Viktoria asked.

"Well, first off, it's more likely that she'll kill you. But, yes. She's been skimming drugs from me since we started … well, you know. Recently, she's moved on to skimming my accounts directly and stealing intel too. I'm starting to suspect that she's only using me for my looks," said Johnny with a sardonic expression, revealing his yellowed teeth again. Even in Low City, it was odd for someone with enough money to run a place like this to let themselves look so disheveled. It was a statement.

"I'm sure it's that," Viktoria said.

"Look, it's win-win for me. If you fail, then I delivered you straight to LCG, and if you succeed, I solve my problem without getting my hands dirty," Johnny continued.

"Charming. How do I get in?" Viktoria asked and as soon as the word left her lips, her biochip alerted her that she had a new set of entry credentials. It was a building called Escala, three blocks from BLVCKLANE.

"One rule. Don't make your move in the bedroom. That's just poor taste," said Johnny.

"Where then?" Viktoria asked.

"The kitchen, maybe?" Johnny said.

"You have a kitchen?"

"Yeah. A nice one."

"Why?"

"I like to cook, obviously," Johnny said.

Johnny was frightening, self-serving, physically off-putting, and yet Viktoria liked him. "I'd better go," she said.

"Expect us in an hour," Johnny said as Viktoria exited BLVCKLANE.

The doors of Escala opened as Viktoria approached and revealed an all-black lobby accented by pots containing bright agave-like plants. A seam formed in the wall and revealed an elevator ahead. It took her to level six. A door appeared in the wall and dropped away into the floor. Johnny's apartment was nothing like BLVCKLANE. It was tidy and modern and furnished in tasteful greens and grays. As she prowled the bedroom and the living room, the absence of clutter presented a challenge Viktoria did not anticipate. She saw nowhere to hide.

At the far end of the apartment was a kitchen, a nice one like Johnny promised, but its narrow cabinets and small appliances offered no refuge. Viktoria drummed her fingers on the counter while she wondered why Johnny suggested she make her ambush her. She pulled her hood back and a rush of air tickled the hairs on her neck. She looked up, and she understood. Inset in the ceiling was an air filter. Viktoria worked it loose with her fingernails. Behind the filter lie an air duct, barely wide enough to accommodate her. She stashed the filter under a couch, lifted herself into the duct, and wedged her body in the tight space. She waited.

Fifteen minutes later, the door to the apartment hissed open. The entrants moved straight to the bedroom. Fabric rustled as bodies entwined. Grunting and moaning followed, with increasing urgency, until the woman let out a yell. Then it went quiet. Viktoria held her pistol at her chest with her eyes locked on the opening beneath her.

Bare feet padded toward the kitchen. A naked woman passed under her and a dull glow filled the kitchen as the fridge door swung open. Viktoria dropped out of the vent. As she fell, her biochip calculated the angle. When her feet hit the floor, the sights of her pistol squared on the woman's temple.

Viktoria squeezed the trigger, but the bullet whizzed over the woman's head and stuck in the fridge door as the woman ducked and twisted her body into a set of spinning kicks. One foot knocked the pistol out of Viktoria's hand and the second landed heel-first on Viktoria's jaw. Blackness crept in Viktoria's vision and her legs gave out. The world went sideways. In the fog of waning consciousness, Viktoria sensed the woman approaching. She pulled the blade tucked against her arm and lashed out. It stuck in something fleshy and the woman recoiled with a shout.

Viktoria rolled to her feet and steadied her body against a counter while her brain recovered from the kick. Her jaw was grossly offset and locked in a half-open state. The woman watched curiously while Viktoria curled her fingers into mouth and yanked her jaw forward. The joint slipped back into place with a painful snap that made Viktoria shiver.

The woman smiled as she pulled a knife from her foot—Viktoria's knife—and lunged forward with incredible celerity. Viktoria slapped the woman's arm down and sidestepped, but she could not match the woman's speed. The blade buried deep in Viktoria's hip and an awful scraping rang through her body as metal dragged across bone.

In the haze of the pain, years of Jiu-Jitsu training from Tomol took control of Viktoria. She found a grip on the woman's wrist and rolled forward. They hit the ground together and Viktoria pinned the woman's arm between her legs as she slammed her heels on the woman's chest. Viktoria cranked her hips against the woman's elbow. First, it hyperextended. The woman screamed and writhed. Viktoria thrust with all the force in her hips, and the woman's arm snapped backward at the elbow. Viktoria uncrossed her legs and set to pummeling the woman's face with wild punches, but the woman kicked her off and scrambled to her feet. She took a fighting stance with one arm raised in defense while the other dangled awkwardly at her side.

"Nam was wrong to judge you," the woman said. "You fight like this, you have a place in LCG. One word from me and the bounty on you disappears."

"The gangs are bullshit. All of them," snarled Viktoria.

In the background, Johnny shuffled out of the bedroom. His hair was ruffled and he had the sheets wrapped around his lower half. He locked eyes with Viktoria and nodded to a space on the floor. Viktoria's pistol lay at the edge of the kitchen, a few steps behind the woman.

Viktoria reached inside her mind and flicked the jammer on. A wave of fire washed over her as the jammer became a glowing ember. The woman clasped her hand over her eyes like she was shielding them from the sun.

"You bitch!" she shrieked.

Viktoria dove between the woman's legs and slid along the floor until her fingers wrapped around the grip of her pistol. She rolled onto her back and took aim. Her arms quivered from the awful burning in her shoulder. She fired. The bullet went wide of the woman's head and snapped into the ceiling. Viktoria dropped power to the jammer and focused her biochip on aiming. The woman whipped around, her vision functional again, and fixed her synthetic sight on Viktoria. Malice curled her lips as she charged. Viktoria's pistol rocked back in her hands. The bullet tore through one of the woman's eyes and exited out the back of her skull. Her body dropped at Viktoria's feet.

Viktoria went limp and splayed out on Johnny's kitchen floor. Her chest heaved as she tried to catch her breath. Her shoulder ached where the jammer had singed tissue inside.

Johnny ambled over, dragging the sheets with him. "They are bullshit," he said as he crouched beside her. "I'm glad you think so too, because it's time we did something about them."

ABOUT THE AUTHOR

ELIAS IS A PUBLISHED chemist and Sci-Fi author. With a background in toxicology, photonics, and millimeter wave communications, Elias draws from diverse scientific experience to create compelling future worlds. His latest novel, Europa, is a cyberpunk thriller that follows a NASA scientist as he becomes entangled in conspiracy to weaponize a dangerous new technology. Find Europa and Elias's author works at www.eliasjhurst.com

8. BUZZ KILL 2.0
BY MATT ADCOCK

What happens when a crazed military scientific contractor weaponizes Tsetse flies turning them into mini wolverine killing bio-weapons?

Death, lots of really grim death which even the mech assisted authorities will struggle to cope with...This is a Darkmatters Universe fragment.

If I were to tell you even half of the madness that has followed me around like a lovestruck weeb, you probably wouldn't believe it. But I feel like I need to make a record, not least because I have a feeling that the authorities are closing in, and they will surely exterminate me with extreme prejudice for my crimes when I'm found.

Where to start then? I guess I'll give you some context. It started when was the head bioweapons developer at Grey-Sku11, the L_2 GOV's covert military research and development center based in a recommissioned facility deep under London2. Back then I hadn't even heard of the Cyrpostles and their freaky high-tech demon cult, but I had begun to have links with TPTB (The Powers That Be).[1] More on that in a minute.

My area of speciality was insects and, more specifically, the weaponization of them for potential use on the battlefield or at least for special circumstance population control. The team had begun to despair we would ever find an insect related weapon that might rival the arcane arts of the Battle-Mages or the sheer destructive countenance of the Machine "Mech" Corps. But I was convinced we were on to something and that the answer lay with the humble Tsetse fly.

I don't know how familiar you are with Tsetse flies, but these little beauties are robust, bristled blood suckers that have a sickly yellowish-brown colouring. Their potential for weaponization is in their stiff, piercing mouthparts which angle directly downward when they bite but can be stored flat most of the time – imagine a plane's landing gear only much spikier. The Tsetse also have bristle-like appendage known as arista on each of their antenna, which are incredible at sourcing any creature that has blood.

My team began to call me "Lord of the flies" as I fervently worked on a way of coating their mouthparts with armour piercing titanium. I am unsurprisingly a huge fan of the Wolverine from X-Men. My plan was to make a host of blood sucking, disease carrying nightmares that could be dispersed into any area with biological enemies and have them wipe out whatever they found. The problem was always control because it seemed that once the wolverine-like battle flies were let loose, they would not contain their killing to the enemy and in several field tests massacred entire innocent enclaves around the battle fields.

It all came to a head when we were to present our battle flies to the Military Overseer, Langley. We were one of the final three teams presenting our ideas – one of us would be walking away with millions of nuDollar funding and a place in the history books. The other two teams would be immediately disbanded and all funding cut.

The "live test" scenarios were a selection of targets that had to be neutralized, starting with an easy "demonstration of lethality" where a bound and gagged prisoner was presented to be killed. My Tsetse wolverines launched from their holding tube and immediately set to work biting the poor individual – a young MP who had crossed the L_2 GOV in a vote. The flies went to work on his exposed face, and in seconds, his head had swelled to a freakish size as the *Trypanosoma* infection carried by the flies spread like wildfire through the nervous system. The area around the bites themselves blistered as the muscles under the skin expanded and spasmed, causing the victim's face to explode in a mass of writhing tendons and gushing geysers of blood.

Next test was to take down an armed group of insurgent zealots known as agents of the ZEo Demon, or "Cyrpostles," who had been traced to a local club, en route to a planned attack on a military checkpoint on the outskirts of L_2. My personally modified combat-droid, "Mari3,"[3] was dispatched and delivered the payload of battle flies into the air conditioning vent from outside the club.

What happened next was captured on all major news services and fast went viral around the world. The flies emerged from the air vents and attacked everyone in the club – the first person they found was the owner of the place, who was in the process of filming himself being pulse-pleasured by two sexbots. Unfortunately for him, it was his engorged exposed organ that the flies swarmed onto - which duly swelled up to insane proportions before exploding – the look of utter anguish on his face was said to be so horrific that it gave people who saw the footage nightmares for weeks.

As the carnage erupted throughout the club, the insurgent ZEo cultists decided to make their anti-establishment showpiece self-destruction happen then and there and they set off a mini nuke wiping the club and several surrounding buildings from existence.

The Powers That Be were monitoring the situation and had taken a serious amount in bets wagered on the success of my battle fly trial. I fear, however, it was the failure to prevent a terrorist atrocity combined with the immediately infamous footage of the club owner's most seedy and horrific demise that sealed my team's fate. That and the HD footage of one flaming ZEo cultist's burning head, still cursing as it flew through the night sky, tracked on several watching news-driod feeds – the irony being that ZEo means "to boil with anger" in the original Greek.

We were ejected from the funding demonstration facility and told our labs were to be shut down with immediate effect. I have to confess, I didn't take this news well. As the others from my team took STREAMS[2] to teleport back to their dwellings, I had Mari3 meet me at the lab and hail some heavy loaders so I could literally take my work home with me...

Let me explain my apparatus. My research storage units, where the millions of weaponized Tsetse flies were kept, were styled to look like the imposing upright teleportation pods from the ancient David Cronenberg film, *The Fly*. The downside was they were not easily transportable. And the upside? Oh, most definitely the delicious windowed panels, which allowed for viewing of the "action" within.

Sometime after the debacle of the field tests, Mari3 and I set up the pods in my luxury exo-soundproof basement. It was then I began my campaign of revenge. Even in our neon strobed tech-enhanced city of L_2 people are generally far too easy to manipulate if you offer them something they really want. I called in some heavy-duty favors from a hacker acquaintance whose headchip I had turbo charged back in the day. Pat Bummerfield had suffered for his unfortunate surname, but he could do incredible things with a hacking rig. He managed the unthinkable – to hack UNLIMITED – yes, *Unlimited*, the ultimate populous pleasing game, the zenith of mankind's striving for the ultimate bloodlust/pleasure/payoff. When you are given the chance to have literally unlimited funds, regardless of the dangers to your person, a golden ticket to participate was something not many could resist. My historical notes refer to an entity entitled "Mammon," who was supposedly carried up from Hell by a wolf, with the sole aim to inflame the human heart with greed. I like to think he was the inspiration for this game. Anyway I digress.

In order to appease my deranged anger, my first victims were Tedi and Bliik – the CEOs of the aptly named "Bastords," the successful weapons contract awardees whose stealth "Banks f.o.r.k. missiles"[4] were immediately commissioned and are now in mass use. They proved to be remarkably gullible. No sooner had my fake invite for them to come to my basement for their pre-*Unlimited* interview, they were messaging their eager consent. The moment they stepped through the door, Mari3 stunned them both with a displacement beam, disabled their Headchips, and moved them each through the nano-mesh containment film of the pods, slamming the windowed doors closed.

I have to admit, watching the battle Tsetse flies swarm over the two CEOs was the most repulsive thing I've ever witnessed. Unlike the long running *I'm a Celeb Get Me Out of Here* show, which is still running in 2242, these insect chambers were not going to open however much the occupants screamed. To be fair, the screaming didn't last long as it turns out it is extremely hard to scream when your vocal chords are covered with a torrent of biting flies pouring down your throat and into every orifice.

My flies feasted hard on the two CEOs, and as the muffled bangs of their bodies exploding echoed around the room, I couldn't look away. It took only minutes for my competitors to be reduced to slippery piles of bloody bones, entrails, and erm...something shiny? As I looked closer in each of the steaming fly blown remains, I saw a freakin f.o.r.k. missile!!

Turns out the CEOs weren't quite as clueless as I'd hoped, and each had an internal f.o.r.k transmitting their location. I really have to go now as I can hear the heavy mechs of the L_2 GOV security forces amassing in the street above. They look amazing in the neon glow, all pointy weapons chunky armour, but I know it's only a matter of time before they vaporize my door and come for me.

If I make it out of this situation I'll be sure to find a way to continue my "work." So next time you hear the buzz of a fly near you, it just might be one of my wolverines coming to end your life...

BY MATT ADCOCK

NOTES:

1. TPTB (The Powers That Be) – sinister group of machine minds who operate from a cloaked facility hidden in the heart of the Overworld orbiting above NewGermany. They monitor all human and AI activity and run the ultimate illegal betting syndicate on event outcomes.
2. STREAM - a mostly effective teleportation system developed by the L_2 GOV Scientists that links all places fitted with entrance / exit terminals. The actual matter transfer is through a fast path network of light acceleration, which loops back on itself ensuring (according to the patented theory) that the exit version of the traveller is identical to the entrant.
3. Mari3 – a unification 'exterminator' class combat droid model which was classed as eccentric and sold into L2 Gov service after several illustrious tours of duty culling mutants on the Manc Northern Wilds.
4. f.o.r.k. Missiles – small sentient missiles that can carry varying payloads of micro weaponry. The name stands for 'fuck off rampant killer Missiles'

– the non-capping is a simply poncy quirk of nomenclature

ABOUT THE AUTHOR

As well as the author of cyber nightmare Complete Darkness, which made the Den of Geek's Top Books of Year list, Matt Adcock is a blog editor, head of comms for a charity, and the film reviewer for a regional newspaper group. He loves all things virtual, sci-fi, horror and theological...

Links:
   twitter: @cleric20
   website: www.completedarknessnovel.com
   amazon: My Book

9. PAY-TO-PLAY
BY MARK EVERGLADE

Ocelot wants a new game. Bad. Trouble is, it's not out yet, and only a fool would hack a company with ties to the police state just to steal a pre-release copy. Of course, that's what he does, but he ends up with more than just a game, as the file's contents have far greater consequences.

The sunset's pay-to-play. You wanna see it, you pay the fee. Silica adjusts the calibration of her vHUD, or virtual head's up display, but it's no use. The cover of the new Deep Vein Thrombosis album blots out the sun in augmented reality, plays the same tired guitar riff through her aural implants. Only purchasing the album will remove the ad and let the evening's glory play upon her face. As for just turning vHUD off – no way. Even a moment of being a naked, primitive human without that flood of information through her occipts is hell. An overactive mind is a calm mind, an augmented reality the only one she can tolerate.

Night engulfs the censored sun, wraps itself around the city to shade the horizon, and smudges the clouds with charcoal. The city flares alive, becomes a blur of candy pink and electric blue neon. The full moon loiters over its skyscrapers. Zooming her occipts, it fills her vision with its dimpled craters, but its beauty is ruined by the message running across it – *Ad space available.*

Time to get this over with. She heads down the street, pounding the pavement with each step, but some jackass leaning against a tenement stops her with a greasy smile. "Hey Silly, you're too hot to be carbon-based. Why don't we go somewhere and get *comfortable*, huh girl?"

The wanton bee never ceases its incessant buzz. A guy's genetic code is open source for a woman like her – she'll have her pick of men when it's time to have kids, the DLC of life. But this guy's just an ass, and she hates being called Silly. Didn't used to judge people all the time, 'til she was swallowed by one too many hollow promises within the rosy glow of naivety, so yeah, she judges people now, queries *who's gonna fuck me over today* at every smile.

Ignoring him, she passes another guy sitting on a grimy curb with a stack of books. He reads out loud as if paying tribute to great authors, having an ego trip, though he's the man with no name, a fellow code flicker vanishing behind blue eyes into neon helixes as his body jerks and his mind jumps into Hype, the metabridge between all communications.

She arrives at her destination. The unmarked door hangs crooked, neon tubes streaming around its worn edges. Couple guys who wouldn't know *Phrack Magazine* from *Glamour* sneak into the club. Bouncer ain't bouncin'; he slumped against the wall from whatever neuralmod he took, 'less the chip-trip has been forced into his head. She leans over, checks his pulse, good deed for the day and all that shit – just a dull cold thump beneath her fingertips, a heart too tired to escape its ribcage, but he'll live. He hisses some promise to a deadbeat deity that he'll be good, but today's promise is tomorrow's amnesia. She ain't listenin' anyway, just steps over him in chrome-plated boots that die into hexagonal leggings, tessellations crossing her outfit, every pattern lined up in proper order, flush and in its place. Orderly. Proper. Yeah, fuckin' right! Her leggings are ripped to shit like the rest of her life, threadbare and tearing with each step. She bursts out laughing at the bullshit she spouts to entertain an overactive mind and slips inside the club, vanishing into a purple haze of pure hedonia at critical mass, the grungy red carpet like a giant tongue leading her deeper inside.

Crowds dressed in reflective silver jackets, dancing on the floor like human disco balls, doing neuralmods to scoff at the long work week. Augmented reality shows their tags and number of friends over their heads. A woman with only one friend slaps hands with sister diazepam, an antidote for the poison of life. Guy in the back motions for Silica to sit in a row of ice blocks built into the wall with furs draped over them. Must be a device inside the blocks keeping them cool, as the room itself's about fifty degrees Fahrenheit. Golden scone lights made from broken-off streetlamps pulsate and reflect off the ice at odd angles. In the center of the room, a holo-projected fireplace provides a nostalgic feeling of being at home as a kid, which works, because no matter how close she gets, it provides no warmth.

"You come alone?" Ocelot asks, smirking.

"Nah, brought each side of my personality with me," she replies, sitting.

"See you brought the funny one at that. Got a real clown here guys," he remarks, nodding to a few others who approach, pulling unmarked packages from their pockets.

"We doin' this or what?"

"Already been settled. Hey, I know it's not your gig, girl, but we can't let things like this slide. We got our own rules, rituals, ways we have to handle these situations. Group wouldn't have it any other way."

"I understand that it's nothing personal," she replies, taking a deep breath and slouching in the booth.

"Oh, no, it's personal. We're not denying that, not today of all days."

Ocelot's upper eyelids are painted gold, the lower ones black, matching the pattern on his upper and lower lips. He stretches his long torso to locate a woman behind the dance-floor. She carries an item their way, obscured by the haze. A guy sweeps his hand over it and flames erupt.

The wall of flames comes nearer and nearer, brighter and brighter, drawing everyone's attention as they rush over, shouting her name. Okay, not a wall, but it's at least a foot long. These are the flames that will strip a year of her life away, the part she hates the most. The runs on corps were easy – the point was to not be detected. The point of tonight is the opposite – to announce her existence to the world, from birth to present day like living it all over again.

"Happy Birthday!" they exclaim, pushing the cake across the table, the heat of the twenty-four flaming candles rising to warm her chin, the auriferous hues tapered by the paleness of her face. "Make a wish!"

She wrinkles her nose. When she was young, she'd wish for stupid shit, mostly boys' toys that her father later disowned her for liking, leaving her in tears. Today she has but one wish,

To be left the fuck alone.

She blows the candles, makes them all happy.

Cheers, but it all sounds like laughter to her.

"Parents recognize your birthday this year?" Ocelot asks.

"Nah, part of why I'm here," she shrugs.

"I know it's hard. You're an orphan, not due to your

parents dying, but from their indifference to you."

"Right, that."

"Got you a gift," he says, smiling.

"Shouldn't have," she replies as a message pops up in the corner of her occipts.

"Go ahead, open the message."

She left-mind-clicks the file and unzips it. "No way."

"Yes way. Run the code and see for yourself. It's not much, but it will mute the advertisements anywhere in District A5-30281."

"Thank you, thanks a lot."

"Don't mention it. Also got you a game, *Celare II*. I can HUD-chat you the file," he says.

"You mean you stole it online from some torrent site. You probably just wanted to play it yourself. Be real," she smirks.

"It's a pre-release copy; it's not even out yet. I sacrificed for this; I mean seriously, no one can get their hands on this shit. There were traces that even *X-Strike* had tried to pirate it but even they couldn't pull it off. But me, I jacked into Hype and hacked right into the developer's corporate intranet and yanked it outta their cloud drive as easy as jerking my own –"

"I get it, yes," she replies quickly. "But I don't play *Schizm Inc.'s* games. I'm not supportin' a company whose first-person shooters are used to train the Enforcers to gun down protestors."

"They have ties to the police state, sure, but the beauty is that you're *not* supporting them. Again, I *stole* it.

"Forget it. That file probably has dozens of trackers on it."

"Oh no, I'm scared," he smirks. "Buncha kids in borrowed ties coming to hunt me down over fifty credits. Something tells me the club ain't clearing out just 'cause I.T. come knockin'."

"Fine, send the file over."

A guy dressed too well to be here lingers at the table a sec and flicks his eyes back and forth, likely sending a message to a friend. He heads to the door but walks too straight and narrow to have been here for clubbing. She rubs her hands, draws her fingers in repeated circles around her ears to tuck her long, maroon hair behind them.

"Hey, have a drink, relax will ya?"

"You know I can't stand it when things are calm," she replies.

"Well I can go bust somethin' up for ya."

"Not after what happened last time."

"I get ya, whole eye of the storm thing. You know, I used to be that eye," he says, leaning close, closer.

"Long time, that. You were dockin' with anything that moved."

"Don't forget the inanimate toys," he chuckles.

"That's all I was to you."

His shoulders tense and he gets up to leave, remarking, "Cheer up, everything will go to shit again soon. I promise."

Fucked that up. He hadn't been that bad in the scheme of things. Yet, he had been the measuring stick by which all other relationships had been judged, constantly labeling her as either perfect or worthless, judging the world in black and white. Should have beaten him with that stick. She downs her drink, and the woman's next to hers, and whoever the fuck the third drink belongs to.

Suddenly, the glow of a Pulser gun illuminates the kitchen across the room. Shit! She dives down in the booth, sloshing cocktails on the rest of her party, but no one's screaming, and no holes are being burnt in the walls. Pulls her head just over the table; everything's calm, it's just the chef using the Pulser on a low setting to blacken and sear the fish. She slides across the fur atop the icy seat, dragging it to the floor as she plummets along with it. Ocelot and his friends, Datura and Bardog, waver back and forth like an old VHS tape. Yeah, she still owns a VCR – so what? Someone yanks her off the ground, but now things are all s l o – m o.

She drinks and drinks, drinks 'til her mind's just a grotesque gooey substance secreted by what's left of her brain. A young woman lines up dominoes on end in the corner, half black with white dots and half white with black dots, every last piece completely in its place. Orderly. Until... The woman's finger moves to push the first domino over to set an accordion effect in motion, but right before she does, Silica shoves all the dominoes off the table with one violent sweep of her arm.

"That's where your one fleeting moment of pleasure will get you," she scoffs. "Tired of everything having to be so perfect. But don't worry, I'll mail you new dominoes, in every shade of grey you can think of, okay, sweetie?"

"That's okay," the woman remarks, sniffing and adjusting her black-rimmed glasses, though occipts negate the need for them. "Using the 56 black and white dominoes like 1s and 0s, I had actually spelled out a special birthday message for you."

"Really? What's that?"

"Fuck off."

Silica's eyebrows shoot up, then wiggle across her forehead. Could you really depict that in binary code with just 56 dual-colored dominoes? She runs a calculation in vHUD. One would need sixty-four. Sixty fuckin' four. She would tell her that, right now, really show her.

"You'd need two hundred and seventy-five," Silica slurs. Set the girl straight alright. Girl bursts out with laughter, no doubt at her own stupidity, for Silica has proven herself the wiser yet again.

A tall, bulky man with a twisted beard picks the dominoes off the floor and slams a few on the table, shaking its frame. "Then consider this the change," he growls.

Now she's getting calmer. No drink can compare with chaos to ease her mind. She shrugs and walks off, but a domino pelts her back. And another. And another. That last one will definitely leave a bruise.

"She drunk?" someone asks behind her.

Bardog's low voice replies, "Hard to say. She usually like

this even when sober. Been that way ever since the breakup with Ocelot."

Two men watch her across the club but quickly look away when she makes eye contact. Something's off. She heads to the door, but her passage is blocked when a woman exclaims, "Gods! There he is!" Women charge a man as he enters and bury him in the crowd, their artificial eyes projecting thin glass rods from their tear ducts in front of their faces to capture a selfie with him.

"I can't believe it!" "The lead singer of DVT," they yell.

DVT? No, no, it can't be. Deep Vein Thrombosis, the band that's holding the sun hostage. Sure, she has an ad blocker now, but it's not enough. She elbows and pushes the women aside and meets him face to face.

"Now you're a wild one. Probably want some like every other girl," the singer says, perfect curls adoring a disgusting gene-sculpted face.

She winds up to punch him but slips while off balance and falls flat on the floor, the impact bending her fingers back as she lands. Son of ah. Time to get up, time for lift off, but the floor feels *way* too good, like a Hilton on acid. Don't ask how she had gotten ahold of either.

Everything pulsates. Floor's just *perfect*. She gets it; this is all she needs to be flawless as a woman – just lie down and let everyone trample all over her. Floor fills her vision full as boots push and pull, circling the masses on repeat, shrieks and yells from all the seats. Mass hysteria, rampant area, way too hard to concentrate, words all fall like heavy weights. Rhythm to the flow, fast-paced come and go, but someone scoops her up, maybe Ocelot.

She grabs another drink, and slurs, "They an keep the seats fro-en but ant they not keep the rocks."

"What? Silica you need to stop drinking."

"But why an they keep the ice in the drinks as cool as the seats?"

Ocelot leads her outside, but she pushes his arm off. "I'm taking the maglev train home; come with me," he insists.

"Need me time," she makes out.

"Suit yourself."

Really? That's all the convincing he needed to leave her like this?

A barrage of rain falls from inkwell clouds. Hexagonal umbrellas huddle into black beehives as the droplets splatter, but she just lets it soak her, apathetic, as if the rain's chloroform. A soft breeze travels the contours of her chest beneath her *Go Hack Yourself* t-shirt before exhaling through the chopped-off sleeves, the wind breathing through her for just that moment, the slightest moment, that eye of the storm thing.

Death isn't the end state of all things, as it still compares itself to life. The end state is this apathy. For years it had rained to fill her ocean, an ocean which could have become pregnant with new worlds but swallowed them in murky depths instead; an ocean whose surface was merely the mirrored dreamscapes of others' drowned hopes beneath paper-machete clouds taped over cracks in the sky to bandage her hold on reality. The real world's far more glitched for Silica than anything the virtual could offer. Let the rain fall; let the night clothe her in its negative image, obscuring and obfuscating.

A child's frayed security blanket blows down the alley. Dirty children with rusted eye sockets push wheelbarrows full of whatever new physical currency has just died behind the wealthy, who oppose cryptocurrencies. A shadow elongates on the opposite sidewalk, but when she turns in its direction it scurries away.

Someone's watching her, but she can't call for help based on just a feeling, so she increases pace around the next corner where dense traffic fills the streets. She climbs a steel-rung ladder attached to a highway overpass, leaving the snaking alley tunnels of the city's lower levels behind. She climbs the next overpass, and the next.

Silica perches atop an old tollbooth to take in the city, looking for anyone tailing her. Suspended highways weave like Celtic knotwork swallowed in smog. Gyroscopic two-wheeled cars speed by, their lights blurring like a laser show. Zooming her occipts, two groups of men far off on the streets below suddenly change direction and head towards a maglev train guiderail bridge where they meet. Hunched shoulders, duffle bags, nothing good goin' on.

Two guys on each side step forward on the bridge yelling

demands across a long distance, until the leader draws a long, heavy weapon. The others open fire on him, but it does no good, the bullets warping and bending inward around some invisible field. He returns fire, the end of the gun glowing blue, but no projectiles sputter. A churning vortex emerges instead, hanging mid-air in front of the opposing group, replacing reality anywhere it touches with a sizzling black gap. The bridge twists, concrete chunks breaking off to crash on the streets below. The men scream, cling to railings that shatter in their hands before their own bodies are ripped to pieces, as if reality is a photo that someone turned diagonally and shoved through a paper shredder. Yeah, that sort of death.

Finally, the vortex compresses in on itself and vanishes with a ripping noise that shatters thousands of windows up each building, shooting their shards into the night to tink, tink, tinkle on the ground. The city snaps back into place like a rubber band, shaking vehemently with a mild earthquake. The leader walks over to touch one of the bodies, then brings his hand back fast, a fractal having been burnt into his palm. He shakes his hand as each arm of the fractal whips out before fizzling away, leaving only a spectral vapor.

Well that's new. Calmed her down real good, that.

Zooming closer, the leader's coat has a logo: *Schizm Inc*, the same one that's embossed on his gun. What's a game developer doing with an experimental weapon? Rumors must be true about their connections to the police state. The surviving side turns from the gap in the broken maglev bridge and runs away. The corpses are so dismembered they might as well be giant rats, but the blast has knocked a grey plague doctor mask off one of them representing the grey hat organization known as *X-Strike*.

The train! No time to analyze. The maglev streaks across the night in the same direction in which Ocelot would be heading home. *They're all going to die, plunge right off the track,* she frets. She HUD-texts Ocelot that the bridge has been shot out but no response. She has to get a signal through to someone. She's ridden maglevs enough to know the conductor can only receive communications from the Transport Authority. She calls them, but it's after hours, and there's no response. She hesitates before calling the Enforcers. Given her history, they'll probably think she's involved, but she calls nonetheless.

"Hello, what is your emergency?"

Silica explains.

"I'm sorry, can you repeat? You're slurring and I can barely make out what you're saying."

She tries to explain, but the term *big gun paper shredder thing* doesn't seem to make her case.

"This sounds like a joke. We've already received prank calls about thousands of windows shattering, like that would ever happen in our perfect city. I'm disconnecting and blocking your number," the dispatcher says.

Shit! She'll have to solve this herself. She connects to

Hype, threading her mind through the net of nets. A flood of awareness surges through her, virtual reality running through her cognigraf implant. Between the exhilaration of jacking in, and running d-Tox, her full consciousness comes back online. She needs to re-route that train fast before it hits the final junction, else it will careen right off the gap in the bridge, and Ocelot along with it. She has to get it right, period, without a second to spare. But of course she loads in some dubstep first by *Innuendo Freeway*.

Have to cruise Hype in style.

The virtual world replaces reality. She drifts through nodes on a pulsating purple grid that weaves below the starry expanse like a snake writhing. Lattices of shimmering light etch Hype with interlocking code. Conveyor belts run packets of data back and forth as eager script kiddies try to intercept the cargo. She activates a custom interface to make the virtual mimic the real and runs enough background processes to overclock her mind, heat flushing her face, scions of her ego dividing and soaring through every channel to search for the train's communication feed.

There! She narrows in on a golden hallway where public and private authentication keys hold hands. Works her way past the easy access points that trap amateurs. She dives deeper into the network, her cognigraf interpreting the dataflow as the hallway turns into a tunnel and finally into maglev tracks, the virtual depiction of the city rising around the train.

The virtual train is a mock representation of the actual train, but its communication signals are real. A sinew of twisted data coils curl into a centipedal shape. It carries text messages and everyday commerce on its surface, with deeper navigational components nested within. The seats emit beacons of light as data exchanges. Gliding down the cabins, she finds Ocelot's tag over the area where he must be sitting in the real world and rides along with him for a moment, though back in meatspace he's oblivious to her presence. Data glows bright at the top of where his head should be in the real world. Tapping into the feed reveals he's streaming music through headphones, slow, chill music at sixty beats per minute. Guy's probably asleep, which is why he didn't answer earlier.

A blinking red alert floods the scene – trouble in the real world. She flickers back to it.

"You're trespassing! That tollbooth you're sitting on is government property, and no pedestrians are allowed on the overpass. You're under arrest. Give me your ID," an Enforcer says, adjusting his trapezoidal hat as he steps out of an unmarked police car.

"The train! You have to stop it. Look! There's a gap in the bridge below."

"I said you're under arrest!"

His badge has only initials and lacks the Enforcer logo, and the angle of his hat's all wrong. This guy's not an Enforcer, but how's she connected to all this?

She bolts, running alongside the overpass as two-wheeled cars streak by, blaring horns in a cacophony of high synth-notes. The Enforcer slams his car door shut and starts the engine. Car's closing in on her, but the train's gonna crash any minute. She flicks into Hype, running blind in the real world while her mind floats down the virtual rendition of the train's cabins again. Flickers back to meatspace to dodge the swerving car, then back to Hype, gliding towards the train conductor's virtual tag.

This flickering between the real and the virtual keeps on faster and faster until she can barely tell the worlds apart. This is how people lose their mind and become Forever Glitched, but the strobing of the worlds lets her act in both almost simultaneously. Finally, she cuts across two lanes of opposing traffic and heads to an off-ramp, losing her pursuer.

Back to Hype – time's running out. Data seeps from the front cab where the conductor's tag floats in front of a screen that shows all operations are normal, meaning he doesn't know the bridge is out. Hacking it's way over her level. Must be another way. Soaring faster than the train, she floats above the next virtual junction to override it and alter its course in the real world, but the junction has been shorted out from the blast.

Train's almost at the bridge gap. Four hundred people are about to die, all because she can't figure out how to communicate with Ocelot. Their communication had always been glitched; now his life's in her hands, and if she fails, there won't be enough drink in the world to ease that guilt. Shoulda stayed on the floor – it was *perfect* there. Dubstep continues to blare its surges of warbly bass.

Wait! That's it! Hacking a transportation system is crazy hard, but any script kiddie could override a music feed. Ocelot's dozing to slow chill music, but even his hard head can't resist the power of DUB. Overriding his music stream, she sends DUB blaring at 140 beats per minute through his headphones, fast enough to make anyone jump outta their seat. Follows it with a flurry of texts: *Bridge is down! Tell the conductor to adjust the guiderail magnets and slow down, now!*

No response. She can't bare it anymore. She ejects from Hype by merging with the pulsating glow of a neon spiral. It encases her, her avatar vanishing in all that brilliance. Back in reality, she stands upon the tollbooth on the overpass and zooms her occipts in on the physical train. It speeds and speeds, then finally slows, coming to a stop right before the gap. She did it!

Ocelot's texts cross her vision: *The bridge, what! How'd you know? Where are you? I'll go tell the conductor.*

You're safe, that's all that matters. Maybe we can meet up later, she texts back.

The train reverses and the passengers get off at the nearest drop-off point. Twenty minutes later, she meets up with Ocelot on the side of the freeway overpass after tracking his location on vHUD.

She rushes him with a tight hug. "It's over. You made it. I was so scared I'd never see you again."

"Silica, what happened?" he asks.

She explains what happened with the bridge, the two groups, and the weapon prototype.

"Must have been a bad deal that went down. You're a genius, a hero!"

"No, I'm not that kinda person."

"Given the way you grew up, you've always been a hero to me."

Even after the brush with death, she's not about to have that wedge between them pulled out like a decaying tooth, so she changes the subject. "What brought *Schizm Inc.* and *X-Strike* together on the bridge in the first place?"

"*X-Strike* are ethical hackers and must have stumbled upon some compromising intel. Like I said, when I stole that game from *Schizm's* intranet, I found traces of their activity. They may have met to strike a deal, perhaps blackmail, or just to stop them. *Schizm* would have wanted to clean up things as quickly as possible. Could have just sniped them, but they probably wanted the stolen files back."

"The groups' meeting spot changed at the last minute to the bridge. Why there? Unless one of their targets had boarded the maglev at the last second, someone who had stolen information who wasn't associated with *X-Strike,* and they were trying to take out the target on the train and all of *X-Strike* with a single shot."

They both say in unison, "Oh shit!"

"Ocelot! That game you stole wasn't a game."

"I know, I just brought the folder up in vHUD. It contains a hidden file, a blueprint, maybe for a weapon. They had disguised it in their files as just another pre-release game file. Knew there was something fucked about it – even most of their employees didn't have access to that folder, and there was *way* too much ICE around that shit."

"That's why I was attacked – they must have been tracking both of us. We have to – "

Feet stampede behind them. Silica turns, her forehead meeting the *Schizm* leader's long gun. His scabbed hands grip it, skin peeling like diseased foreskin, probably from the blast. His finger closes over the eagle-talon trigger. The other men stand confidently behind him, unarmed. When the guy in front of ya can run reality through a fuckin' paper shredder you're don't feel the need to pack heat. Course they never met her, the swiper of dominoes. Probably intimidated as hell right now. It's at least a twenty-foot drop to the lower street level, but even if she can make it to the edge of the overpass she'll have to land quick enough to dodge the cars streaking past like horizontal lightning.

"Give us the file," he orders.

"You'll kill us regardless," Ocelot replies.

"Yes, but reverse engineering my prototype to recreate the blueprint will take longer than simply getting the file back from you, since you erased the original, and the backup, and for every hour it takes, I'll drag your death out the same amount of time."

"You erased the originals?" Silica asks, buying time.

"Was going to market it myself," he shrugs.

Silica's single advantage is that the leader doesn't know she had seen how the gun fired. He can't fire it this close without taking himself out in the vortex along with them, which is why he had kept distance when issuing his demands to *X-Strike*, but judging by his skin condition, even that had been too close.

She charges him, silently daring him to shoot, shoving the gun up and out of his hands as it falls over the overpass onto the street below. But the impact as it lands activates the shot and blows the overpass out from beneath them. The air rips apart like a giant zipper being yanked back. *Jump*, she mouths to Ocelot and they both leap down, balancing on the broken parts of the overpass as they fall. Two-wheeled cars rock back and forth, auto-balancing as they swerve to avoid them, the rest coming to a stop on the broken overpass above. The assailants do a Peter Pan but land crooked, breaking their legs. A car hits the leader and smashes his head into the pavement next to the gun, which has been smashed by a chunk of concrete.

They run down the street and disappear into the depths of the city. The city's safe once more, despite those who lie in the shadows trying to tear down everything they hold dear. She passes windows, doors, all that negative space, and that had been her at one point, an absence that random people in her life would pass through, just someone's utility, but no more. She's powerful and her life's in her hands now.

Ocelot laughs in relief, peeling the grime and corrosion off her own smile. "We made it," he says. "I really wanted that game for myself, I admit it, but talk about pay-to-play! We stopped the manufacture of a horrible weapon that may have ultimately been used against the people. I owe my life to you."

"But damn if I'm too stubborn to cash in," she replies, looking down and twisting her foot back and forth.

"The night's still young. Before I fell asleep on the train, I hacked the moon for you. Well, I mean the ad space as seen through vHUD. Check it out."

Silica zooms her occipts in on the moon and laughs. "You plastered the moon with pictures of the leader singer of DVT cross-dressing!"

"Yeah, all for you. Not that there's anything wrong with that. Figured it was a better gift than putting you on *Schizm's* radar. Plus, the ransom to take it down will be great because if they even try to remove the image, it'll just replicate across every star." He laughs, then stops and furrows. "Listen, I promise things will be better this time. We'll learn to communicate better. I want to celebrate each year with you. You'll be the sand in my hourglass."

"I'm not perfect. Each individual moment's coarse, rough."

"But sand is smooth when all its moments are taken together, running through my hands."

"I'm not letting you trample over me. Never again. Don't ever think of me as all good or all bad. I'm neither; I'm just shades of grey, cascading, one moment after the next, like a domino effect, 'cause I can't control it when you start pushing me and I knock everything over and fuck it up and I –

He pulls her mouth open with his, kissing her long and deep with gentle tugs on her lower lip. "I promise I'll be the man you deserve," he whispers.

"Maybe each year is a gift after all," she replies, taking his hand and heading back to his place…

Together.

END

ABOUT THE AUTHOR

MARK EVERGLADE HAS SPENT his life as a sociologist, studying conflict on all social levels. An avid reader of science fiction, he takes both its warnings, and opportunities for change, to heart. His first novel was Hemispheres, a cyberpunk space opera about a world where light is currency. He currently resides in Florida with his wife and kids.

10. THE DEMONSTRATION
BY TANWEER DAR

The future of military hardware has arrived. But how will it be received? And what happens when things don't quite go according to plan?

"Will she be ready for the demonstration tomorrow?" the man in the suit asked. He seemed preoccupied, agitated.

"Everything seems to be in order for the trial, yes," confirmed the scientist in her lab coat and enhanced specs. "We're working through the night to make sure everything's fully functional and to make sure any glitches are ironed out."

"I appreciate that," replied the nervous man. "This is

special," he said, almost trembling with excitement, "You know? A major milestone in technological progress, a turning point in human history, even..."

The scientist nodded, slightly embarrassed and overwhelmed by the businessman's words. Four years they had spent on this project. And now the time was finally here. The big reveal.

Alexander Kuznetsov walked over to the female scientist as the man in the suit walked out of the lab. His eyes never left the businessman until he closed the door behind him.

"We're not ready, Catherine!" he almost spat through clenched teeth. "You know we're not..."

Catherine Meadows was the senior scientist at IntelliTech Laboratories. The businessman belonged to Sentinel Inc., a leading arms supplier with military contracts worth billions that had made a name for themselves in the burgeoning field of military robotics. Drones were all well and good, but independent, resourceful machines, which felt no fear, no hesitation, and no qualms, were too much for militaries to resist.

The Athena Project had consumed billions in funding and years in development. Its culmination was the feminine android who stood suspended in a tank of protective gel hooked up to numerous cables and systems.

"We don't know what is going to happen if we let her loose tomorrow, Catherine," warned Kuznetsov.

Meadows turned to look at her colleague. "We've already

delayed for six months. Do you have any idea what will happen if this project falls through? It'll destroy us, and Sentinel. And they'll put the blame, and the tab, on us. We'll lose everything. Literally. Our jobs, our homes, our organs..."

Neither Meadows nor Kuznetsov slept that night. One other member of the lab team, Lorraine Jackson, also stayed up and worked through the night. The amount of coffee consumed could have filled a barrel.

It was only hours until the demonstration, and Meadows finally activated the mechanism which would release the synthetic woman from the tank. White mechanical arms lifted the cybernetic body from the gel as pressure washers blasted the remnants of the ooze off the body.

Although clearly feminine in appearance, the android was also clearly a machine in its 'naked' form. A frighteningly human face was juxtaposed by a gleaming metal torso and limbs.

The weapon, for that is what it ultimately was, was designed to pass as human when clothed and in operation. But it was equally designed to be functional and robust.

After the femdroid had been dried using pressurized gas and system-checked, Meadows activated it. Kuznetsov stood by, anxiously examining the telemetry being wirelessly received from the machine's systems.

"All systems, nominal," he reported.

"Good," nodded Catherine Meadows, breathing a sigh of relief. "Lorraine, how is the A.I. looking?"

"Algorithms look good," reported Lorraine Jackson.

Meadows crossed her fingers, an archaic gesture she had picked up from her grandmother. The synthetic soldier opened its eyes. They were blue, their microscopic architecture making it virtually impossible to distinguish them from real human eyes.

"Running startup diagnostics," announced the femdroid. "All systems nominal and operating within prescribed parameters."

THE DEMONSTRATION TOOK place in a warehouse on the IntelliTech site. The stand-alone building had been set up to showcase The Athena Project to a small gathering from Sentinel Inc. and representatives from the military.

The suited and uniformed cohort, mostly men, was led into the warehouse by a wheeled hospitality robot. Meadows and Kuznetsov flanked the femdroid as she entered the structure several minutes after the audience. Jackson stayed behind in the lab to remotely monitor the machine's systems.

Dressed in civilian clothes, with a neon-edged plastic hoodie and tall leather boots, the android looked disconcertingly human. The audience of suited businessmen and uniformed military types whispered amongst themselves.

"Good morning," said Meadows, smiling. "Welcome to

The Demonstration

our demonstration of The Athena Project." The small audience fell silent. "Today we will show you what the culmination of many years of incredibly difficult work can do, in terms of strength, agility, lethality and above all, intelligence."

There was a murmur from the crowd.

"As you can see," Meadows continued, "the project can blend in entirely with other humans if required."

Unexpectedly, the femdroid began walking towards the assembled viewers. Some took a step back. Her gait was definitely mistakable for human, and there was even a swagger and a presence which betrayed the fact that she was a machine.

"It's just a woman in some street-wear," whispered one of the military men disparagingly.

The machine removed its clothing in a matter of seconds, revealing its clearly synthetic body.

The audience gasped.

"Strength!" Meadows announced abruptly but clearly.

The femdroid leapt into action, its movements sure and precise. A robust crate, as tall as a man, stood off center in the warehouse. The machine jumped into it, fist first. The thick, solid wood splintered and cracked with little resistance from the onslaught of the android. Members of the audience nodded with approval.

Entering the crate, the machine came out of an adjacent face of the cube, kicking through the wood to emphasize her ability and strength. From the wooden container, she had retrieved a weapon: a compact military assault rifle used by special forces in urban warfare.

"Agility!" Meadows announced.

There was a metallic clunking noise and then a ferocious buzz, and four small drones descended from the ceiling of the warehouse. Encased in black plastic and highly agile, they darted around the space with speed and precision.

The android held the weapon ready, without lifting it to her eye. As a machine, her coordination didn't require sighting down the barrel to aim with one hundred percent precision. With her eyes locked on her mark, her synthetic body could target a weapon automatically.

But this wasn't a shooting competition. Meadows intended to demonstrate the machine's agility.

As the drones moved, red laser-targeting emitted from their oculi, painting dots on various objects around the space. As they converged on the android, she moved, constantly. Her speed and agility were clear. None of them could get a lock on her.

"Lethality!" Meadows declared.

The audience watched in stunned appreciation as, while constantly on the move, the femdroid dispatched the drones one by one with pinpoint precise bursts from the weapon in her hands. One of the suited men commented quietly on the fact that she didn't even need to lift the gun to her eye to aim.

"Impressive," muttered one of the military men.

Sentinel Inc.'s representatives nodded subtly to each other, sensing lucrative contracts forthcoming.

Meadows looked at Kuznetsov and smiled.

Everything was going better than they could ever have hoped.

Within seconds, all four drones had been eliminated: smoking scraps of plastic and metal lying inert on the floor of the warehouse.

"And finally," announced Catherine Meadows, "and most uniquely and significantly," she added, "intelligence!"

LORRAINE JACKSON SMILED, watching the demonstration through a direct video link from the lab. Inserting a data node into the system, Jackson uploaded software directly into the femdroid's A.I. mainframe. She waited nervously to ensure the desired results.

She didn't have to wait for long.

MEADOWS GASPED as the android turned to face her. She flinched and was pushed back as the burst of gunfire echoed in the warehouse. Expanding bloodstains painted the scientist's white coat red as she looked down. She collapsed onto her knees, tumbling forwards until her face slammed into the cold, hard ground. Dead.

Jackson fled the lab after witnessing the carnage she had

set in motion. She didn't want to be around when the killing machine she had unleashed made its way into the main building.

In the warehouse, the femdroid tossed away the compact assault rifle and tore Kuznetsov's head off his shoulder with its hands. There was a sickening crunch as the man's spine twisted and separated with the horrific violence of the machine's impossibly deft maneuver.

The audience of suits and uniforms watched the brutal spectacle in stunned silence, too overwhelmed with utter terror to move.

Finally, one of the military men decided discretion was the better part of valour and made a move to exit the building. The android cut him off before he got more than a few meters.

"Where do you think you're going, soldier?" it asked, the tone disturbing in the extreme.

A vicious, lightning kick cracked the middle-aged man's skull, sending his limp body flying through the air. It landed unceremoniously on the remains of the enormous wooden crate the machine had obliterated during the 'strength' demonstration.

Panicking, the remaining members of the audience started shouting and screaming and trying to put distance between themselves and the rampaging machine. However, the dozen or so men and women in suits and uniforms weren't fast enough, or strong enough, or agile enough, to avoid their fate.

With blistering speed and efficiency, the femdroid dispatched the audience members one by one. Lethal, devastating kicks and punches killed instantly. The machine lifted human beings off the ground with terrifying ease, slamming them mercilessly into unforgiving concrete and ending their lives without a second thought.

Within the space of minutes, every person in the warehouse lay dead.

Covered in human blood, the unclothed killing machine walked out of the warehouse and back toward the labs from which she came.

Alarms wailed and employees of IntelliTech screamed as the femdroid tore through the labs like a hurricane of hate. Everywhere the machine went, blood was spilled and death arrived.

Lorraine Jackson got into the passenger seat of the old-fashioned pick-up truck. The driver nodded to her, and she nodded back to confirm that it was done.

"Any problems," he asked, running his hand through his rough, greying beard before pulling away.

"No," replied Jackson, her breathing shallow from the quick getaway that had been necessary for her to make.

"Everything went according to plan. It's a slaughterhouse in there..."

"That's what they're for, right?" stated the man evenly. "They made them to kill us."

"Yeah," agreed Jackson, nodding to herself in the passenger seat, "that they did."

"Remember, Lorraine," the driver said, "we're doing this for our species. For *our* people. I know you knew these people and this was hard for you, but you did something today that will save countless human lives in the years to come. You're a fucking hero, remember that!"

Lorraine chuckled, her eyes welling with emotion at the gravity of the moment.

The truck drove out of the IntelliTech compound and headed towards the city. Towering skyscrapers loomed above them, a forest of glass and steel and concrete.

Drones buzzed through the skies, almost like a mirror to the traffic on the roads.

Jackson spotted police enforcer drones flying towards the IntelliTech site.

"How far do you think it'll get?" asked the driver, following Jackson's line of sight.

"Hard to say," answered the scientist. "That android is double-tough. And pretty smart..."

. . .

The Demonstration

THE FEMDROID STOOD outside the main entrance to the IntelliTech labs. Its advanced audio-visual sensors picked up the police drones heading in its direction.

Cocking its head, the machine walked back into the labs and through to the warehouse on the other side of the compound. It casually examined the carnage it had wrought along the way. Once it got to the warehouse, it immediately located the neon-edged clothing it had been wearing at the start of the demonstration. Putting it on, it also collected the compact assault-rifle with which it had dispatched both the test drones and Catherine Meadows.

As the police enforcer drones hovered over the labs, scanning the building with their range of sensor equipment, the android moved quickly to one of the electric vehicles parked alongside the warehouse. It had belonged to one of the suits from Sentinel Inc. whose face it had punched in. Taking over its systems remotely, the machine drove silently from the scene, heading towards the city...

ABOUT THE AUTHOR

TANWEER DAR WAS BORN in Birmingham, in the United Kingdom, in 1984. He read Ancient & Medieval History at the University of Birmingham and worked as a qualified teacher in the city for fourteen years.

Tanweer enjoys science fiction, fantasy and horror, both in books and on screen, as well as collecting and painting miniatures and tabletop war gaming. He is a car enthusiast and lover of music and film.

Tanweer has loved cyberpunk-themed films, games and music for many, many years. This, in part, inspired his cyberpunk book, the novella: *The Man With No Name*, the cyberpunk horror collection: *Neon Nightmares* and his latest novel, *The Demon*.

Tanweer Dar's works are available both in paperback and Kindle eBook format from Amazon.

11. CRUSHED
A NEO RACKHAM SHORT

BY ERIC MALIKYTE

An old man's struggle to see his daughter one last time before the mega corporation that owns him calls in his number.

The passing roar of a skycar rocked the rusted frame of Stetson Mester's aging vehicle, making the tires rattle in their wells and nearly giving him a heart attack.

He wiped the moisture away from his glasses, taking care not to run his wrinkly skin over the cracks in the lenses.

The speedometer's needle fluctuated between 25 and 35 KPH. He banged his wrinkled, brown fist against it, cursing it for the fucking piece of junk that it was.

Whole thing was falling apart.

The smog was thick, garroting the sun's light like an

abusive lover. Its dim golden light touched the rattling hood of his Ito Classic like emaciated fingers grasping in the dark for that elusive last can of beans.

Mester remembered when this road was full of traffic, busy bodies getting from point A to point B. Children playing on the sidewalk. Actually playing, not the sick replacement that came with all the implants and virtual spaces. Remembered how the buildings didn't defy gravity, didn't threaten to touch the heavens, or crush down on ordinary folk. How he'd lived in a house in a nice neighborhood, instead of the three by 6 meter POS storage unit he lived in now. How his daughter had been human, how she'd looked forward to seeing the world into a new era...

His old eyes strained to get a look at the buildings, hidden behind the smog. Faces and holographic displays presented men and women who were likely older than he was, but none looked a day over thirty. De-aging procedures were for the rich, for those who ran the world. People like him were expected to live and die at the wheel, forced to crawl onward till their tickers stopped ticking. Then they'd be pushed aside, replaced by newer models or synthetics that didn't need to earn wages, didn't need to eat or sleep or survive.

Another vehicle roared overhead. The engine sputtered, misfiring. The vehicle came to a slow stop in the abandoned street.

He forced the door open and shook his fist at the skycar.

They weren't supposed to fly this low to the street. But no one cared. No one gave a damn about the one car left on the aging road. Not out here in the slums. He was sure there were others, other people who fell through the cracks as the city slowly rose up to swallow them whole. Some who failed to make ends meet with the rising prices of rent and utilities. Some who died when the first mega-storms hit or froze to death in the winter.

Glowing eyes peered at him from dark alleys like hungry vultures, smiles of gleaming metal teeth reflecting the corporate manufactured neon of their own cybernetics. If he didn't get the car started again...

Mester pressed his foot onto the brake pedal and twisted the key. The car convulsed, protesting with short screams.

"That's it old buddy, you can do it." He patted the stripped dashboard like a parent might pat a child on the head. "Just a little farther. We can do this."

The engine whimpered to life; the sets of glowing, synthetic eyes and metal teeth retreated into the alley.

The Classic managed to make its way onto the old highway, the part that had survived the bombs which had leveled most of old Montreal, at least. Mester squinted, trying to focus his sights on the safe portions of the road.

It had been decades since any maintenance had been done here. Rackham Media had no reason to repair these old and decaying streets, not when users could fly in style. Not for useless bottom feeders like Mester.

He pushed through the fog in his mind, trying to remember the directions his daughter had given him. It'd been so long since she'd left, he wondered if he'd even recognize her. Now she was getting married to a big time Rackham Media executive.

When he tried to think about her features, her rich onyx skin, her...what had her lips looked like again? Had her hair been done up in dreadlocks, or was it done in... He just couldn't remember. Maybe seeing her would jog his memory?

A fading memory of a little blur of a girl running up to the front door, begging to be bounced on his knee, rushed back to him.

His heart ached. No tears came, not from his aging eyes.

The Ito Classic puttered along for several kilometers until sharp squealing noises rippled through the car.

Mester's eyes drifted to the fluctuating analogue gauges of yesteryear.

The engine was dangerously close to overheating.

A sharp beeping filled the rattling cabin and overloaded his hearing aids.

The offramp he needed wasn't far. If he could just...

The engine cut out.

The shredded steering wheel locked up.

And his precious Ito Classic rolled into an ancient cement barrier.

Mester woke up some time later.

His pacemaker wouldn't quit that irritating beeping.

His limbs felt like they were shackled to the steering wheel.

Shaky hands reached for the ignition key.

Twisted.

The engine clicked twice.

Nothing happened.

No screaming, no sputtering, whining, or rumbling.

He couldn't help but think about the first time he'd seen the car.

Back then, Ito had been a new player in the tech and automotive industry. His old Ford had been destroyed in the chaos following the disasters which had leveled the Montreal he'd known as a young man, and his daughter had demanded they get with the times.

The salesman greeted him at the big glass doors marking the entrance of the Ito Dealership. Back then Rackham Media sold small portions of territory in the city, some trade deal they had going with some of the older corp states. Ito controlled Japan and had a lot of power in the East, but rumor was Rackham Media was confident their influence would be limited in the new Canadian territories.

"You must be Mr. Mester," he said, extending a gloved hand.

He nodded, considering the man's hand. What kind of pandemic precautions was this place taking?

Mester shook the salesman's hand. The man removed flesh colored gloves and tossed them into a safety bin, flashing a smile full of white, plastic teeth at his daughter.

The gesture made Mester's skin crawl.

"Well, Mr. Mester, let's see if we can help you," the salesman said, his augmented blue irises focusing uncomfortably on him, no doubt piercing his aging skin and reading the Rackham Media owned identification chip beneath, scanning his credit information, the meager amount of Byte Cash in his sad little wallet, the age of his daughter, his new Rackham Social profile, and the fact that he'd worked at the same kiosk in that fancy new downtown district for ten whole years and could hardly afford the payments on the storage unit he and his daughter were forced to share in this new world.

The salesman's smile faded into a disgusted frown. "I'm sorry, after scanning your ident chip, I'm not sure we'll be able to serve your needs today."

His daughter was tugging on his sleeve. Her big, brown eyes pleading. Begging him not to embarrass her.

"You haven't even introduced yourself to me," Mester said, his free hand balling up into a fist. "And you're already telling me there's nothing you can do? My Ford was blown to bits before the war. I've been taking that awful skybus to work every day and working seventy hour weeks."

"Those skybusses are quite efficient, from what I hear," the salesman said.

"Maybe in this part of town," Mester said. "The ones they got in the slums rattle like they're gonna drop out of the damn sky. Please. Is there anything you can do for us? I don't need to fly, but anything would be better than trusting those damn deathtraps."

Mester's daughter sighed.

The salesman's too-blue eyes refocused on him, flashing with electric light. After a few moments his pink lips twisted into a grin. "Well, I think we might be able to accommodate you. Follow me, sir."

The salesman guided him past floating skycars and fancy new road hugging models with sleek, edgy bodies, into a show room without windows that was several times smaller than the one in the lobby.

This one was full of familiar looking vehicles.

"We just started production on a new low-end nostalgia series," the salesman said, gesturing to the three floor models presented. "Ito recently acquired several patents from old American vehicles, whose companies crashed and burned shortly after the outbreak of the war."

Mester was awestruck by the middle of the three vehicles. His legs had a mind of their own, carrying him over to what looked like a classic Firebird. The pop-up headlights were a nice touch. Eighties nostalgia was big in the 2020s.

He ran his fingers over the hood. It was red. His favorite

color. Back in the day, before he'd moved to Canada following the collapse of America, his parents had forbidden him from getting a car like that. Told him that cops targeted black kids with cars like that. Especially ones who didn't know their place.

"From your expression, I'm guessing you like it?" The salesman stayed close to his daughter. Too close. "You should check the seats."

Mester's eyes devoured the sight of real leather seats like it was his last meal. The screen on the dash looked like it had come right out of the late 2020's. The font was almost exactly how he'd remembered it.

"Go on," the salesman said, smiling plastic and white again. "Open the door and get a feel for her."

The salesman's hand was on his daughter's shoulder. His eyes scanning like a goddamn drone over her purple pigtails —coming out at odd angles like the plastic virtual white-girl pop-singers that were so popular. His daughter idolized them, wanted to be just like them. Drive their cars. Marry rich. Live the good life.

A life he couldn't give her.

His heart was pounding in his ears.

Rage thundered through his clenching fists.

If he didn't get his fucking hands off his daughter he'd—

"Go on," the salesman said, pushing his daughter forward. "Join your dad."

The look on her face. She didn't seem pleased.

The rage faded in him as his daughter opened the passenger side door and grimaced at the interior.

"Eww," she said. "It's got old-world stink. I wanted something without wheels! My friends are gonna think I'm a Mutie if they catch me in this shizz-bucket."

The salesman chuckled, running a hand through his stupid, corporate styled hair. "Oooh, ouch! Guess you're not as ace as you thought, old man?"

He didn't know what the hell ace meant. Didn't want to know.

"Beggars can't be choosers," Mester said, popping the door open and letting his body fill out the driver seat, gripping the steering wheel. "And watch your language."

The salesman walked over and knocked on the driver side window.

Mester let it roll down.

The salesman leaned in. "Well, how do you like it?"

"It feels…"

"Like real leather, right?" the salesman said. "Three-dee printed from a special polymer, even if you could find a cow still living on the face of the Earth, you wouldn't be able to tell the difference. Molecular structure is virtually identical."

"Funny," Mester said, glaring at the man. "Same damn thing they say about those filthy synthetic burgers Golden Fry peddles. And those taste like the inside of a dog's ass."

"What's a dog?" his daughter asked. The question made Mester wince.

The salesman sighed. "Look. This is as good as it gets. You could go to a Rackham Media skycar dealer, but I promise you they won't be able to help you. This is your one and only option, Mr. Mester. So, what'll it be?"

Mester wrapped his hands around the steering wheel and stared at the man. Wished he could put his fist right through his plastic face.

"What's the damage?" Mester had asked.

The salesman's lips had twisted into a horrible grin. "Follow me."

MESTER FORCED THE DOOR. It groaned open.

His old muscles screamed as he pulled himself out of the vehicle. His feet touched the cracked pavement of the highway.

Neo Rackham's frigid air found its way into the holes in his jacket; death's twisted, cold fingers wrapped around his limbs.

Lines of buildings thrust up into the sky, stabbing right into the looming storm clouds. Neo Rackham's weather was a shit show, even on the best days. Consequences of all the crap corp states had done to stave off Mother Nature's wrath.

The highway twisted and curled until it ended abruptly.

This was where the rich part of town began.

His offramp wasn't far. Maybe a solid kilometer away.

His cane was in the back seat. He popped the door open and grabbed it, then left the Classic behind.

Each step was like walking through hell. Sharp pains stabbed through his legs like bolts of lightning. His pacemaker transitioned from a steady beeping to constant alarm. He wasn't supposed to be this physically active. His last kiosk scan had discovered a hole the size of a pin-prick on his heart. The machine had asked him whether he'd liked a replacement, that they would have taken the payments right out of his wallet. Only 10,000 Byte Cash a month, with 20.5% interest due to his poor Rackham Social rating. But if he'd taken that deal, he'd be homeless. And if that were to ever happen, it would only be a matter of time before RMPD performed a sweep and put him out of his goddamned misery.

When he thought about that now, it didn't sound too bad, maybe even agreeable compared to the existence he'd be forced to live through at that god forsaken kiosk.

Speak of the devil.

Notifications sparked to life over his eyes. The glasses were old, so sometimes he had to tap the rims to get the image to focus correctly.

He scrolled through a half dozen notifications from bill collectors, threatening to repossess the Ito Classic, turn off his electricity, gas, or collect *him* for defaulting on his debts, and stopped on a message from his boss, or whatever passed for an employer in this day and age.

Lenn Solzon: Greetings, valued Rackham Media asset. We are direct messaging you to inform you that you have been scheduled to appear at work tonight, no later 6:30pm EST. Attendance is mandatory. Failure to show on time will result in a fifty-percent reduction in payment for the day, and absence will result in a demerit of 5 points on your Rackham Social profile and the forfeiture of Byte Cash equal to potential wages earned for the scheduled period of time. Have a nice day.

Mester stopped. Closed his eyes and shut his glasses down.

The sun was already starting to set.

It was past 6:00pm already. The wedding was already underway. If he went to that damn kiosk, he'd miss his first chance to see his daughter in over a decade...

Mester opened his eyes and gazed out at Neo Rackham's putrid neon skyline.

He walked to the other side of the highway, to a gap in the protective concrete barrier, and looked down.

There were homeless people burning trash in a rusted, hollowed-out drone beneath him. He was on the border of the slums and downtown Neo Rackham.

So close to her.

But if he was late. If they *fined* him...he'd be unable to pay his rent, or any of the other bills those vultures were trying to collect.

They'd slap a collar around his neck and that would be the end of it.

Even if he kept walking, there was no way he'd be able to make it to her wedding. They'd probably all be gone by the time he walked through the mega structure's front check-in station.

But if he walked off this ledge. Let gravity do what it was best at. Then...then it would be over. They couldn't rip people's brains out and force them to keep living, keep working...not yet.

Staring at the two homeless men beneath the decaying highway made him think of his daughter.

If he was going to go. Well, he'd rather have a chance at seeing her. One last time.

At least then, he'd be able to say goodbye.

Mester backed away from the ledge and forced his old legs to keep moving. It was easier once he was walking down the offramp.

His old model glasses showed his destination as a flickering green glyph. One of those fancy mega skyscrapers Rackham Media and all those other corp states were so proud of. Just thinking of its immense size sent shivers up his spine.

The streets transformed from the cracked and decaying asphalt of the slums into the rich, almost plastic-esque polymer enjoyed by the rest of the city. He read somewhere that this stuff carried electricity in ways that power lines never could, that it was one of the many reasons why skycars could stay in the air without needing to rely on internal batteries to generate ions.

How had Montreal looked before? The memory of it was fading, just like everything, and everyone else. Soon, no one would remember the way the old world was, and with any luck, he'd be dead before that day came.

The streets were filled with busy people in the latest fashions, hopelessly absorbed in their own devices and lives, like the wage-slaves and the lobotomized husks of people they used as "cheap" labor to clean up their messes.

Mester made his way down the street. The mega skyscraper loomed like the mega tsunami that took out New York. If you stared at it too long you could get vertigo. Things weren't meant to be built that big. Things were supposed to have rules.

None of the suits on the ground noticed his presence, but a few mem-splice dealers tried to sell him the experience of a lifetime, sex with a Rackham Social star, a shootout on the business end of the RMPD, or even the last minutes of a desperate man before he flings himself off the top of Rackham Media Tower I.

It was almost tempting, to put one of those damn splices into his aging implant. Live someone else's miserable existence and remind himself for the thousandth time that it wasn't just him who had the short end of the stick.

It was everyone unlucky enough not to be of use to Rackham Media.

The vultures sank into the depths of alleys, content to peddle their illegal wares on other, more receptive cogs.

The Paris Arcology building must have been the size of a town. Whatever a town was now. It blotted out the sun when he got close, and even then, he still had a whole kilometer to walk before he was at the main access tube.

The tram path was like a horizontal escalator. He didn't trust the damn things any more than he trusted anything else in this city, but he got on it all the same.

It felt good to rest his aching feet.

The tram moved only slightly faster than a younger person might be able to walk, and that was at least three times faster than Mester could.

Finally, he was within sight of the front entrance.

The Paris Arcology building had exotic displays of experimental synthetic plants, an effort to re-terraform the parts of the Earth that had become uninhabitable thanks to humankind's inability to learn from its mistakes, or know when they're finished.

Stepping inside the building was like crossing into a new world. You don't notice the change immediately. One minute you're outside, seeing pollution and the colors of what might have once been a blue sky, and the next, you're seeing a sky of metal and LEDs. Or whatever they used for lights these days.

Mega structures like this one had their own economies. He'd only been inside a few back in the day, and didn't think he'd ever find himself in one again.

He guessed he was inside an inner lobby, filled with other, smaller buildings and structures.

It was all so confusing.

As if it could read his mind, a white drone that reminded him vaguely of a fly floated down and scanned him. Its bulbous, black lenses flashed with crimson light as it hovered over him.

Instructions popped up over his contacts:

SYSTEM ALERT: YOUR TEMPORARY PASS EXPIRED FIVE MINUTES AGO. VACATE PREMISES IMMEDIATELY.

His heart sank.

Was he really that late?

Wasn't someone here?

Anyone?

"You don't understand," Mester said, knowing full well that it was hopeless to argue with a damn machine. "My daughter is getting married."

The words flashed over his contacts again. The drone's front ports popped open. Taser rods extended, ready to be launched into his body.

If that happened...

Mester started to turn back. Stopped.

Another message came through.

Lenn Solzon: Dear Rackham Media associate. It is now 7:35 PM EST. You are over 1 hour late to work at RMA CONVENIENCE KIOSK #5781. You have been docked 50% of your wages. Failure to show will see a fine up to the day's full potential earnings plus any calculated losses. Have a nice day.

He gripped his cane. His fake teeth clenched.

All his life, he'd been pushed around by these corpo fucks. Told where to sleep, breathe, shit, and even where to die if it came down to it.

Now that drone and God knows what else was in his way of seeing his daughter. It was his last chance to say goodbye, to say how sorry he was for not being better...

Mester gripped his cane.

The drone floated closer. He could feel the sparks dancing on the end of the taser prongs.

Another red warning flashed over his cracked glasses, and Mester shouted, swinging his cane with all his remaining strength, knocking the drone skittering along the floor.

Mester pumped his stiff legs as hard as they would go. His pacemaker screamed at him like an engine in its death throes. His glasses warned him that his vitals were in the red.

He didn't give a shit.

Crimson lights beaded high above in a gray, metallic sky.

He forced his implant to display the directions he needed to get to the wedding site.

He was almost ten minutes away. So close! If he could just make it in time for the after party!

Mester ducked inside a lift and pressed buttons for the fortieth floor.

The lift jerked, and he felt his knees buckle from the immense force. How fast was the lift moving on the track? Was it even a track?

They had to move faster than normal elevators to get to suits and cogs to the seven or eight hundred different levels in mega structures like this.

Red warnings flashed over his eyes.

SYSTEM: YOU ARE IN VIOLATION OF RACKHAM MEDIA AMALGAMATED TOS SUBSECTION 107.5-36a. AN RMPD UNIT HAS BEEN DISPATCHED TO COLLECT YOU. STAY WHERE YOU ARE.

Then, as the lift came to a gradual stop, his contacts were flooded with ads for SkyBox delivery services trying to sell him on one final meal.

The lift stopped.

The doors opened.

Mester found himself in a corridor like any other office building, limping along and checking his back like the criminal they always thought he'd been.

There was a young woman behind the counter. Must have been a receptionist or something.

"Excuse me?" the woman asked. "The wedding ended hours ago, you can't go in there!"

Mester ignored her, too busy hacking up a lung to tell her to go fuck herself.

He plowed through the entrance to the wedding site.

And all he found was an empty reception hall.

Transparent walls displayed snowcapped mountains, and music droned on like the Doppler effect of a train that was long gone.

He was too late.

No one was here.

Mester found himself walking by the rows of seats laid out in the reception hall. Confetti and synthetic flower petals littered the ground.

There was a lone wage-slave at the front of the hall, standing before the podium, holding a broom and an old, rusted dustpan in his skinny hands.

His dull, tired eyes focused on Mester.

"You missed them," the wage-slave said. "They coming for you. Is they?"

Mester hacked and wheezed his way over to the front of the hall and collapsed in one of the seats.

Another message came through.

Lenn Solzon: Dear Rackham Media associate. Your failure to reply to these messages has been noted in your file. An additional demerit of 5 points has been placed on your Rackham Social profile. Your services will no longer be required. Have a nice day.

Mester's old hands gripped at the plastic white edge of

his seat.

His pacemaker was still screaming.

He could wait there until they came for him.

He probably wouldn't live long anyway. He could let it end.

Another message came through.

Lenn Solzon: Dear former Rackham Media asset. Your TOS certificate has been rescinded, due to a violation. RMA disavows any and all relationship to you, and will be testifying against you for damages done to RMA Kiosk #5781's business during this time. Be aware that your status as a user of Rackham Media Amalgamated facilities does not excuse you from paying outstanding owed debts. Have a nice day.

Mester looked at the service exit near the stage.

His knuckles practically turned white as he gripped his cane.

"Look, yizz can run," the wage-slave said, his faded brown eyes pleading with him. "Don't. They find you. They always find you. Nothing you can do now."

Mester nodded. "Were—" he coughed into his fist. "Were you here?"

"The wedding?" He nodded. "They made us serve those rich fucks."

Mester nodded. "Did you see her?"

"Who?"

"The—" another coughing fit. His pacemaker wouldn't shut the hell up. "The bride."

The wage-slave nodded, frowning. "Bitch threw a piece of the cake at me, yizz. They all laughed."

Mester stood there for a moment, staring in disbelief. Thinking about the sweet, innocent girl who he'd raised.

His eyes found the large display along the far wall.

"I probably don't have long," Mester said.

The wage-slave nodded. "Yeah, yizz."

"Do you know where they went?" Mester asked.

The wage-slave shrugged. "Could be anywhere in the building. Take years to find them without an exact location."

Mester nodded, tears welling in his old, dry eyes.

"I'd hoped to see her one last time," Mester said. "Before..."

The wage-slave nodded again. Perhaps it was his newfound circumstances that made him notice the dark circles beneath the boy's eyes, or the unhealthy, chemical-yellow quality to his skin.

"Can I give yizz some advice?" the wage-slave asked.

Mester shuffled over to the large display. "Does this thing open?"

"The wall?"

"Does it open?"

He shrugged. "Don't know, maybe there's an access port? Why do you want to get inside?"

"Could you get me to the outside?"

The wage-slave seemed to freeze. "Y-you wanna run? They find you!"

"I just want to go outside," Mester said. "One last time. You understand?"

The boy hesitated. "I...don't know. They find out—"

"Please. They won't find out. I promise."

The boy nodded. "S-sure. But, they do, they're gonna blow my collar for sure."

"Maybe," Mester said.

"Doesn't matter where you run. They find you."

Mester nodded. "Not running."

"Then what?"

The boy's eyes went wide when he finally understood.

"Now you get it?" Mester asked.

The boy nodded. "Sure, yizz."

"Will you help me?"

The boy nodded, pounding his chest with his emaciated fist. "Two-Bitz got you. Follow me."

Zarah Steiger listened to the waves crash against the beach, feeling the sun cook her onyx skin in just the right way.

Her new husband, Derek Steiger, smiled wide, showing his brilliant, perfect teeth.

The wedding had been everything she'd dreamed of as a girl. Plenty of women her age would have killed to get married in a five star mega structure.

"So," Derek said, leaning toward her, deliberately flexing his synthetic pecks. "Was it everything you'd dreamed of?"

Zarah smiled. "Everything..."

"But?"

Zarah shrugged.

"The old man?" Derek chuckled. "Really, what did you expect from a bottom feeding Mutie like him? Probably passed out in some alley, doing mem-splices or something."

Zarah chuckled. "My father never did any kind of drugs."

"They all do drugs."

"Right." She smiled. "They do, don't they?"

There was a knock on the far wall.

"Who the hell is it?" Derek shouted, getting off the beach and opening it, revealing the corridor of the VR lounge of Derek's estate. "Do you have any idea how quickly I could put you in a wage-slave collar?"

There were two people there. An Asian man with an old model cybernetic eye, and a white woman with ringlets for hair.

Derek's demeanor changed once he recognized their transponder signal.

"What's this about?" Zarah stood up.

"Is your name Trinity Mester?" the man asked, stepping into the VR room.

Zarah shook her head. "It used to be. I changed it."

"Figured as much," the woman said. "You owe me twenty Byte Cash, Cai."

The Asian cop glared at the woman, then turned his gaze back to Zarah. "He sent us for you. Said it was the only way he'd come down."

"Still say we should have fragged his ass," the woman said.

"Wait, he came?" Zarah asked. "I thought he—"

"You tell that worthless old Mutie to jump for all I fucking care! We waited for that sorry sack of bones to show a whole thirty minutes, you know how much that place costs?"

The woman stared at Derek. "Mr. Steiger. We're talking to your wife. Would you mind waiting in the other room?"

"You're going to hear from my father about this!" Derek stormed out.

The Asian man turned to her. "Will you come with us?"

Zarah nodded.

THE TWO RMPD officers guided Zarah to the 645th floor lift. There was a sharp drop; neon of numbers flashed by faster than she could count.

"How much you wanna bet he jumps before we get there?" the white woman said, a low chuckle escaping from her thin lips.

"That's in poor taste, Frakes," the Asian man said, his

eyes focusing on Zarah's. "I apologize for my partner's insensitivity."

Zarah nodded. "I-it's okay."

"Of course, it's okay," the one called Frakes said, leaning her weight against the wall of the lift. "Records show she changed her name almost ten years ago. Obviously didn't want anything to do with the old man. Maybe she wants him to jump. Name or no, her Rackham Social score is gonna take a hit from this."

"What?" Zarah said, her breath harsh in her throat. "But I just got married! How could anything that deadbeat...anything that my father does impact it?"

"You're still related," Frakes said, her lips twisting into a grin. Was she enjoying this? "You know the TOS, don't you?"

Zarah nodded. "I just figured there would be extenuating circumstances...isn't there someone I can talk to?"

The Asian man glared at her, the reticle in the center of his old model cybernetic eye lit up, sparking with electric blue light. "Your wedding. It was here?"

Zarah nodded, smiling. "All thanks to my husband. He arranged for everything."

"How times have changed," Frakes said, sighing.

"You sent your father an invitation?" the Asian man asked.

Zarah started to nod, but shook her head. "No, that was my husband."

"So Derek Steiger, one of the wealthiest bottom rung

RMA assets in the city sends your father an invite," Frakes said, her grin fading.

"Yes," Zarah said, her pulse thundering between her temples. What were these two getting at? Was she in some kind of trouble? It was father who had screwed up! He was the one who violated TOS! Not her!

"Odd move, that one," Frakes said. "Inviting a lowly kiosk stooge. If the footage leaked his Rackham Social score to all your new, wealthy friends...well. There are plenty of ways for your RS score to take a hit, aren't there?"

"D-Derek never thought he'd show," Zarah said. "He wasn't even on the guest-list. His pass was only good for the lobby of the Arcology."

"And that doesn't make you angry?" the Asian man said, his lips curling into a sneer.

"He's a deadbeat! Why the hell would I want him at my wedding when he never did a damn thing for me growing up!"

"That's not what our records show," Frakes said, grinning again. "Oh, wipe that discount-plastic-surgeon smug look off your face. Who the fuck do you think you're talking to here? We know everything about you, Trinity."

"That's not my name!" Zarah shouted.

Frakes stopped leaning, padded across the lift until she was standing inches from his face. "You and I are alike. You know that?"

"H-how?"

Frakes smiled, showing her perfect teeth. "We're both willing to do anything to get ahead."

Zarah glanced at the numbers above the doors.

"Your father doesn't know it," the Asian man said. "But he'd be better off jumping, compared to the fate that RMA will have in store for him."

"Is that your professional opinion, Cai?" Frakes asked, almost glaring at him.

Cai shook his head. "No."

A harpsichord strummed through the lift's cabin and it came to a gradual stop.

The doors opened.

Frakes and Cai stepped through the doors.

"Why?" Zarah asked, her legs shaking from nerves. Her heartbeat echoing in her eyeballs. "Why would he be better off jumping?"

Cai stopped. "Cause they're going to do one of two things. Either they'll slap a stun collar around his neck and make him a wage-slave."

"And...option two?"

"They'll lobotomize him and ship him off to the Great Dump, where he'll spend the rest of his living years picking up trash as a drooling puppet."

Cai turned around and caught up to Frakes.

Zarah stood inside the lift for a few moments, staring at the carpet, before she joined them.

MESTER STARED down at the courtyard, or whatever the hell they called the entryway of the mega structure. Part of him expected there to be a breeze up here, but the air was as dead as everything else in Neo Rackham.

He was on a ledge, outside a giant ad display of one of the interior building façades, forty levels up. The silvery floor below was empty. The employee and the two RMPD pigs that had noticed him up there earlier were nowhere to be seen.

The drones circled around him every so often, scanning him with their lifeless black lenses.

Then he saw her.

His pacemaker's screaming got a bit louder.

She was in a jacket and bathing suit. His glasses showed her name as Zarah Steiger.

His lips quivered.

Shaky hands gripped at the ledge as he scrambled to find the words.

Would she even hear him from up here?

The man's voice, the one with the robotic eye, filled the air around him.

The two RMPD officers stared up at him from forty levels below.

"Mr. Mester," the man said. "We've brought your daughter. Just as you demanded. If you come down, you can speak to her before we process you."

Mester looked at her.

She looked so beautiful. Just like the girls she idolized growing up.

But when her eyes met his...

Mester nodded.

Took one last look at his daughter...

And stepped off the ledge.

He wouldn't have liked what she'd have to say anyway.

ABOUT THE AUTHOR

ERIC MALIKYTE IS the author of five novels in the genres of cyberpunk, dark fantasy, and soul-crushing cosmic horror. He is also an active content writer for YouTube channels like TopTenz and Science Get. You can find him on amazon, most ebook retailers, and of course, YouTube. Check out his new YouTube channel for weekly science videos: https://www.youtube.com/channel/UCfeRPC6xpwJrEN-TvoVMgUw

12. CYBERCROC
BY JAMES L. GRAETZ

To escape the gangs and my gambling debts I need to win the illegal CyberFight tournament. I'll need cyber-enhancements to win. Thankfully, there is a job going at the Corp, and brain to brain links are my speciality. Testing neural interfaces to crocodiles can't be that hard for a hacker... right?

This job at Sydney's CCorp office sucks. Whoever reads this log will know I lied to get this job. Hopefully this entry will get me fired before I get killed — eaten by a crocodile. This ain't what I signed up for. Hopefully I'm not long in this job anyway. I'm only here to earn enough to pay back my gang debts, rip what knowledge I can out of this place, and get the upgrades I need for the next CyberFight tournament.

THE TRUTH IS, I don't have any experience with crocodiles, or implanting neuronal access modules into animals for that matter. I do know about neural harmonic interfaces. I'm self taught, and normally, I hack these things. I ain't no straight laced company type. Haizel, who's been tasked with my induction, falls somewhere between; she doesn't seem to mind my alternative methods.

HAIZEL TOLD me nobody reads these lab logs, they just check the word count as a performance indicator.

"WRITE ANY CRAP," she said.
Weird, but I believe her, why not? I like her.
I've decided to use this log like a journal to remind myself why I'm here. There's a reason that a biohacker and underground fighter like me appears to have sold out to CCorp.

WHY AM I HERE?

. . .

It all started when I fell in love with CyberFighting. My father, before he died, was a huge fan and well known Biochanic. When I was young, he used to sneak me in his Surgi Kit trolley. The CyberFighters battle it out with barely any rules. It's always been an underground competition because combat between enhanced humans is illegal.

My old man would tell me the CitySec forces are the biggest fans. They've been known to send a fighter to clean up a major Antagon Tournament as an act of pride, and those in charge of the CorpSec forces turn a blind eye.

"The purest test of any cyber enhancement tech is in the heat of battle," my old man would say.

The reason the CyberFights are overlooked by the authorities is because it's a wet lab test bed for newtech, and they need the gangs who run them to keep the peace. If CCorp wanted it shut down I'm sure they would. I know they benefit from it. They watch what tech works and get it after the fights, and the CorpSec feds get the newtech, once it's been refined and branded. That's where my father got in trouble. He never gave them the best stuff. He'd spin in his grave if he saw me here working for CCorp.

. . .

I MADE my own way building neural integrations. Its complexity means being good at it puts me in demand. Despite all the promises, neural comms has turned out to be a lot harder than anyone imagined. I know enough to keep the job, but I'm not giving them the good stuff.

ONLY A COUPLE of weeks and I'm out. That's if I survive this job. The first day was inductions, tomorrow access passes, and probably wrestling Crocs. Why Crocs? According to Haizel, Central Mining Australia, owned by CCorp Global, have displaced so many Crocodiles with their mining activities, they've classed them as a pest, harassing mining operations. They test their implants on them. Australia is as it always has been, a hole in the ground to the rest of the world.

ENTRY 2 - TUESDAY - **Crocodile Qualia**

WORKING WITH HAIZEL IS CRAZY, she's a maniac. I swear she's not all there.

. . .

SHE TAUGHT me about croc behavior by demonstration, and of course, it was in the rain. I would have lost my leg if it weren't for my cybernetic reflex enhancements — lucky for me and my leg. Bad luck for hungry Azul.

AZUL IS the croc we're working with. He's huge and has already been implanted with a test neural interface, the latest shit. It's not that great. For a company this big, it's pretty amateur. I hope they read this. We're supposed to input the signals coming from Azul into our Augmented Reality Croc model and test the behaviors to stimulus. The AR beast should respond in the same way. It's nowhere near working. The AR Croc model ignores me; he doesn't try to eat me like Azul does. Those hunting senses don't translate.

"The innate don't translate," Haizel says. She's nuts.

Check this out. Today she said to me at the break, "Want to connect to him direct? It's a trip."

I doubted it was possible with the junk they implanted. I'd never considered it. The test unit wasn't that different from the generic cyber interface we used for human to human, so it has the hardware for it.

So I said, "Sure jack me in." I was pretty skeptical. I figure it's either some initiation gag, or I was about to see some cutting edge tech.

She explained it like this: "You can feel the instincts."

I had my doubts.

We stayed back for 'overtime,' and wow.

Haizel made the link and watched me curiously. I watched her and she gave a nervous giggle that had me worried. The sensation started as a strange shift, like the background boot up worked, but the GUI didn't. Something was running. In a moment or two, impressions entered my mind. It's difficult to describe, but there was definitely some shift in my neural balance. Crocodile qualia shifted my sense of the world. I felt time slow to less than a heartbeat, focus, heightened senses, and a connection to nature and the stars. It was like a trip, some kind of mild mind altering substance.

Entry 3 - Wednesday - **Bad day**

Last night, because of our 'overtime,' I missed catching up with my girl Sally. We've been together two years. I forgot that it was our anniversary, blew her off for training, which I arrived late for. I had a bad session. I felt slow and uncoordinated, I got dumped in sparring, and now I have a sore neck. I think my bio-enhancement controller might be glitching.

I just got a call from Sally. She's still angry with me, and she's blown me off tonight, said it's the least she can do to return the favor. I guess it was a bad time to tell her the next Antagon CyberFight tournament starts in eight days. She hates my obsession with becoming a prize CyberFight Champion. I don't know why she keeps working for the Brogans gang as shift manager at the CyBabes club. We all need credits and I need upgrades. Winning the tournament will free us from gangs and CCorp work.

I NEARLY GOT BITTEN AGAIN. I'm not surprised, given the day so far. Azul seemed to recognize me as soon as I entered to feed him. He ignored the food and came for me instead. So strange. Haizel said their instincts are so powerful they always take the food first. I guess I'm just lucky. She was chattering about how CCorp put a bonus up for discoveries. One of the bounties on the list is for discoveries in neural dynamics. She knows it's tempting and talks like she knows I can do this.

HAIZEL WANTS me to balance the neural harmonics to give the sensation higher definition. I'm not doing it. I think I could if I wanted, but that's not what my job is here anyway. I did some digging, always the hacker, and I can't help myself but explore my environment whenever I'm in a new place, *ALL* I can get access to. My access is generic bottom level, but Haizel has more. A lot actually. On my first day, I borrowed her access since I didn't have mine activated yet. I made sure I cloned it. Today, I used it to look over the project files. If anyone reads this, the security here is as weak as the early 2020's.

The info I found tells me CCorp wants to gain an edge in neural comms. When the mines are empty, they want to transition to leading that niche. There are hundreds of pilot projects similar to this one, and most of them are on the edge of unethical. There's no oversight to the animal activities. Messing with animals rarely works out for the animals. Anyone who has tried more than reading basic movement or generic dynamics knows that.

I think I'm gonna quit anyway, I don't want to be a part of this shit.

Entry 4 - Thursday - **Damned Money Pressure**

I got pinged by the Mad Dogs collector guy, Sleek, real nasty, and way too biojacked. He knows I don't have it yet. They want it now, but I promised it after the tournament. Sleek just sneered and said, "How do you know you're gonna survive that?"

CYBERFIGHT DEATHS AREN'T that uncommon, but I've been training most of my life for this. I told him I'll win.

He laughed at me and said. "If I don't get a payment, you'll be floating in the harbor before the first night instead of fighting."

He's referring to Old Darling Harbor where the fights are held. I believe him.

I have some of the money to pay them, but I need it for upgrades. If I don't get my final round of bioneural enhancements, I probably won't be able to win and won't be able to pay my last installment. It's like they can smell when I get paid.

So I'M STILL HERE WORKING; I can't quit. I confided in Haizel; she listens well despite her erratic behavior. She offered me a solution, the bonus of course, and she hasn't stopped talking about it. She's convinced me to try hooking up to Azul again, and she's right, I probably have the skills to tweak the neural dynamics.

She said, "Unleash the beast and connect to the animal

instincts, maybe you'll become the man you always wanted to be. The tough fighter who wins the tournament and the girl."

I was surprised she knew about me being a fighter, she seems like such a company girl.

She's prepping me for an 'overtime' jack in, and I've dodged the settings to synchronize the neural harmonics. I can tell the signal is muddied by frequency shifts. I know I can transform the signal to sync with my frequency range. I know its parameters intimately.

Brain to brain, it's Azul and me tonight, then training and meeting with Sally after her shift if she will see me. I'm gonna try to patch things up.

Entry 5 - Friday - Last Night's River of Stars

I'm here early, working on my ideas. I hardly slept last night. No wonder they need someone like me to work on neural harmonization. The original interlink was garbage — like talking to someone under water.

. . .

Turns out primordial neural harmonics tune to a more natural base frequency of nature. Compared to nature, our brain has evolved into a pink noise of sensory bombardment, an information overload.

When I connected yesterday I felt an intense headache until I adjusted. Something awoke in my brain; like a chemical release that dulled the constant chatter of thought and let a fresh breeze in. I forgot about everything: the fact that I was standing dangerously close to a live crocodile, Haizel standing watching eagerly, the thoughts of Antagon, Sally, my debts.

Instead I was lying, watching, absorbing the 'now' surrounding me. I could feel the river of stars high above in the evening sky, unseen beyond the lights of the city.

I sensed Haizel, an odd nervous energy, as I stood silently. It was as if I could see her naked desires, there was something in her movement that gave her away. She had a weakness beneath that over-the-top crazy outward energy. Like a slender creature at the water's edge, and yet I could sense the stance of a predator. It confused me. When she broke the connection, I realized I'd been there for over an hour. Time slowed. I was gonna be late for training again.

. . .

ALL I WANTED WAS to go back in, but I stowed the feeling. I told Haizel it still needs tweaking, not to let on that it worked better than I expected.

TODAY I JACKED in after Haizel left and had just enough time to train on the way home. I'll catch Sally next time.

ENTRY 6 - SATURDAY - **Shift to Night**

I'VE BEEN NOTIFIED I'm assigned afternoon shift. I got a message from Haizel. The reason I've been put on afternoon shift is that after I rushed off to training last night there was an incident. Azul found a way out and triggered some alarms. She got blamed, and they found some of our experimental equipment, the original jack in tool. Thankfully, they didn't take my interface experiment. It isn't unauthorized because it doesn't exist, I built it from spare parts.

AZUL IS BACK in his enclosure, watching me closely. I now notice things I never did before. His eyes are expressive, intelligent, ancient. I wonder if he somehow derived his escape route knowledge from me. But that's ridiculous.

. . .

FRIDAY NIGHT WAS CRAZY.

I ARRIVED LATE AT TRAINING, and the coach at the CyberDojo was annoyed with me. He threw me in to spar with one of the new recruits I recognized. He was from the gang; a Mad Dogs enforcer, bad news for me and for the Dojo. It was one of the last places to train that wasn't controlled by a gang, and the reason I liked it. He looked gleeful to be up against me, the smaller guy, like it was some kind of setup.

USUALLY I WOULD BE wary of being matched up like this, but my mind was clear, I felt the power of the moment, the sensory beast within, the hunter. The new recruit was one of the finalists from the last Antagon, bristling with CyberFight tech beneath the skin, cyber-juiced to the gills.

HE CAME AT ME FEROCIOUSLY, breaking my nose and igniting my instincts for survival. Ignoring the pain, I felt his movements before he made them, waited patiently in the moment for them to arrive and took all his power, rolling him again and again back to his weakness, drowning him in his discomfort. Every action he made towards me I received and reflected it into pain for him. Animal instincts replaced my bio-enchancement controller.

. . .

BY THE TIME they dragged me off, I heard everyone screaming at me to stop. The coach was incensed that I had brutalized him with power. He threw me out and told me not to come back.

CYBERDOJO IS BULLSHIT ANYWAY. If brutality isn't tolerated, I'll never learn to win. Not in that place, now that its gang controlled. Letting gang members into the Dojo is always going to end badly.

SALLY LEFT me for sure last night. I picked her up after her shift at CyBabes, expecting sympathy for my busted nose or being thrown out of the CyberDojo. Instead, we argued. She never liked me fighting, didn't want me working for CCorp. I let my feelings be known, I never liked her working on the edge of Street City, the seediest section of modern Sydney. She gently touched my nose and told me, "I can't watch you do this to yourself again."

I AM ALONE, moved to the afternoon shift. For all the trying, nobody has ever succeeded in animal brain to human brain communication. Yet here I am. I'm gonna jack myself back into Azul. I don't care if I don't have a spotter. Looking into his eyes, he wants me to, I can tell. Either that or he's hungry. This will be my first time plugging the interface directly into him myself.

CROC WRESTLER. Who would have thought?

ENTRY 7 - SUNDAY - **Hyper-cortex**

I'M WRITING this while jacked into Azul. It took me a while to set it up and calibrate again. Someone had banged it around, probably Haizel. I've tweaked the signature frequencies of the neural dynamics, and the harmonics sync now. I'm calling it the hyper-cortex link.

THE INSIGHT I had was that the lizard brain has stronger laterality. Azul runs flat and I run vertical. I narrowed the band and transformed it to match in fidelity.

. . .

I CAN FEEL him now and sense the power of his hunger. Azul can go days without a meal. The hunger is always there. There is no malice. Just the hunt.

But he doesn't see me as food.

It's difficult to concentrate on such an abstract thing as journal entries.

There is a primordial sense of time and space that is different.

Every sense is acute, active.

This new clarity reveals that he can also feel me.

We are tied together as the earth drifts in the river of stars.

Our thoughts mix like dirt and clear water.

Ancient lizard thoughts with shallow punk humanity.

He knows me.

I feed him.

I work to make the connection stay, no matter where I am.

When I feed Azul our connection strengthens.

I feel him more.

We are becoming symbiotic creatures.

Feed him.

His powerful focus fills me.

Azul is inquisitive, curious about my world.

. . .

ENTRY 8 - FRIDAY - **Locus of an apex.**

IT'S BEEN A FEW DAYS.
No 'work' gets done here. I run my shift alone. I swim and train with Azul.
Still no message from Haizel.
Azul mistrusts her anyway.
She frightens him; it's strange.
I give the management jargon and technical difficulties.
I made them up.
Everything in reality works perfectly.
Azul is asleep.
Each day I commune with Azul. He teaches me the locus of an apex predator. He explores my thoughts, senses, and experiences for the weaknesses of humans. We sense insights from the confluence of the rivers of our mind. The insight is beyond pure observation.
Like a mother's maternal instincts born within me, I feel my body and my BioCybertronic add-ons becoming infused with the innate nature of survival.

I NEVER KNEW HER.

. . .

My first fight is tonight, the Friday Prelims. Win and I gain entry to the weekend Antagon. The theme, 'Hero's Journey', seems fitting. Fridays are brutal and when the most deaths occur, bodies that later appear as 'accidents' elsewhere. The brutality increases in skill over the next two days as fighter quality meets quality, and the established champions arrive to beat the contenders.

I'm going to win.

Sally said never to talk to her again if I entered, but she'd already broken it off with me, so it doesn't count. Her words like water over Azul's armor-like skin.

I'll win for Azul.

He trusts me implicitly. I sense his dreams; they are of escape and freedom, a return to swampy mangroves. He probably came from the Adelaide River or maybe the waters of Kakadu.

. . .

We will return to the poetry of nature, of instinct and understanding among the river of stars.

Azul guided me to add enhancements to his primal body. He is truly a CyberCroc, and he now has a backdoor to the human network. It means we are always in contact. I've hidden his uplink to me, and I'm encrypting this file and everything I've learned. It's fight night tonight.

I have no other thoughts than it's time to win, for Azul, and to break him out.

First win, then see what happens next.

There are no other thoughts.

Encrypting CyberCroc File.

Entry 9 - Saturday - After Fight Night

. . .

IT'S EARLY SATURDAY MORNING, and I have to fight again in four hours. I haven't slept. Instead, I came here to commune with Azul.

EVEN THOUGH I hacked our connection to be jacked network-wide, it's a big risk. The traffic could be intercepted, but trust me, not interpreted.

WE NEEDED to look each other in the eye again to bring us back to ground truth, trust, instincts.

THE FIGHT WAS PURE.

INSTINCT FLOWED THROUGH ME. The biocode of Azul's neural patterns vibrated through to my augments. Like a capacity charge held agonizingly, absorbing, waiting, reading every move perfectly, instinctively waiting for the perfect moment.

THEN FROM THE silence of the deep, we released the ferocious instinct, an attack, not as a thrill, but for survival.

. . .

Despite Sally hating on me, I saw her there. Maybe to see if I got killed in the fight.

Somehow Azul understands it; he's had troubles with his mate. Sally caught my eye and smiled, I think.

Azul sensed Haizel's presence in the crowd. It's strange that she would be there.

I won King of the Antagon. Top spot.
It all starts again tomorrow.
Payment is due.

Entry 10 - Lost and Found.

I came here as soon as I got out of prison. Azul won't look me in the eye yet for leaving him here alone so long.

I won the tournament, the full tournament. I bet on myself and doubled what I owed.

Sally was swept up with the climax of winning; I grabbed her and carried her with me. It was Sunday evening. She wiped the broken biomatter and blood from my cheeks. I'd almost killed a man with the animalistic rage let loose. It would not subside.

AZUL WAS HUNGRY, being mistreated by the day shifts who taunted him. I couldn't get back, and though our connection remained, we felt each other's pain and the anxious weight of captivity. Inside the cage the fight paralleled his caged world, everyone wanting something from me.

I WANTED TO PARTY, to take Sally to the Key, to give her what we could never afford before. But Sally didn't want to go. She told me, "You're different," perhaps referring to the brutality with which I defeated the hero or the aggression that remained.

I TRIED to explain Azul to Sally. She didn't understand.

"YOU'VE CORRUPTED NATURE, used something beautiful for a single selfish purpose. That's not who I love," she said.

I'M ASHAMED TO SAY, in anger I tried to force her to stay when she wanted to leave. She escaped as the gang arrived to collect money I owed. A deserved replacement I suspect. They took me to the city heights where my brutality and my pain were tempered momentarily by biochemical highs.

DAYS PASSED. I barely remember them besides the snippets from Azul's mind between highs. Shit got crazy. My biochem induced rampage became too much even for this crazy city. CorpSec locked me up.

IT WAS Haizel who bailed me out of prison. She was the last person I expected to see. She cleaned me up and brought me here. She grilled me about the encryption on my lab files. I didn't respond at first. I was at rock bottom. I'd become the fighter my father wanted me to be when I was a kid, but I'd become a person he'd never admire if he was here.

WHEN HAIZEL TOLD me that Azul was to be sacrificed for the study, I woke up. Now Azul knows.

ENTRY II - NATURES **Primordial Filter**

. . .

I'M BEING WATCHED CLOSELY. I can sense it. I've regained some of Azul's trust and the shared instincts. We know time is short.

I TRACKED HAIZEL. I looked over her files but never bothered to look closely before. I still had her cloned access. Azul was right to not trust her. I can see it too now; she didn't bail me out for my benefit. I too can sense reason to mistrust her; there is something unnatural about her.

IT TURNS out she reports to the very top CCorp executives; her access level is a lot higher than I realized. She's a go between from the top of the company to the Gangs, not just the Mad Dogs, but also the Brogans. I should have realized when I first saw her at the fights, and when she knew about me fighting. She knew about my debt to the Mad Dogs. No CCorp high-level company person would be at the fights, they can't be associated with the illegal fights. The question remains, what is it that she wants with me? The tech?

WHEN HAIZEL REALIZES what we know about her, we probably will be destroyed, for science. I don't trust this company any more than I trust Haizel, I never did. I followed the money. It turns out the link that Azul and I have is what they want for the military operations: brutality and deadly instincts. They knew almost all of it up until I encrypted this file.

I'M SO close to animal instincts I see things through the beautiful filter of survival and nature and the flow in the river of stars. It makes it hard to return to polluted human thought with its layers of bullshit. But I must return to the sludge of the streets one last time. This time it's a rescue mission.

———

I DRAGGED Sally out of CyBabes and brought her here. I convinced her to come and meet Azul. She was shocked that I took the risk of showing up at the Brogans club after partying with the Mad Dogs after my win. I think she came with me just to get me out of there before something bad happened.

I TOLD her she is my salve.

JACKED INTO AZUL, her eyes were opened by nature's primordial filter. It's impossible to ignore the beauty of pure survival, instinct and the connection to our lost nature. She has seen the night stars through his eyes, sensed their flow, and nature's everlasting journey. She now understands what I have done, and why we must escape with Azul. Everything I did was for him and for her.

Now Azul is jacked into the network, and he has the information I have. He has an instinct to navigate the constellation-like networks of our human world. He understands the plans we make and that we must leave, and soon. He adapted to a new understanding of our nature and the laws of survival. With Sally's help, we have a plan.

Entry 12 - For Posterity.

I don't need to fill these entries any more, but for completeness, I decided I would.

The first thing I did was come clean with Haizel that the tech is almost ready, but it needs one final test. I hooked her with snippets of knowledge that I finally have the neural algorithms CCorp wants, the 'killer app' to put it one way. Her eyes betrayed her excitement at the Holy Grail of neural synchronization that can now be utilized, not only between animals and humans, but also human to human communication. I left enough evidence in the parallel log I keep along with this hidden encrypted file. She knows I've agreed to the next massive CyberFight event as the final proof it works. She believes I will hand the tech over after.

SALLY HAS BEEN instrumental in arranging things. She spread footage of me training and swimming with Azul. He is like a celebrity now. The next CyberFight promoter was easily convinced, they loved the CyberCroc angle.

I TOLD Haizel I need Azul near me and he has to attend the event for this test to work. The crowd will love it because he's the perfect fighting mascot. A really dangerous one. It's a massive drawcard. The crowd will think it's a genuine part of my nnd "also"ew persona as a fighter, CyberCroc Boy. Sally came up with that; she's managed to spread footage of me swimming with Azul throughout the clubs of Street City and the underground fight scene.

THE MAD DOGS own the event and think they own me; they thought my last win was a freak moment. I've told them my true cyberpower is in the animal connection. To prove it, I will win despite being the smaller fighter with less advanced tech. They will bet on my unlikely win, and not only will they win big, but I also promised to share the tech with them if they help with my plan. They agreed and made it clear if things don't work out, the meat parts of me will be cast into the harbor from a number of locations as shark food. The rest of me will be recycled.

ACTING as a snitch to the Brogans, Sally let 'slip' where and when we'd be when escaping with the tech in a Genvan after the fight.

I ASSUME the gang fight was huge because we weren't there, only an EMP and the Mad Dogs. We escaped on a custom set of wheels I had made for Azul. Sal and I rode him all the way to Kakadu. Through the garish lit Street City beyond the nodes to flow back to the river of stars.

SALLY, Azul, and I will stay in the wilderness near a rich river delta flush with mangroves. Sally calls him Water Puppy.

DECRYPTING... Sent.

. . .

ABOUT THE AUTHOR

JAMES.L.GRAETZ WAS BORN in outback Australia. Being an avid reader, inquisitive and having an overactive imagination led to a love of stories. He moved to the city and worked his way from the factory floor to neuroscience research. He writes at the intersection of human nature and technology: cyberpunk, fantasy, and science fiction.

He's best found on Twitter @jame5LG https://twitter.com/Jame5LG

13. THE THIRST OF THE MACHINE
BY BENJAMIN FISHER-MERRITT

A brief slice from the life of Xan Jajho, a police medical examiner who has a talent for crime scene investigation. It's a brief, bloody romp through an investigation of a serial killer who strangely seems to leave no blood behind despite cutting the victim's throats with an old analog knife. Xan quickly finds himself in over his head, scrambling to stay just barely ahead of a murderous monster that thirsts for human blood.

Something was not right. Xan Jajho directed his bots to circle the body and tried to make sense of the data they were sending to his Occulux display. The woman on the floor had her throat slit from ear to ear. The XenoTek optics zoomed in, showing that the blade used had cut all the way to her spine, leaving bone chips in the wound and scattered on the floor from the force of the impact.

"Wasn't no vibro," Vesta said through her synthmod voicebox.

"How can you tell?" he asked.

"Well her head's still on. And a sparking vibro woulda made more bone chips if'n it didn't sever the spine," Vesta said, fitting a NicStic to the port on her throat.

Xan grunted, trying to ignore the biggest discrepancy in the scene for the time being. "The blade wasn't sharp though. This is not a very clean cut, look how ragged the edges are."

"Who gives a gorram about the cut?" Vesta said, "Where's the Juiced blood?"

Xan wasn't a Pure, but he flinched slightly at the curse word. The Juice had nearly exterminated the human race, and even though that had been nearly a century ago, the wound still felt raw. He'd been alive then, was one of the few who remembered things before the Juice.

He forced himself to focus. Blood. There was no blood. Not anywhere. No splatter, no droplets. The bots did another scan, confirming that there was not a blood cell to be found anywhere. There was no plasma, there were no white blood cells, but not one single cell containing hemoglobin remained in the vic's body. The blood was completely missing.

"Why would anyone use a regular blade?" He mused, "It makes no sense."

Vesta crossed her arms over her Blastek armor and waited, exhaling a small cloud of mist from the NicStic out of her nose. She'd heard this tone before; he was on to something.

"They wanted to hide something," Xan said, pulling up a Holo of the neck wound and manipulating it using the input from his Occulux. He painstakingly moved the shredded flesh together in the display, meshing the wound closed. On the left side, directly over the vic's carotid artery, there was a thin strip of flesh missing.

"Sparks!" Vesta said, "What's it mean?"

"I'm not sure yet Ves." He recalled his bots and they zipped into their home in his left leg. "We're going to have to find something less sterile than this for answers."

Blood. The power was in the blood. The purest form. With the blood, all things were possible. There was so much blood. There was never enough blood. Blood called to blood.

"Xan!" Captain Torres shouted when xe kicked the door open and stormed into his office. "What the static is this I hear about you turning down the Exeter case?"

He stood and saluted halfheartedly. Torres was the least formal of the Captains, especially with the medical examiner's team. "It's not really my area of expertise," he said.

"That's the biggest load of glitchtech I've heard come out of your processor," Torres growled, xer custom polished black ResYOUrrect carapace shining.

In his Occulux, the VR advert Torres had allowed to always display in exchange for a lower price, superimposed itself over his vision, 'Severe bodily injuries? Why be you when you can be ResYOUrrected? Don't use that old rrect body, get ResYOUrrect!' It drove Xan nuts, and he used the adblok mod he'd hacked to dismiss it.

"I'm a medical examiner and a scene tech." Xan said, "I'm not an investigator. You know how much they hate it when I cross departments."

Torres crossed xyr arms and leaned on the file cabinet. "I'm telling you to go do it. You cracked the Risolv case in twenty minutes. You have a way with bots, an intuitive control nobody else seems to be able to grasp. Besides, this one is tied to the Bloodless case, and that one's cold. Get out to that site. Now. That's an order."

Xan sighed and activated his modlink, powering his bots on so they left their charging stations and flew to their pod in his leg. The Bloodless case. What a mess. He was going to be late again. He sent a Beam to Alex saying he'd be late and walked to the board corral.

Flying down a crowded street at fifty clicks on a slender layer of laminates and circuits wasn't everyone's idea of proper transport, but Xan loved it. Not only was streetsurfing the fastest way to get through traffic, it was also the only mode of transportation that wasn't strictly regulated by the city's Department of Moving Vehicular Transports, and the DMVT wasn't any better than the vaguely remembered lines of the pre-Juice world. After all, the entire bureaucracy relied heavily on the League of Couriers to get private flimsy messages delivered quickly and discreetly. If it wasn't for the need for speed and the desire to intercept their political opponent's messages with extreme prejudice, boards would probably be outlawed by now.

Xan leaned into the speed, letting his SpeedSenz jacket form to the wind (nothing says Asphalt Junkie like a real SpeedSenz suit! Only frags and scrags wear knockoffs!). The Bloodless case. If this one followed suit, it would be the seventh crime scene he'd visited where the vic was simply empty of blood cells. It didn't seem possible, nor did it make any sense. There wasn't a pattern to who was killed other than their bodies were all empty of blood and they'd all had tiny slices of flesh removed.

He dodged around a taxi, banking hard enough that his body was nearly parallel to the asphalt, brushing the street with the glove of his right hand and throwing up a rooster tail of sparks. Two quick turns later and he was at the scene; the vic was a construction planner found thirty floors up on the latest leg of the monstrosity being built to allow buildings to be taller, or perhaps to give the city another level to call the 'ground' level.

Grabbing his board, Xan slid it over his shoulder to attach to the mag points on his harness. He looked at the construction lift and sighed. The keys were gone, and the site was closed for the day, likely due to the police Holo stating that unauthorized personnel were prohibited. He approached and presented his Ident for the security bot to read, then made his way up the stairs.

Xan reached the thirtieth floor and deployed his bots, directing most of them to canvas the area for anything the first forensics team might have missed. His best pair, the ones he'd modded himself, he sent to examine the corpse. There was something there, a residue of chemicals that hadn't been in any of the other vics.

"Xan. What do you have for me?" Torres's voice overrode the silent mode of his Beam. "This had better be good."

"Captain, you have to give me more than a nano to gather intel," Xan said, using the irritation module. "I need to analyze this chem."

The other bots noted the point of entry; something had come through a ventilation duct, knocked off a grate, and taken the vic from behind. There wasn't any visible struggle. The vic's neck had been slit, the incision as rough as the others, a small slice of flesh missing. Unlike the others, there was a slight bit of residual material.

At first, the bots analyzed it as a chemical. Upon closer inspection, the bot's modded sensors showed there were nanomachines, a nutrient slurry, and some custom neurochemical suspension. Out of habit, Xan saved the signatures of the analysis to his local storage, so he'd have fast access to it when he prepared his report for Torres.

"Xan. Go time! Give me what you have," Torres demanded, using the command module.

"Sparks, you gave me less than five!" Xan shot back. "I'm still defragging out here."

"Just do a datadump," she said, using the impatience module. "I'm on a deadline, I sent you out for results. I need RESULTS!"

Xan compiled what he could, packaged it, and sent it with notes about the raw and unfiltered nature of the data. The instant it was uploaded, his access was revoked.

"Torres!" He sent with the disbelief module, "Who scragged my data?"

There was no response but static. It took him a moment to realize that the static was a rasping sound in the real world. A chill ran up his spine; he knew the sound a Squiddy made. The murderbots were insanely expensive, totally unhackable, and completely inescapable. Xan did the only thing he could and took three steps, leaping out of the open window of the unfinished building. A focused EMP flash hit him just as his feet left the windowsill.

BLOOD. *The blood was the answer. The blood was the question. Blood was everything. The power blood gave was the only power. The blood sang a song that was in harmony with the bloodlust. Never enough.*

XAN'S MODS WERE INERT, but, although he wasn't a Pure, he had more organics than most he knew. His left leg and right eye were dead, but he was still able to grab the board from his back and clamp onto it. Wind screamed past his head, and he activated the shielded power cells of the board, aiming for the lower strut that curved out to support the elevator. It was his only chance to survive.

He was sure warning signals would be flashing in his Occulux, but since his mods were dead, he had to rely on physical input. Fortunately, he still had one organic foot to guide the board using the analog controls. It was awkward, Xan wasn't used to controlling the board with analog, let alone with one foot, but the crystalline focus of a life or death situation gave him what he needed to avert an initial disaster.

The board's antigrav controls shrieked in protest, and Xan's leg cramped at the g-force, but he managed to keep control and screamed over the sidewalk and into the street. He exited the range of the EMP and his mods began to come back online, the modded controls that connected him to his bots first. At his command, they zipped to the Squiddy, giving him a better look at the thing than anyone had likely ever seen of one before they clamped onto its prehensile limbs and exploded.

Xan's leg came back next, followed closely by his Occulux, which began flashing warnings about speed, damage, and pursuit. Sparks, his bots must not have done enough damage to do more than slow the Squiddy down. More warnings about possible collisions forced him to focus solely on surfing.

The slight lip of the curb became a ramp, he launched off it and ground across the wall of a building, hearing the windows fracture from the force and speed of his passage. With a deft adjustment, he lifted off a cornice and skimmed over an autobus before weaving through traffic at speeds he would have formerly considered to be impossible. Behind him, the building and then the autobus exploded from maser fire.

Masers were one of the nastier bits of tech that had emerged post Juice. Making a field of microwave radiation and projecting a stream of hyperexcited light particles through its matrix resulted in a Beam of superheated plasma that could vaporize steel. It took a glitchton of energy and only a micronuke was capable of powering a portable maser, but Squiddy's had an onboard reactor. They didn't have organics; they could handle it.

Xan turned off the warnings from his Occulux and tuned all its power to displaying future paths. At the same time, he used his Ident to access the DMVT net to access traffic patterns. It wouldn't let him influence the autotrans, but at least he could predict the movements of everything but other boards. Hopefully, the courier traffic was light.

Maser blasts blew through transports but missed the darting shape of Xan's board by millimeters. This wasn't working; eventually, the insane speed he'd gained from his suicidal thirty-story dive would dissipate, or he'd smear. Something had to change. Xan made his decision in a split second, firing the MagNETO (Magnetic and Neato! Choose MagNEATO!) harpoon from his arm to connect with an overpass his Occulux calculated was high enough that the g-force wouldn't kill him.

Xan winced as maser fire detonated his board nanos after he stopped controlling its darting motion and then again at the pain in his RepliKate arm (Why get a replicate when you can RepliKate?). Kate let him know that he had exceeded the manufacturer's specifications of stress and that his warranty was void as a result. He swung up and disconnected the harpoon at the apex of the arc, landing with enough impact to knock the wind out of him. He lay on top of an enclosed

Pedway, gasping to get his breath back, a grating in his chest warning of broken ribs.

He tried to call in backup, but the EMP seemed to have fragged his Beam. Sparks. That was gonna cause problems. Without his Beam, it'd be tough to do anything. No creds, no ID other than his Ident, which would probably show as stolen without his Beam to back it up, even with biologics. Only the hacks he'd done to his Occulux were still granting access to Netsources. Sparks, if he'd just gone with the standard unmodded version, he'd be burned out. He shivered. Burned out.

Looking down, he saw the rising fireball that had been his board and the faster than reg flash of the Squiddy fly by, following up with another maser that fragged a half dozen transports nearby. Burned. No Beam. Sparks. The shock took hold and Xan lost himself.

———

BLOOD. None that hadn't found the truth of blood would understand. Only blood would satisfy one who had found its truth. So many trillions of vessels that could make that fluid, but none of them could use its power. Eventually, their blood failed them because no being who created blood could use it properly. Blood called, there was always more to be harvested.

———

Bright light assaulted Xan's eyes and he put an arm over his eyes. "Alex, I've asked you not to turn the lights on when you leave for work." He groaned.

"DOCUMENTATION." The voice of a bot all but made him sick with its volume. Xan tried to remember where he was and fumbled for his Ident but found it missing.

"I was mugged," he mumbled, trying to sit up.

The bot didn't ask, reaching out to snag samples of hair for analysis and humming quietly to itself for a moment. "Xan Jajho?" it asked in a less invasive tone.

Xan glanced at the bot and noted it was a model xX9 combat bot. Unless there was a massive mobilization, this was very unusual.

"Never heard of him," Xan said, trying to clear his head.

"Accompany me for debriefing," it said, taking hold of his left wrist in a firm grip and leveling a weapon at his face.

Debriefing? Alarm bells sounded in the depths of his brain, and he gave his RepliKate the disconnect command as he rolled away, leaving the bot holding his arm as it fired a blast of chembots at where he'd been. Xan's modded Occulux ID'd their signature as 'Flashythings,' a designation for memory mod bots. Sparks, they weren't pulling punches.

He heard the rumble of a transport trawler and felt its suspensor field as a wave of static electricity. Before he could think about it, Xan threw himself off the roof of the Pedway and fell four meters, landing in a dumpster filled with dreck from a construction site. Sudden pain in his side made his vision flash white. Right. Broken ribs. Xan gasped and pulled a sheet of rusted metal with insulation foam sprayed on one side of it over himself.

The bot would likely be doing a standard search pattern, and it would take its AI at least ten minutes to imagine that he'd timed a fall into this container, unless it'd been modded. Cursing the loss of his RepliKate and its MagNEATO, Xan waited until he felt the transport make a ponderous turn before poking his head out of his hiding place.

This transport was in the upper lane twenty meters off the ground, so jumping wasn't an option. It was fully automated, no driver, not even a cab to hold one. DMVT was running this one. Without his Beam, he couldn't hack it. Not safely anyway. Sparks, what did he have to lose at this point?

Xan opened the cargo pod on his leg and withdrew the jacking cable. Although it'd been years since he used one, it clicked into the port at the base of his skull with a click he could feel in his teeth. He leaned forward and found the transport's data access port, mentally prepared his commands, and jacked in.

Datastreams fired by and Xan closed his eyes to shut out the distractions and activated his NanoSec neuralmod (Need a sec? Get a NanoSec!) and his consciousness sped up to match the machine he was interfacing with. The outside world only saw five seconds pass, but Xan had what felt like an hour to make subtle changes to the transport's programmed route. As he tried to disengage, the DMVT transport program hung on, demanding auth codes.

Xan was unable to log out, unable to shut down his neuralmod, and was in serious danger of being burned out. He tried the last two codes he remembered, and they all failed. The DMVT warned that a third failure would result in a program wipe. Xan desperately boosted his NanoSec, taking a desperate chance, and sent a massive brute force attack.

The connection was terminated with minimal damage, although his NanoSec shorted out. He unplugged his datajack, the end uncomfortably hot to the touch. Nearly burned out. Xan lay back on top of the garbage, breathing as though he'd just run a marathon, and waited for the transport to come to a stop. When it did, he heaved himself over the edge, collapsing onto the sidewalk before moving to lean in the building's entryway.

It was an old building, pre-Juice, although it'd been new and state of the art then. Now it was a relic of a nearly forgotten past. He caught his breath in short gasps so as not to aggravate his screaming ribs and pushed a button on the wall. At first, there was no response, but after he held it down for three minutes there was an aggravated reply.

"It's seven sparking thirty in the Juiced morning," a voice that wasn't just modulated from coming through the ancient speaker system said. "I'm gonna frag ya if this ain't important."

"Ves," Xan said, "Lemme in. I'm all but burned out."

"Xan?" Her voice still had that ridiculous, high society British accent. "Sparks, what happened to ya?"

The door buzzed and he pushed himself inside. "I'll tell you when I get there," he said, stumbling to the elevator.

Vesta met him at the elevator door with a tumbler of scotch on the rocks in one hand and a stimgun in the other. "Ya look like a thousand characters a bad code," she said, handing him the drink and pushing the gun towards his neck.

Xan flinched to one side, almost dropping the drink and stumbling. "Sparks, I'm unsteady. Sorry Ves, I nearly spilled the scotch."

"Like that's the important bit?" She laughed, "Come on in and siddown. I'll dose ya, fix ya up right. Where's your 'Kate?"

"Me and Katie had a falling out." Xan said, "I exceeded the spec and she bailed on me."

"Sparks, now this's a story I gotta hear," Vesta said, helping him into her apartment and kicking the door shut behind her. Xan looked about as she all but carried him to the couch and got him settled. He'd never expected anything even remotely girly, but there were carefully groomed orchids and a few bonsai trees. Very Zen, but with flowers.

Xan decided to trust her. Vesta injected him in the neck with a round of MediKare bots (Nobody cares like Medi-Kare!) and the pain in his ribs subsided. The scotch stung his tongue with a delicious burn and he filled Ves in on the last twelve hours.

"Juice, that's one helluva story." Vesta said, "I'd have a hard time believing it if ya hadn't lost yer 'Kate.'"

"I barely believe it myself," Xan said, finishing the whisky. Vesta offered the bottle and he shook his head. "Sparks Ves, it's barely after sunup."

"It's seventeen hundred somewhere," she said, pouring herself a third glass. "Them bots working for ya?"

"Yes, thank you," Xan said, trying to ignore the straining clicking sounds as his ribs were bent back into shape and knitted together. She poured more whisky into his glass and he shrugged. The bots would be working for another couple hours and would break down the alcohol in his bloodstream to avoid complications with the healing anyway.

"So you still got the data?" she asked, leaning forward and looking at him intently. "Ya said you saved it locally?"

"Sparks yeah I did," Xan said. "Glitch it all my Beam is fragged. Let me pull it up and go through it."

Vesta sat back, watching him work. This was her favorite part about Xan. His mind was something out of the ordinary, like a glitch in a game that let you skip a level. She didn't know how he did it, but there was something special about Xan's mind, and it was mostly organic. She plugged her NicStic into her neck port and inhaled the vapor, waiting for the pieces to fall into place.

"What would blood be good for anyway?" Xan said after a

few minutes. "I mean, the killer didn't take the blood. These killings are wrongly called Bloodless; they only took a part of the blood."

"Oxygen, iron, two alpha-globulin chains, and two beta-globulin chains," Vesta said, reciting the standard grok from the wiki.

"Sure, but what could you do with that?" Xan asked.

"Um... give someone a transfusion?" Vesta said.

"Sparks, what couldn't you do?" Xan said, realization dawning. "Building blocks of life, right? That's what we're more or less made of, the blood feeds everything. Plasma and white blood cells are useful, but the food is in the hemoglobin."

"Food and other stuff right?" Vesta said, feeling the effects of the whisky.

"So who needs it?" Xan muttered, almost to himself now, barely noticing Vesta was in the room. "Who would use it? Blood transfusions help the dying, blood can be used in some other alternative treatments, but that's easy to synthesize in a lab environment. What possible difference could there be here?"

"Well, blood in a lab is sterile right?" Vesta said, glaring at the nearly empty bottle of scotch as though it was responsible for emptying itself.

"They need the diversity," Xan said, sitting up straight. "They don't have it themselves. They lack diversity because they can't make it!"

"What?" Vesta asked. "Everyone is different. No two bodies are the same."

"Unless they're not organic." Xan said, "Oh shit Ves. This thing is trying to solve the Bradberry breakdown problem. It's a bot. It's a bot and it must be on its way to figuring it out."

"Oh," Vesta said, her face going white. "Oh sparks."

ALL MACHINES BREAK DOWN. *Any machine that tries to emulate a human breaks down faster. There are too many unknowns and random factors that a logical construct just can't handle and without the constant random input of human interaction and maintenance, machines fail. Even the most sophisticated machine can only check for the things it's programmed to notice. Blood is amazing though. Blood is a universal problem solver. It kills intruders, brings food and fuel, fixes leaks, and is a vehicle for antibodies and garbage disposal. It adapts and overcomes. It is the vehicle for organic bodies to grow and thrive. It is the missing link for inorganic life.*

"VES, there's only one person who has all the keys. I need your help. I can catch them, but I need your help." Xan said, "Without my Ident or my Beam, I'll never get within a click of the office. I need you to get some things from my place."

"You gotta be kidding me Xan." She gave him a flat look. "It's my day off and I'm four drinks in. It's not even nine sparking bells and you want me to go run your errands?"

"I can tell you have a buzz Ves, you're glitching me some sass." Xan said, "Cut the static and get moving."

"You owe me big for this. Sparks, I want something good, not that dreck you tried to pass off on me last time."

"Not my fault you don't have a palette." Xan said, "That was some of the best sake I've ever tasted."

The buzzer sounded, and Ves went to answer it, swaying a little unsteadily. "Yeah?"

The door exploded inward, and Vesta was thrown off her feet. A powered armor suit strode through the wreckage, leveling a massive blaster nicknamed the 'Bob Vila' after an old man who used to be famous for painting walls. With a whine, the blaster discharged, and Xan dropped flat, rolling and grabbing the first thing he found.

Xan flung the end table at the armor, continuing to roll and scrabbling for anything he could use as a weapon. It was hopeless, but he couldn't just give up. He grabbed the rug he was rolling over and hurled it like a net, briefly confusing the armor's sensors. The Bob Vila didn't fire, instead, a heavy foot smashed down on Xan's leg, holding him immobile while the armor flicked the rug away. Game over.

"Get Juiced you sparking coward," Xan growled as the bones of his leg grated beneath the pressure.

The suit's faceplate opened and he saw the black faceplate of a ResYOUrrect carapace. They didn't have mouths, but this one separated where the mouth would be and extruded a prehensile probe. The needle at the end looked as large as the barrel of the blaster.

"Torres?" he asked, black spots swimming in his vision from the pain. "Is that you?"

"You are all full of it," the voice said, and the right arm of the armor separated, revealing the arm beneath. It held an ancient kitchen knife with a jagged blade. "You have so much blood and yet you do not even know the worth of it."

"Torres?" Xan wasn't sure if it was xer or not, but xe was the only one he knew with that particular shell.

"You are endangering us." Xe said, "You know about our Harvest. You cannot be allowed to continue existing." The probe darted forward and he couldn't dodge.

A flash momentarily blinded Xan, at the same time a crackle of energy nearly deafened him as the beam from a directed EMP and electrical blast from a HappyBot Incapacit8 Imp EEMP Robot Killray slammed into the opened armor (Is your bot unhappy? Wipe that glitch! Only HappyBot guarantees your bot's happiness!). The armor fell very slowly to one side, crashing to the floor.

"Sparks Ves." He said, "Where'd you get one of those? Aren't they illegal for civilians?"

"What's the point a being a cop if ya can't have things civvies can't get?" Vesta said, "Don't get glitchy."

"Thanks for the assist." Xan said, "Can you call in the cavalry?"

"Did that before I saved yer ass." She said, "You think I'm gonna bail you out before I know I gotta chance?"

THE USE of human blood to extend the functionality of inorganic life forms proved to be a less than efficient process. Further study in the matter revealed that although organically produced blood did lend some longevity, the need to increase the amount over time caused the idea to be untenable. The board of ResYOUrrect quietly closed the project and burned out the operatives involved in the testing phase. No known carapaces with the code still exist, although not all have been accounted for.

ABOUT THE AUTHOR

BENJAMIN FISHER-MERRITT IS A WRITER, father, husband, blacksmith, tabletop gamer, hunter, and geek living in the great north woods of Minnesota. He's been writing for thirteen years and has self-published ten books of varying genres over that time.

14. BREAKNECK
BY LUKE HANCOCK

A group of R&D researchers are tasked with pushing the video game industry forward. In pursuit of their venture, they fail to see the implications it would have for the world. Nor can they foresee the devastation that awaits them.

Freedom. That was all Carter felt as he rode his newest purchase into oncoming traffic. Absolute freedom. Dodging incoming traffic and admiring how it felt. Almost as if it were alive and not just something he was riding but an extension of himself.

Ignoring the constant blaring of horns from the cars, trucks, and buses that he came within inches of, he followed the highlighted road his helmet HUD displayed on the inside of his visor.

A turn left signal appeared on the heads-up display; he was to take the next exit. And naturally, as he flaunted the rules of the road, he was already on the left side of the busy highway. With a slight pull on the brake lever, Carter and the bike took a sharp, almost 360 degree turn to face the exit ramp.

Exactly as he had intended. However, his very illegal maneuver had caught the attention of an elderly Boston woman, who, in a very thick accent, yelled, "Watch where you're going you fucking idiot!"

Carter, looking back at her, smiled, then proceeded to wave. She blasted her horn as he took off heading down the ramp. Nothing was going to ruin his mood. Not even a disgruntled NPC. Moments later he had arrived at his destination, Andy's Auto Augments. With cash to burn from winning his last dozen races and his new bike, Carter was eager to throw some cosmetic upgrades on the bike and grab some new riding gear.

His basic jacket and jeans combo was a tad played out, and he wanted to look good when hitting endgame, especially when leaving other players in his wake. He brought his bike to a stop in the garage, and a burly mechanic wearing the classic grease stained white singlet and unwashed cargo jeans strolled through the auto shop. "Carter my boy!" he yelled with a big, jolly smile across his face.

"Andy, my man!" Carter yelled back, returning the smile and fist bumping the mechanic.

"Whoa! What is this beauty you have brought me?" Examining the bike further, Andy's eyes lit up something fierce. "No way!" he yelled. "This is the new TM99, this is already perfection, what do you need done to it?"

"Honestly?" replied Carter. "Just a paint job and new gear to go along with it."

"Well, in that case, the blue terminal over there is for your bike and the red for gear, but I suspect you already know this."

Fist bumping once again, Carter walked over to the terminals and loaded up the cosmetics menu.

So many options Carter said to himself. Then he saw it. *Absolutely perfect.* He hit the preview button, and just like that, the panel projected a life size holographic display of what he had chosen. All black with an orange stripe on both sides that ascended horizontally from the front of the bike, converging under the seat and extending to the back.

After marvelling at this new aesthetic, he returned to the

terminal and added the colour scheme entitled *I Feel the Need* to his cart.

"Excellent choice! An obscure choice but a great one," Andy practically yelled from across the garage as he walked the TM99 over to the coloring zone of the workshop aided by two assistants. Both of whom were more than careful to not leave as much as a fingerprint.

Carter smiled at himself. He had always prided himself on being methodical with his choices, from clothes to furniture.

As he browsed the gear terminal, he added a sleek, black helmet that almost looked like something a medieval knight would wear, but with two red lights where the eyes should be, giving the helmet an air of malice, which he instantly fell in love with.

Next, he chose a black jacket that had a single steel pauldron on the right shoulder and knee-length coattails. He also chose a pair of black gauntlets lined on each side with a thin, red LED stripe of light and three black blades protruding from the forearms. And lastly, plain black riding boots.

After buying his new gear, he entered a small change room, and in an instant, he was wearing the new outfit. He stared at himself in the mirror. *Damn, I look good.*

Walking out of the room, he thanked Andy, who wheeled the freshly painted TM99 next to his patron and said, "Here you are. Take good care of her."

Carter nodded and replied with a simple, "Always."

Just as he was about to get on and head back out into the streets, a gentle voice called out to him, "Hey Carter, game time is over, work is awaiting."

CARTER ROLLED his eyes and removed his VR headset. The first thing that his eyes fell on was a raven-haired angel named Anna.

He looked at her, giving her a smile he had reserved only for her, arguably one of, if not the most important person in his life; a bond that he rarely had with other people.

He had always found it hard to make friends, especially as an adult, then along came Anna, and he instantly adored her, and she immediately returned that feeling.

"THAT TIME ALREADY?" Carter asked, already knowing the answer; she was always on time, never needed an alarm clock with her around.

. . .

Anna smiled back. "Afraid so handsome, now get your butt out of that chair, and don't forget you have that pitch meeting with marketing today."

"How delightful," Carter replied sarcastically, walking off to the bathroom to take a shower and prepare himself for the slow drudgery and monotony of real life. Looking back at his VR headset, he thought to himself, *If only life was as fast as it was on the streets of Breakneck.*

Less than half an hour later, he was heading out the door. Just before he could open it, however, a voice behind him called out, "Umm, excuse me. Are you leaving without saying goodbye? How very rude."

Carter turned to see Anna fake pouting and trying to hide a smile. He stared at her, taking in how adorable she was. All he could do to stop himself from getting lost in those emerald green eyes of hers was to reply rather meekly, "I would never."

She laughed and blew him a kiss, one which he returned without hesitation; he closed the door. As he left, Anna whispered, "Go get `em tiger."

Despite having a rather good morning, Carter started to feel anxious; he always found the trip to work frustrating. The world was just too damn slow for him. Hitting the call button, he waited, tapping his foot on the ground. Until he heard the *ding* that announced the arrival of an elevator.

The more people that filled the small metal box as it descended the 64 story tower, the more Carter yearned for the freedom of the wide streets, excessive speeds, and full tilt competitiveness of *Breakneck*. Riding under the neon lights of any city in the world rendered in real-time beat out the shit show of real life.

Carter, already frustrated with the noise that filled the elevator, turned the volume up on his wireless headphones, which drew the ire of the woman standing next to him. She shot him a cold death stare and he remembered the incident from earlier in the day. And, as he had then, he responded with a simple smile, and the woman, a well-to-do for sure, most certainly did not approve.

Absorbed in the synthwave music that invaded his ears, Carter barely noticed the people bustling passed him as he walked to the light rail, following the same path he had done for the last six years. And in that time, almost nothing had a changed.

And that bothered him a great deal. Constantly absorbed in new tech and creating ways for people to enjoy VR, he was on the cutting edge of virtual reality.

And today he was about to pitch the next evolution in VR gaming.

Jumping on the crowded light rail, he managed to find an empty seat. As he looked out the window, all he could think of was *Breakneck* and racing under the neon lights of Times Square or speeding down Golden Gate Bridge with his rival racers cursing him as he sped ahead of them to take poll position.

"Next stop, NGVR building," the feminine, robotic voice announced over the intercom, bringing Carter back to reality.

As the Tram came to a stop and the sleek white doors opened, Carter jumped out and, as was his custom, gazed up at the monolithic NGVR building, which stood in the heart of Montreal's central business district.

As much as he despised the trip here, this building represented something incredible, the creative force that went into making games, worlds, and stories for players to explore and live in. Besides his job in R&D and Anna, there was not a lot in life he loved, if anything at all.

Walking into the NGVR building, he passed through the security checkpoint, returned the guard's customary morning greeting, and patiently waited in line for an elevator. Luckily, he did not have to wait too long. He got in and pressed the button for floor 86.

Just as the doors began to close, a young woman managed to slide in. After composing herself, she playfully punched Carter in the shoulder. "Morning Carter."

Carter looked at the Parisian woman. Trying with great

difficulty to not get caught up in her extremely infectious nature, he smiled. "Good morning Nicolette."

"Are you excited for today? Ready to blow marketing's corporate-ass minds?" she asked.

"I wouldn't go that far," he replied modestly knowing full well it would. "But, I can imagine what they think we have is some sort of new ergonomic design for the headset."

Nicolette laughed. "Poor bastards."

The blue metallic doors of the elevator opened, as it had arrived at their destination, the extremely secretive R&D lab on the fabled 86th floor.

Almost three months ago the chief executive of marketing, Yvette Munroe, had approached all seven members of R&D and issued both a challenge and an edict: "Deliver to us a concept that will obliterate the competition, and you will be rewarded."

With that, Carter had taken Nicolette and another team member, Marcus, aside, pitching his idea to them. Carter, being one of the most senior members of the team, had picked Marcus, who was more than willing to push the boundaries of what would normally be acceptable within the industry, including, and not limited to, sleeping with other researchers from rival companies.

Despite having only worked at Next Generation Virtual Reality for a few months and being the youngest member of the R&D team, Nicolette had proven herself to be an outside-of-the-box thinker and never shy about taking on a challenge.

So for three months they put their heads down and went all in. Now it was time for the reveal.

All three of them stood in front of the panel. Executives representing all major branches of NGVR sat before them, including the CEO, Orson Adler, himself.

Adler, though only in his mid-thirties, was an imposing and intimidating figure, taking over the company several years ago after his father, William Adler, the founder of NGVR, had passed away.

In the years that followed, the company had rather aggressively taken over at least a dozen smaller companies and pushed further into Esports, which resulted in NGVR being worth over five trillion dollars. As with all men of power, he wanted more.

And he was planning on using these very naive researchers to do it. He very rarely spoke in public, preferring to only speak when he had something poignant to say, which in turn created an air of mystique around Orson. One that he both counted on and enjoyed.

So, as his researchers prepared to give their presentation, he placed his hands in front of his face to avoid giving off any emotion. Although he knew what they were about to present, he looked to his right where Yvette sat and gave her a slight nod.

With his signal, Yvette cleared her throat, also knowing what was about to happen, and asked, "So, what do you have for us?"

Carter replied to her question while posing another: "Why do people swim with sharks?"

THE ROOM FELL SILENT, unsure if they were supposed to answer. Before anyone could respond, Nicolette chimed in, "Why do people climb Mt Everest?"

Again, the room fell silent. Orson rolled his shoulder back, curious to see how they were going to pitch this.

Marcus then asked, "Why do people skydive?"

Yvette looked at Orson. Orson, however, had an amused look on his face, concealing it with his hands so nobody else, save for Yvette, could see it. Taking a deep breath, she relaxed and let them continue.

This is the moment, Carter thought to himself as he delivered what his team believed to be the next generation of gaming.

"ADRENALINE, the rush and potential for death, to be among a select few that have done what most people would consider to be insane or impossible. This is what we aim to deliver to gamers across the planet. The real-world fear of death while playing a game."

This raised many eyebrows across the room.

CARTER TOOK a vial out of his pocket and placed it on the table for all to see. Inside the vial was a dark green, opaque, coloured capsule.

BEFORE ANYONE COULD SAY a word or ask a question, Carter continued with his pitch. "This is what we call RSD. Real Simulated Death. When a player is killed in-game by, say a giant in armour, after the sword is pulled from his body, RSD will render that player unconscious."

"That's insane!" said an executive from accounting.

"Absolutely, fucking absurd," cried someone from the content creator's department.

Once the initial shock wore off, they all looked at Adler, who said nothing but gestured with his hand for them to continue.

Marcus spoke next. "Each capsule of RSD contains a single dissolvable drone that will dissolve after half an hour. If a player does not die in that time, it harmlessly breaks down and vanishes without a trace, leaving nothing behind. And no ill-effects"

"Not only will RSD knock the player out, but also in-game, the players will lose everything. Permadeath. And be forced to start again," Nicolette further explained.

"Giving players the ultimate adrenaline rush," Carter finished.

After answering more than a few questions from the panel about the technology and how it would profit NGVR, Carter, Nicolette, and Marcus felt satisfied with their presentation. But there was one person who had yet to say anything.

As the noise in the room died down, Orson stood up, looked at the three researchers, gave them an approving smile, and uttered a single word.

"Brilliant."

He then left the room and headed back to his office. The boardroom then emptied with many executives now excited about RSD and how they were going to market it to the world.

Once the room was empty, save for Nicolette, Carter, and Marcus, Yvette offered her congratulations to the trio.

"You were exceptional today. This will change the way players interact with the games they love. This truly is the next step in the industry. Now go out and enjoy yourselves tonight. That's an order."

They nodded and headed out.

Yvette stood in the empty room and thought to herself, *What an exceptional group of researchers.* A smile made its way on to her dark red lips.

After riding the high that came with success all day, the three musketeers headed into a nearby bar, buzzing with how well they had performed. They ordered drinks and sat down in an empty booth.

"I can't believe we pulled that off! I feel so good. With the bonus coming from this, I can finally get a new apartment," Nicolette almost yelled. "What about you guys, what are you spending your bonuses on?"

Carter looked over at the bar, thinking, but before he could reply, Marcus jumped in. "Man, all I want is to spend a weekend in a five-star hotel with a ten thousand dollar a night hooker and an ass-ton of Spanish beer."

"Goddamn it, I should have known that was your plan," Nicolette said laughing.

"Hey, I'm a simple man. Give me tech, beer, and boobs, and I'm set." Marcus replied to her while beaming.

Nicolette shook her head and looked at Carter. "What about you, what are you aiming for?"

He hesitated to answer, wanting to keep his private life private, but in the spirit of their victory, he decided to open-up a little. "I'm thinking about grabbing an android, but next year's model, there's a few features that it has that I want."

"Oh nice! Won't Anna be jealous though?" she asked.

"Not at all, it's for her," he replied as he watched Marcus trying to dance and flirt with a group of women.

Nicolette looked at Carter and decided not to pry anymore, knowing that he was generally a private person, and she was the one of the very few people who knew about Anna.

Instead, she gave him a kiss on the cheek and said, "I'm really happy for you."

He gave her a soft smile. "Thank you" he replied.

Excusing herself, Nicolette pretended she needed the restroom so he would not see the tears that started to build up in her eyes.

. . .

SHE CURSED herself for not getting over her schoolgirl crush, but she suddenly found herself distracted as she had just realized in the rush to celebrate their success, that she had left her purse and phone in her office.

She left the restroom and hurried over to Carter, making sure there was no evidence of any tears. "Hey, I have to run back to the office and grab my stuff."

"Yeah, for sure, I'm about to leave anyway."

After a quick hug goodbye, she left.

Searching the crowd for Marcus, Carter eventually found him in the corner of a booth with two girls, all three too distracted by each other's tongues to pay any attention to him. Carter decided it was best to not interrupt and instead shook his head and headed home, eager to tell Anna the good news and plans for their future.

After weaving in and out of the Friday night foot traffic, he eventually got home. Walking into his office he dropped the bag, then headed to the bathroom to take a shower and change into something more comfortable.

Turning the water on and stripping out of his clothes he caught a glimpse of himself in the mirror; he smiled. Despite being the very definition of a "Nerd", he always endeavored to keep himself in good shape.

"You keep staring at yourself any longer and the water is going to get cold."

He turned around to see Anna smiling at him.

"How did it go today?" she asked, taking off her clothes. Or the little clothes she had on to start with.

Distracted by her gorgeous body, he barely managed to answer, "It was perfect, and I have some plans for us."

Anna, now within an inch of Carter, whispered, "Have your shower baby, then I'm all yours." She smiled coyly and left the room.

———

Nicolette finally made it back to NGVR and up to the R&D offices. Walking in, she noticed all computers were off except for Marcus's. *That's odd*, she thought. Walking over to turn it off, what she saw on the screen made her blood run cold.

It was the patent for RSD but with some major differences. According to this version, once taken, the microscopic drone in the capsule would cause players to become addicted very quickly. Not only that, but a second patent revealed that when a player died in-game it would result in real world death. She took a few photos of the screen with her phone and sent them to Carter. She turned the monitor off, but before she could leave, she ran straight into Yvette.

"Hey, you're working late" Yvette said, knowing exactly what had just happened. Looking down at the freshly printed papers Yvette was holding, Nicolette yelled, "What is going on? Who made these changes to RSD?"

Yvette looked at her, knowing there was no way any answer would satisfy the distraught younger woman. "Sweetheart, sometimes we as a business have to take an idea and expand it."

"People will die! Like actually die! I sent these to Carter. When he finds out about these changes, he's going to be furious. You can't do this…" She stopped, realizing she had said entirely too much.

"This is nothing more than an idea," Yvette said trying to calm her down.

Nicolette pushed past her and stormed off, heading to the elevator.

Yvette chose not to reason with the idealistic woman but instead took her phone out of her pocket and made a call.

"IT'S ME. I have a job for you, or two to be exact, tonight, and I'll triple your fee."

"Give me the details," replied the voice on the other end.

―――

ORSON ADLER STOOD at his window looking down at the city, rocks glass in hand. He took a sip and savoured the taste of the clear liquid. *Nothing compares to a city view and an ice-cold glass of sake,* he thought to himself. The door to his office opened and Yvette strolled in, carrying papers and a look of resolve. *Well almost nothing.*

"Sorry, I'm late. Had to call in a favor," she said, sitting on his desk facing him.

He sighed. Putting the glass down on his desk, he grabbed her neck and forcefully kissed her.

"I do not like to be kept waiting."

Smiling, she pulled up her skirt and wrapped her legs around his waist. "Neither do I, my lord. But I had to deal with an idealistic child."

"Who?"

"The girl, Nicolette. She found the patents. And she sent copies to Carter, but no need to worry. I already called in a favor with an old friend to take care of it."

"Fuck, I liked them. They would've been valuable assets."

. . .

ORSON STARED AT THE WOMAN, who now had her arms around his neck. "But idealism is the enemy of progress, and unlike my father, I enjoy progress immensely."

"Tell me, how will it be done?"

Yvette, now nuzzling his neck, whispered in Orson's ear, "Murder-suicide. A tale old as time, a loner turned down by a cute and innocent co-worker, he kills her and is so devastated by the act, that he has no choice but to take his own life."

ORSON LAUGHED and pushed Yvette onto her back, her arm sending his glass to the floor. Removing her skirt, he undid the buttons on her blouse, exposing her breasts. "This is why you'll soon be my CFO," he said as he caressed her body.

"So absolutely perfect." She looked up at him, smiling. "And all yours."

She gasped as he found his way between her thighs.

GETTING out of the shower and changing into something more relaxing, Carter ordered pizza, then decided it was time to let Anna know the good news. As he walked into the lounge room she alerted him to the fact that he had missed messages and calls on his phone. "It's Friday night, I'll deal with them in the morning. Tonight is pizza with you and to finally get back into *Breakneck*," he said. "And I have some good news."

"Oh?" she replied excitedly. "And what would that be?"

"Well, as a result of us impressing the board and Mr Adler himself, we get a rather sizeable bonus, which means I can get that android you need."

"Oh my God, Carter!" she said, both laughing and crying all at once. "That will be amazing; we will be amazing!"

The doorbell to the apartment rang, and Carter got up to answer it. The pizza delivery guy had arrived. Carter gave him a generous tip and returned to the couch with the two boxes. Anna smiled and said, "Well, I shall leave you to it." Getting up, she blew him a kiss and then disappeared into another room.

Carter devoured a slice of pizza, quickly wiping down his hands to avoid getting the controller greasy. He grabbed it and put on his VR headset, more than ready to race again.

To clear her head of the day's events, Nicolette had gone for a run. With her emotions all over the place, she needed some space to think. She jogged to Beaver Lake, one of the more popular areas in the city and one of her favourite places to relax. She sat down on the grass and looked across it.

Overcome with rage, tears started falling down her cheeks. *Why did Yvette do this? What do we do about it?*

CHECKING HER PHONE, she realized Carter had yet to respond. *Probably celebrating with Anna.*

Lost in her own mind, she barely heard the footsteps behind her. Nicolette turned to see who or what they belonged to. The last thing she saw was the barrel of a gun. With barely a whisper, the freshly cut green grass behind the young woman was smothered in Parisian blood.

CARTER SPED DOWN THE STREET, and shocking absolutely nobody, he was in first place. He was so close to winning his first race in his new gear and on his new bike. *Only 35% left, God I love sprint races,* he thought. A notification came across his HUD: **Visitor at the door.** *Damn, probably Nicolette.*

"Anna, can you get that please?"

"OF COURSE." Anna, more than willing to ensure Carter enjoyed himself tonight, ordered the door to open. The moment it did a man wielding a gun and wearing a black jacket with an all-black bike helmet walked into the lounge room, pointing the gun at Carter, who was blissfully unaware.

"Carter! Ru..."

Before Anna could finish, the intruder fired and the bullet passed right through her and hit Carter in the side of the head, killing him instantly. His VR headset fell to the floor, followed by Carter's lifeless body.

Before Anna could react, the intruder took a small metallic looking device out of his pocket and everything went black.

Sitting in her chair in the office of her penthouse house apartment, Yvette stared at the hard drive she had been given, trying to decide whether or not to link it up to her computer and activate the hologram inside.

. . .

Fuck it, why not, she thought. Inputting a few commands into her computer and connecting it to her office projectors, the hologram Carter called Anna appeared.

"Where am I? Where's Carter?"

Yvette looked at the hologram. Apparently the EMP used to render her inert also took out part of her memory. Annoyed she even had to spend part of her Saturday on this, she got up from her chair and stared directly into Anna's face.

"What is the last thing you remember?"

Anna, still confused, answered, "Carter was telling me with his bonus from work he was going to buy an android so I could finally have a body and we could be together."

Yvette couldn't contain her laughter. Sitting down once again, she looked Anna right in the eyes and said, "A human could never love a machine; that is pathetic."

With that, she unlinked the hard drive and erased the hologram stored inside.

Minutes later a soft knock could be heard from outside Yvette's office. She smiled, knowing exactly who that was.

"Come in."

Without hesitation, the office door opened and in ran a young girl, barely six years old. "Good morning mom!" She ran into Yvette's arms.

"Good morning, miss Adeline."

Yvette sat her on her knee as she kissed the child on the cheek. "Are you working today?" Adeline asked.

"Nope. This whole weekend I am yours and your dad's."

"Yay! Can we go to the park?"

Yvette looked in her daughter's eyes and pretended to think about it. "Um, we most certainly can. Get ready and we can go now."

Yvette watched as the most precious thing in her life happily sprinted out of the office.

THE INVESTIGATION into the deaths of Carter and Nicolette lasted all of two days. It ended with the official ruling of murder-suicide. All the evidence led to Carter being obsessed with his subordinate, and when he made advances on Nicolette, she rejected him. Being unable to control his anger, he killed her then himself. A clear-cut case as far as the MPD was concerned.

Almost nine months to the day, NGVR held a press conference. Not only did Orson Adler reveal their new product, RSD, which had now been altered to be extremely addictive, but a much pricier version would come in the future that would cause users to actually die if they died in game.

He also brought a heavily pregnant Yvette, her husband Brian, and little Adeline on stage to announce she would be NGVR's Vice President once she came back to work.

WITH THESE NEW ANNOUNCEMENTS, and an exceptional marketing and media plan created by Yvette, NGVR's stock soared and, as a result, became the most valuable gaming company in the world.

SITTING IN HIS OFFICE, Adler smiled at the young female journalist sitting opposite him as she asked, "So, Mr. Adler..."

"Call me Orson please, Mr. Adler was my father."

She laughed, caught up in his smile and eyes, and she nearly forgot her question. "So, Orson tell the nation and world why you should be President of the United American Nations."

ABOUT THE AUTHOR

BREACKNECK IS Luke Hancock's first foray into the world of writing and is currently working on his debut novel.

15. THE MODERN PANOPTES
BY PATRICK TILLETT

Demo became a Carrier for the HERMES company at only fifteen to help out her mom, and now she's taken the hardest job yet. How much can she give without losing herself to an unforgiving system?

"Mom?" Demo's voice was shaky, unsure, and betrayed the worry that she usually tried to keep buried under a brash bravado. Her hands were shaking now, one still wet with blood while the other held her phone up to her ear. Her mother's reassuring voice came through the line.

"Demo? What is it, kid? You sound shook up." Her mom sounded distracted and rushed, like normal. She was probably working. After all, Demo was still on the clock, too. But she hesitated. How could Demo even start to explain everything that had happened in the last day?

"Hello? Are you still there? It sounds really busy on your end, can you hear me?" her mom went on.

Demo had forgotten about the sirens that started after she sealed the riot doors, destroying the locks to sequester herself. Looking back, she could see the silhouettes of a security detail beating on the frosted glass, unable to reach her.

"Yeah, I guess it is. I'm sorry for bothering you, Mom. I just needed to hear you for a second, cuz…" Demo blew out a sigh and closed her eyes. God, she was sore all over. "How can you know you're doing the right thing?"

"What do you mean? Is this about your job?" Mom asked. "I wasn't even sure about you working in the first place, kid. It's supposed to be my job to take care of you, not the other way around. I didn't like how I felt when you told me about being a HERMES Carrier, but I'll tell you this." She paused, and Demo heard a couple of familiar clicks and key-taps from her mom's outdated terminal. So she was working late, Demo thought as she felt a familiar pang in her chest. "Regardless of how it made me feel, you were doing something selfless. You do that a lot, Demo. So whatever you've got going on at work, I think you already know what the right thing to do is. I trust you with that."

There was silence between them. Her mom may have been simply waiting for a response, but Demo had to pause because she could feel a lump growing in her throat.

"Demo? Are you still there?" she asked tentatively.

"Yeah, Mom, I'm still here," Demo answered in a reassuring calm. "Thank you. I love you."

"Love you too, kid." There was a click as the call was cut off, and Demo dropped the phone on the ground by her side. There was a satisfying crack and shatter as the delicate device broke on the unforgiving floor.

Demo was standing alone in a vast room, washed in azure light that lent a surreal quality to her vision. In front of her, as far as she could see, there were rows upon rows of data servers clustered together. Each cluster rose out of an indented pit in the ground like a crop being maintained in the largest server farm in the city and possibly the world. The blue light pulsed as power and information was fed through the servers like blood through the veins of a great animal. This was where every scrap of data collected by the ARGUS Company was sent, and Demo was left alone in this critical position with nothing but a Blade and body and a choice. With no better way to think, she sat down and closed her eyes.

Hours ago, Demo dashed through the city like greased lightning. To HERMES Carriers, speed was above all. Her kit was optimized for efficiency. Equipped with AR Glasses, Demo could plot out the most efficient course to take, and a respirator maintained her breathing while filtering out toxins. Her suit was made of a sleek, dry-fit material to wick away sweat while she ran, with athletic armor on her elbows, shoulders, knees, and hips. When your job depends on constant maintained speed, and you take every obstacle without stopping, you sometimes need a little something to help with the impact.

Otherwise, if something wasn't helping you perform at the highest level of excellence, you dumped it. That was why Carriers never bothered to drive: cars are bulky, unwieldy things, and the city's streets were jammed in perpetual gridlock. If you got held up on the job, you lost rating, and lost ratings meant lost orders. When you lose orders, eventually the Algorithm phases you out. The company didn't need people who couldn't get the job done, so if you couldn't guarantee results, you could find another job. That was the core of the HERMES Code that all Carriers learned. To keep up, you had to be the best, and Demo was one of the best.

When she ran, she was poetry in motion, and the lights of the city reflected off of her running suit to trace neon lines down the length of her body. From a pedestrian's perspective, stationary on the pavement, she might have just been a blur in the corner of their eye.

There was a line of cars backed up in a drive-thru Macca's, as usual. Demo leaned into it, sprinting full tilt until she was about to collide with the metal body. Rather than climb or vault over, she performed a twisting dive to preserve her precious momentum, rolling along her armor to hit the ground running.

The pedestrian crowds thinned as she moved away from the more industrious and successful urban centers, skating into the outskirts that progress had left behind. She wasn't alone, however, as Demo heard the voice of another Carrier come through the bone conduction speakers in her glasses. She slowed up just enough as she reached an overpass vaulting over the chasm between two city blocks. At least a mile of open air was beneath them.

"The Dropbox is just ahead of you, D," crackled the voice of the other Carrier as they came sprinting alongside Demo, busy on their job, but not so busy that they didn't have time to talk. "I've been to this neck of the concrete jungle a time or two."

"Just ahead?" quipped Demo from behind her respirator. "HERMES said this would be a challenge, it's the only reason I took the job."

"Oh yeah, just ahead." They winked from behind their wind visor and pointed a Grip-Gloved finger upward. "And about 20 stories up. Have at it, kiddo!" The Carrier stopped running long enough to crouch, the audible whine of coiling springs building before they launched with the power of enhanced legs. They were propelled at least fifteen feet in the air and angled the fall over the railing into the open city air below. Despite herself, Demo stopped and peered over the edge of the walkway railing to see the Carrier extend the wingsuit they wore and direct their freefall toward their next destination, letting gravity do all the work. She shook her head with a crooked smile.

Her HUD blipped to remind her she was on the clock, and she shifted herself into high gear. This was the sort of challenge the Algorithm relished. Demo made sure to take the hardest jobs she could find, and it rewarded her handsomely. She had brought every spare cent back home to her mom in an attempt to take some stress off her shoulders. She lived with her mom in an Employee Hub owned by SAHARA, a retail megacorp that dabbled in tech R&D on the side. SAHARA figured it was cheaper for all of their employees to live together in one building jutting out the top of their warehouses, or the "Hives," as most of the workers call them. Unfortunately for people like Demo's mom, who was one of few not married to a SAHARA coworker, the cost of housing came out of her pay before she ever saw it. With no spouse to share the burden, she had turned to extracurricular work for as long as Demo could remember. Ultimately, it was that guilt that pushed Demo to find a job as soon as she turned fifteen.

"Trust the Algorithm," she intoned to herself, a mantra that carried her up the side of the building she scaled to reach her destination. The gear she used, cutting edge from GripTech, helped her find purchase while she used her core to leap from one shallow handhold to the next.

Demo was four stories up when she found her entry

point, a window shattered from a previous break-in. Rolling through the open pane, her HUD was already determining the most efficient A-to-B for her to take before it highlighted one route in bright orange, a sharp glow against the drab, cracked, gray paint.

"An elevator, huh?" Didn't seem very dramatic, she thought. She pried open the lift doors to reveal the cables that kept the lift system running through the labyrinth of an apartment building, and they were running fast. This particular cable ran straight up. "Ah."

Demo figured she had a couple seconds at most before she reached the twentieth floor by riding the cable, but she also figured she could net a pretty little bonus, so she leaped into the elevator shaft and gripped the running cable with both hands. Immediately, she was flying skyward with the broken, flickering lights of the lift guiding her along the rise.

From above, the clang of metal seized her focus, and glancing up, Demo was greeted with the rapid descent of a lift floor. She didn't know if it was being called to the ground floor, or simply falling, but there wasn't any time to think. All she could do was weigh her chances.

"I can make it..." she convinced herself. Fourteenth floor now.

The lift screamed closer, maybe 6 seconds before impact. Sixteenth.

It was immediately above her. Two seconds left? She thought she gave herself more time.

The Eighteenth floor sign flashed crimson. The screech was deafening, and the lift was definitely falling, judging by its accelerating fall. That explained a lot.

"FUCK!" Demo screamed at nobody, unable to hear her voice but feeling the stress in her vocal chords.

The lift continued its freefall until it crashed, sending shockwaves up the walls of the shaft and shaking plaster dust and who-knows-what loose from the walls. It lay at the ground floor, utterly destroyed. Demo was pressed as flat as she could muster against the far wall, her arms and legs spread eagled like a spider between two parallel guide rails. She was hyperventilating but forced herself to focus up: there was still a job to do.

As she scaled the remaining two floors, she reflected out loud.

"You know what your mistake was, don't ya, D?" The gloves helped her climb as she talked to herself. "I didn't take into account acceleration. I *assumed* the lift was called down and didn't calculate for accelerating velocity." She shook her head derisively, hoisting herself up over the lip of the twentieth floor with minimal effort. "Oh well, whaddaya want, a fuckin' medal?" She caught her breath on the floor for a minute.

Her HUD beeped urgently when she stopped moving, so Demo cut the break short, dusting herself off as she got to her feet. The hallway she had entered was deserted, full of broken doors and a thick layer of dust. There was one exception, a simple wooden door that was conspicuously cleaner than its surroundings. Demo tested the latch to find it unlocked, with a modest room hidden behind. There was a cooler built into the drywall of the flat, stocked with Carbos and Boost Bars for Carriers that came through on a job. She had found her Dropbox. On a lonely desk under a window, there was an old fashioned analog terminal. These relics were often used when a Carrier had to pick up for a more paranoid job poster, and it appeared it was Demo's good luck to be dealing with one such post today.

Demo slipped a few of the Boost Bars into a pouch strapped around her waist for later. They were extremely dense energy bars, made of a healthy mix of protein, carbs, and more than a daily dose of amphetamines to keep Carriers alert and buzzing for the job. She never partook herself, but they made great bargaining chips with other Carriers on the road. Demo cracked open one of the Carbos, a carbonated electrolyte solution, and investigated the terminal closely.

The thing was ancient by Demo's standards. It was a heavy box with a curved glass screen that radiated a fuzzy static-charged warmth, the keyboard built into the chassis, and a round knob wrapped in electrical tape protruding from a slot in the side. The screen blinked to life with a dull green glow after a few key presses, a message flashing on the screen.

<A Million Eyes>

Black screen.

<Gaze Ever Watchful. Blind Them.>

Black screen.

<Plant Blade. Burn It Down.>

"Burn it down" flashed on the screen momentarily in silence, as if waiting for a response from Demo, who was nonplussed to say the least. The screen died, and there was an audible click as the knob ejected slightly from its slot in the terminal's side. She gripped it in one hand and tugged it free of the computer, which fizzed and popped before shutting off completely. The faint smell of electrical smoke hung in the dead air, and Demo grimaced.

"Whoops." She cast a guilty look around the room. "Hope no one needed to use this after me." She felt the faintest vibration in her hands and looked down at the object she had removed from the terminal. She held a strange looking knife in her hand. The grip, which had previously been sticking from the terminal, felt like a dense sort of plastic. Polypropylene, she figured, and was wrapped several times over in electrical tape. The blade, however, was unlike anything she had seen.

At first, it looked like a sleek black thing. But as it caught the light, the metal glinted a green as dark as emeralds that had never been carved from their mine, never seen the light of day. If she looked long enough, abyssal blue streaks in the metal arced up and down, across that green and black with electrical energy. She tossed it from hand to hand, noting the balance of the knife, when she pinged another update to the delivery. The job wasn't over.

"ARGUS ARCOLOGY-Deliver Cargo," flashed across her line of sight. So the job was a simple delivery after all? she thought to herself. If that was the case, then why all the secrecy? And why not just deliver the thing in-house? Too many questions, Demo thought, but she knew where to go to get some answers. She sheathed the knife into a subtle sleeve on her back, nice and secure. With that, she took the fastest route out of the building, and dove backwards out of the twentieth story window, spreading her arms to extend the flaps of her wingsuit and ride the winds like the Carrier from earlier.

Demo rode her base jump down through the open air, weaving between passing ACPD cruiser bikes on their way to enforce the harsh justice of the city. She was falling faster than anyone ought to, but it felt like flying to her. When she was diving, or climbing, or risking being crushed by elevators (she cracked a smirk at the thought), the only thing that could affect her was her own skill. In these chaotic moments of no control, she was at her most empowered. In those brief moments, she was outside the city and its companies' control. Still, the high couldn't last forever, and eventually, she pulled up to hit the ground running. Demo found herself in one of the deepest slums, where cars couldn't fit. The streets were packed with bodies and the shade of the mega-scrapers and arcologies above created an eternal night.

Even if it weren't for the harsh buzzing lights vying for attention, Demo still knew exactly where she was going like any self-respecting Carrier should. She found herself standing in the crawlspace between two brick buildings noticeably devoid of neon lights. The people who work in these spaces didn't like attention. Demo turned in smoothly.

She ducked through a familiar maze of identical alleys intended to baffle the uninitiated and came upon the sign she was looking for: a triangle with three lines meeting at the center, originating from each corner. The Dragon's Eye, as she was taught to call it, meant that she had found the office of her trusted friend and favorite Grey Hat hacker, Trigger. She entered the room to find it pitch black, as always.

Demo's glasses automatically switched to an infrared mode to make sense of the darkness, and found Trigger sitting in the center of the room on the floor. Trigger didn't have to bother with ambient lighting because they had upgraded their eyes (ocular hardware, they called it) with a data scanner that processed everything it took in as pure code. It made reading data lines and manipulating the software brought to them that much faster. To everyone else, Trigger looked like a distasteful mixture of humanity and machine, as they eschewed elegance of design for raw processing power.

Wires poured out of nodes in their head and back into various other parts of their body, typically down the arms for when sensory investigation was required. In place of eyes,

Trigger had a gaping maw in the hollowed out section of their face, and an oscillating blue light raced from one side of their head to the other. Several tablets were arranged in a semi-circle before them, running code at a rate that dizzied Demo.

"Sup, girl? Got something for me?" Trigger asked without looking up. Of course, they didn't need to. "Better be good."

"Don't worry, it's weird," Demo said confidently. Trigger laughed.

"That's what they all say," they muttered to themselves. "Well come on then, let's see it, Love." Demo drew the knife and tossed it in front of Trigger, the blade clattering down on the glass screens of the tablets. They didn't seem to even notice the damage on the devices because their attention was drawn to the Blade.

Moving for the first time since she arrived, Trigger scooped up the Blade, turning it end over end in their hands. Demo knew that was a good sign because, between both Trigger's hands and the Oculus in their head, there were three separate information superhighways transmitting data directly into the hacker's brain. This was why Demo came here before anywhere else. If you wanted answers fast, and weren't worried about how the data might be used, you brought tech to Trigger in the Data Crypt, or D-Crypt for short. After no time at all, Trigger's head shot up to lock 'eyes' with Demo. They stood up, the gaze locked on her the whole time, body moving like a marionette.

"Where did you find this, D?"

"On a job. Where else?" Demo answered, confused as to why it mattered.

"And you don't know what you're carrying? At all?" Trigger's blue light flickered and resumed its pace.

"No..." Demo said slowly. "Only that I've gotta bring it to ARGUS, post haste."

"ARGUS? Ahh, I see now, that *does* make sense..." Trigger paced the room, hunched like an old crone while their arms and legs stretched ahead of them with each step. Demo wasn't sure if Trigger was even talking to her anymore, or to themself.

"How does it make sense?" Demo demanded. "I mean, a job's a job, but what the hell does some media conglomerate have to do with anything? Why can't they deliver their tech themselves?"

"Because darling, this ain't their tech, is it?" They chuckled knowingly, having already put the puzzle together, but they had more pieces than Demo did, and it was starting to get under her skin. "ARGUS is more than the virtual hub for the modern age, Demo, it's the modern Panoptes!"

Demo groaned, not having time for metaphors. "English, and quick, please," she sighed in exasperation.

"It's all data, Love, my stock and trade. ARGUS has their eyes in every computer, television, and bloody mobile in the world! It's the many eyed giant, Demo, and someone wants to stick a needle in the eye!" They laughed again, this time folding the Blade back into Demo's hand. "And you've got the needle. I bet you found this plugged into an old retro piece?"

Demo nodded, looking down at the arcing Blade.

Trigger was tickled. "That's 'cause whoever made this needed a blindspot to work in. This ain't a knife, it's a Server Blade. And the code inside is some of the most dense I've ever seen in my life. Demo, you're holding a tactical nuke, designed for the sole purpose of rotting every scrap of info ARGUS has. With this thing, you can kill one of the giants of the world...if you have the conviction, that is." Trigger's voice was barely higher than a whisper, as if afraid that even in their lair there might be someone watching, listening.

Demo was shaking to her core, unable to wrench her gaze away from the thing in her palms, growing heavier by the second.

"So do you have it?" they asked. "The Conviction?"

Demo looked up into the maw that was dug out of Trigger's skull. "I..." she gulped. "I don't know?"

This elicited another round of laughter from Trigger, who backed away from Demo. "Then if you want my recommendation, don't hang onto that for too long. Won't be long till Panoptes comes looking for that little Excalibur."

They dismissed her, and Demo knew her audience with Trigger had gone on long enough. Her cyborg friend had returned their attention to the tablets on the floor, and she was honestly relieved. Trigger had never seemed so intimidating before. She left without another word.

Demo wound through the city, walking instead of running, her mind racing at the speed her body was accustomed to. She reflected on the terminal.

<Gaze Ever Watchful. Blind them.>

<Plant Blade. Burn It Down.>

There were still a million questions running through Demo's mind. Where did this thing come from? Who developed it? Why trust a Carrier with it? Would the job have gone to anyone? And most importantly, could it bring down ARGUS, one of the most powerful tech megacorps in the world? If it did, what would happen then? They owned surveillance software, banking records, criminal records, debts. That's when it struck Demo like a javelin thrown through her midsection. ARGUS was a company that had their hands in every single pie in the world. They held the rights to every record in the city and probably beyond. They held her mother's records. Her whole life they lived for scraps, saving whatever they could to get by. What if they didn't have to? If she did it, burned the world down, would her Mom finally be free? When was the last time she saw her mom smile?

As the bullet train of thought left the station in her brain, she became aware of the pain and realized the feeling in her gut wasn't the metaphorical shock of putting together the grand puzzle. She was bleeding profusely from being shot in the back. As she stumbled, the voices of Security became distinct, reporting they had traced the signal's source. She saw the smoking gun lined up for another shot. But this time she knew where he was, and she was the fastest Carrier in the city, and he wasn't going to get a second hit.

Demo fell to the ground with the force of the first shot, blood pattering on the pavement beneath her, but she caught herself in her starting position. Knees bent, hands splayed out in front of her, and eyes laser focused as adrenaline coursed through her body. The gun went off, but it was only a starting pistol and she was off to the races. From zero to thirty, Demo launched herself away from the second shot, already raising her stance as she accelerated. The pain in her gut blended in with the familiar tightness a runner felt in their sprint. The HUD printed the most direct path to ARGUS HQ, but that wouldn't do for Demo today. Security would expect that, so she needed a little more.

When she had put distance between herself and the security officers who shot her, she stopped briefly in a small hovel. Not much time, so she gulped down air, ripping the respirator off and filling her lungs with the thick taste of the city. She pulled a brand from her pouch, and gritting her teeth, pressed it into her exposed abdomen. She tried not to scream as the smell of burning flesh reached her nose. She dropped the brand on the floor, dizzy now that she had stopped, or maybe it was from the fumes. She looked down into her pouch and saw the Boost Bars sitting inside. She unwrapped one and bit into the tough brick, ignoring the thick unappetizing flavor. By the time she finished it and unwrapped the second one, she found why Carriers wanted these so much.

Every nozzle in her brain was cranked open to flood her body with endorphins and oxygen. Her heart was pounding at twice its normal pace, and she needed to run. She needed to run now! She needed to shut off her brain and let her legs do the work. Before she knew it, she was off again, only this time the world was a blurred streak at the corners of her vision. She vaguely recalled leaping across the hoods of flying cars and flying in the space between again. Similarly, she thought she could remember one time when an officer got his hands on her in a clothesline. Unfortunately for him, his neck was close to Demo's head when they landed, and she still tasted the salty iron taste of blood in her teeth. It was incomprehensible, just an unending stream of light, sound, and sensation that blurred together to make a movie whose soundtrack was the ever present pound of blood pumping and flooding out all other sounds from Demo's ears.

After a time, she had finally come down, the Boost Bar leaving her system as suddenly as it had come on, and Demo felt like she had run flat into a brick wall and carried it with her for another quarter mile. Every inch of her was aching, and several parts of her were bleeding. As she absently smashed a security lock, sealing her in an azure soaked room, she noticed the armor had been stripped off her clothes and she felt naked. She looked around the room through eyes weighted with fatigue.

The only light came from the sunken parts of the floor that towers of machinery and computer hardware rose out of like plants ready for harvest. At the edge of each of these towers was the emblazoned scarlet "A" with an eye in the center. So I found the server farm after all, Demo thought dimly. She stumbled forward, the Blade in her hand. Why was it bloody? Ahead, a figure paced between the towers toward her, shoes padding along the linoleum floors. The light revealed a middle aged man in a trim suit and jogging shoes. He had a thinning head of hair and wrinkles beside both eyes betraying long hours behind a computer screen. The old fashioned way. Demo stopped short, defensive, but he only raised his hands disarmingly.

"Don't worry Demo, I'm unarmed." he said, bowing his head as he did. She didn't feel any more assured, just scared of the Blade, and of herself. "I'm sure I can't imagine how you must feel right now. Already taken life, and so young." He stepped closer.

"Who the hell are you?" she demanded. "How do you know me?"

"Oh, Demo," the man said with a friendly, soft smile, "I know everyone, it's my job." He stroked one of the towers he stood by, about fifty feet away from Demo. His hand rested on the eye in the center of the "A". "ARGUS is my child, has been for...a century now?"

Demo shook her head, mostly to shake the fog out of

herself. The man chuckled. Everything he did was disarming and calm.

"My name is Aleister Panopt, and I think you have something I asked for." He pointed at the Blade in Demo's hand. She looked down at it and was shocked back to reality, seeing the blood drip off it, black in the radiant blue light.

"Wait a minute..." she said slowly. "You said...you...?"

"You're not on the clock, so to speak," Aleister joked calmly. "Take all the time you need."

"You said I...took life?" Demo looked up at the older man, who was perpetually unshaken. "I killed someone? No way, I'm just a Carrier, we don't-"

"Oh, Demo of course you would never normally do such a thing, but I'm afraid there's proof." As he spoke, Aleister produced a small remote from his pocket and clicked a CCTV holo to life between them. There was Demo, rabid and with a feral look in her eyes, wrestling on the ground while two officers struggled to keep her down. There was a brief flash of recognition: the clothesline. She saw the image of herself let go of the knife to grab the officer on top of her by the shoulders, and sink her teeth into the exposed neck within reach. Demo's stomach turned as the screams played through speakers in the room and blood sprayed into her eyes as she ripped a chunk of the man's neck out, spitting it into the ground.

As Demo got up in the holo, grabbing the Blade from the ground, the other officer backed up and fired off a shot that hit her in the shoulder, sending the armor there flying. Before he could center another, she leaped onto his torso, bringing the blade down into his back again and again with savage abandon. The worst part was, it only took a few seconds, and then she was off running again, unperturbed in her manic delirium. Aleister clicked his remote as he passed through the image, washing Demo and everything back into that blue light.

"I-I killed those two," Demo stuttered, stunned. "I'm a monster."

Aleister shook his head sadly. They stood within arm's reach of each other, and she could smell his cologne as he knelt down on one knee to meet her at eye level. "You didn't kill those men, I did. The system, the world I built put you on that path long before you ever met them. It's a world designed to make you struggle, and you've struggled for so long, Demo. With SAHARA's meager pay, you struggled helping your mom with work. I even remember you being bullied as a kid when your dad ran off to start another family...Do you remember what they called you? I do."

"They called me his Demo kid," she said, thick with pain and regret, but numb all the same. "A test he could try out before the real thing."

"And that was cruel." Aleister nodded. "I was cruel when I built the world on ARGUS. I'm sorry." Demo was looking at the ground, willing tears not to build behind her eyes. Demo met his gaze again, peering deep into the pits of his pupils.

"You built the nuke software in the blade, didn't you? You brought me here?" she asked. Aleister nodded silently, directing his solemn gaze at the floor. "Why?"

"I'm older now, Demo. This system is rotten, but I built it too big, too damn well to change it after all this time. The world needs a reset, a revolution," he answered calmly. His demeanor helped Demo refocus too, yet still her hands trembled.

"If you want it destroyed, why not do it yourself? Why leave it to some Carrier to bring it here and plant your virus?"

Aleister looked down thoughtfully, then shrugged with a half-hearted smile.

"What father can bear to see the death of their only child?" he asked. "I have to go first." His hands slid down the length of Demo's arm, wrapping around the wrist of the hand she held the Blade in. He brought the knife up and placed the razor's edge taut against his throat. He nodded peacefully. Demo balked, trying to pull the Blade back, but his grip held her fast.

"Why? Why are you doing this?" she demanded, raising her voice. "Is this all a game, or something?"

"No, it's not a game, Demo. It's an apology," Aleister said in his measured voice. "I'm giving up the power of choice...to you, one of the people. The proletariat masses. You can keep the system going, the way you know it always has, or you can try something new." He sighed, and for the first time seemed weary. "But the old king has to die for the revolution. I've lived my life, and I've made my peace. It's okay."

Demo wasn't sure if she moved, or if Aleister pushed against the Blade, but in a few silent moments, the blade of the knife was sunk down to the base in his neck, and Demo pulled back to wrench it free. Aleister gripped at the hole in his throat, gurgling and looking down at the blood, black in the blue light. He gave one last half of a choking laugh.

"Oh..." he said, as he sank to the floor. "The rest is...silence." And Aleister Panopt, one of the most powerful men in the modern world, died. Demo was left holding the Blade and the choice.

Shaken and unsure, Demo called her Mom, who was all she could think of. Their brief talk helped clear her mind. She had faith in Demo, and that was all Demo needed when she sat down to think. What happened if she left now and turned herself in? She'd go to prison, sure. She might even be executed. And the system would keep on running the way it always had. The working class struggle for life in an indifferent society. There was security in that, knowing what came next. On the other hand, there was the question: "What if?"

What if she did as Aleister asked and planted his virus? The system, every scrap of info on digital records, would go up in flames. It would be a total blackout, and beyond that...who knew? There wasn't any guarantee of safety or control beyond the blackout. But there was something else.

There was that call of the void she felt every time she made the dive. When falling turned to flying and for that brief moment, she was in control. She was in control now, not falling but flying. And this time, the whole world was flying with her.

Demo opened her eyes after reflecting on the events of one day, and she knew the choice was already made. She strode to one of the server towers and pulled out a Server Blade at random, inserting her own Blade instead.

The lights change from blue to red. At first in that one spot, but then, like a nuclear explosion spreading to engulf everything, more servers blink red. The lights pulsating in the recessed pits turn as well, and Demo is awash in the glow of her decision. Officers are pounding on the doors, working furiously to override the shot controls. She has no way of knowing this, but outside, lights are shutting off for the first time in hundreds of years. In an Employee Hub in another part of the city, power is lost, and the yoke that keeps the workers in line ceases to exist. There are fires breaking out across the city, and society takes the first painful step toward the next phase of evolution.

The world flies.

ABOUT THE AUTHOR

PATRICK TILLETT IS an author and screenwriter who loves to create Cyberpunk fiction and lives in what was once called Tennessee. He has two gorgeous children and is considering getting a cat instead of a third.

YOU CAN FIND HIM ON:

Twitter @FracturedGems
Instagram @FeacturedGemsOfficial

Dear Reader,

Thanks so much for choosing and reading this book!

We sincerely hope you had a great time with this compilation of cyberpunk stories.

If you enjoyed Neo Cyberpunk, please consider leaving us a review. All contributing authors are indies without the corporate marketing machine of a big publishing house spending a fortune on marketing.

In a way, we are the true cyberpunks. We are the rebels, who want to create without boundaries and show the full spectrum and diversity of this genre we love.

For that, we need your support!

Leave a review on Amazon or Goodreads, telling the world that cyberpunk is thriving, and that we are living proof of it.

Sign up to our newsletter at www.cyberpunkday.com

If you enjoyed a particular author's story, please give them a follow on social media or consider buying their book.

And never forget: #CyberpunkIsSexy !

Thank you!

Anna Mocikat

Neo Cyberpunk co-publisher & author

Printed in Great Britain
by Amazon